The Curveball

a novel

THE CURVEBALL

MEGAN COUSINS

AUTHOR'S NOTE

Thank you for choosing to read *The Curveball*. This is a passion project born of a time in my life when I was struggling with my confidence and body image. It is an Own Voices novel featuring a heroine with Polycystic Ovary Syndrome (PCOS) and the associated pain and physical symptoms; I have based her experiences on some of my own.

I recognize that PCOS is different for everyone with the diagnosis, it doesn't present the same for everyone. My hope is that you will read this with an open mind and an open heart, willing to understand the struggles - not just of this character, but her author as well.

I hope you enjoy.

Content Warnings:

- Death of parents (off page), discussions of grief (on page)
- Anxiety and portrayal of anxiety attacks
- Discussion and portrayal of chronic pain/illness
- Discussion of infertility

This is a work of fiction. Names, characters, places, and incidents are either products of the author's imagination or used fictitiously.

The Curveball © 2022 by Megan Cousins

All rights reserved. No part of this book may be reproduced or transmitted without permission from the copyright owner, except for the use of quotations in book reviews and recommendations.

E-Book Edition, April 2022

Cover Design by Mia Heintzelman & Dot Covers

*To everyone with a glass ceiling to shatter.
Don't let anything stand in your way.*

1

FOOD FOR THE SOUL
PENELOPE

It's raining in New York.

A cool April breeze floats in through the balcony door, filling my apartment with a dampness that chills me to the bone, but I don't care. The oven is on, candles are lit, and my apartment smells like cumin and turmeric and garlic. A chilly day like this calls for a warm meal, and my favorite Indian stew and homemade flatbread is just the thing to warm you up from the inside out.

I push the soft, springy dough in my hands against the cool countertop, kneading and watching the timer on my phone count down. I want to be precise about this bread, just like the women at the Indian market taught me. They were surprised that I'd asked to learn, but welcomed me as one of the family and allowed me to learn a few recipes. I'm trying them on my own for the first time tonight.

Another rumble of thunder shakes the building, and lightning streaks across the sky, breaking my concentration.

"Penelope!" my sister's voice rings out through my otherwise quiet apartment. "Are you paying attention?"

To be perfectly honest? No. I'm not paying attention. At least not to the conversation happening on my computer screen – the weekly Sunday evening video call with my brother Peter and his wife Sofia.

"Are you looking forward to tomorrow?" Sofi asks. Again. Apparently.

Tomorrow. I'm mostly looking forward to tomorrow. Tomorrow everything changes...which may sound dramatic. But it's true.

"It'll be fine," I answer. Trying not to let my frustration show.

"Nell." Oh Peter, the only person who knows how to navigate a crabby Penelope better than anyone else. "You're a brilliant producer. I think you're going to be able to handle a new host joining *On the Field.*

Not just producer.

Executive producer.

I've been at the American Sports Network for two years, and six months ago I was promoted to the top production spot for *On the Field*, the network's only baseball focused show.

On the Field is my dream show.

It's all baseball, all the time. Highlights, live coverage of games, interviews with players, coaches, and executives. In the spring, we cover spring training, in the fall we cover the road to the playoffs. In the off season we talk trade rumors, drafts, and international winter league baseball.

I love being a part of this show.

I love my team.

I love the memories that are tied to it.

I watched *On the Field* every weeknight with my dad when I was a kid. And even when I went to college and then moved to start my career, I would watch it and text him or call after the broadcast to talk about it. Before I was a part of the crew, I'd watch with Peter. And now I can expect a text each night when we go off the air: *Great show tonight, Nellie! I'm proud of you.*

Nellie. My childhood nickname.

I never liked the name Penny. So I chose my own nickname... technically I threatened my brother with bodily harm until he called me something other than Penny. Nell and Nellie stuck. Those I don't mind. Call me Penny and I might kick your shins like I did to Peter when I was a five year old spitfire.

I never would have imagined, when I was a fresh faced local sports reporter – lugging my own equipment to high school games and local semi-pro matches – that I'd ever get to this point, but here I am. I wish dad could see me now. He always believed in me, always believed that I'd make it here. Even when I didn't believe in myself, *he* did. When I'd call home from whatever podunk town I'd been transferred to, after every misogynistic comment lobbed my way, dad would always tell me *hang in there, Nell. Someday you'll shatter the glass.*

That fabled glass ceiling.

So many glass ceilings have broken for women in other fields, but sports? Particularly sports media? It's still a boys club. Women have broken into the upper echelons of academia and politics but in sports media and executive positions, we are few and far between. And it's not that we don't have the qualifications - in some cases we're *overqualified*. We just don't get hired. Whether it's front offices, coaching staff, officiating, and yes, media. Women don't get hired.

So why did I bother? Knowing that this is the case, why even try?

Because I don't give up.

No matter how outrageous the dream or impossible the feat. I. Don't. Quit.

I've *thought* about quitting. I wanted to quit after dad was taken by his cancer; quit and go home to be with mom. Mom talked me out of it, and when she passed not long after dad, I was glad I'd stayed in that job. If only to get me out of my apartment on a regular basis. I needed that routine. Something somewhat normal while my world was in shambles.

When dad got sick I was working in a local station in a teeny tiny

Pennsylvania town. I was discouraged; I'd put in for an open position as a producer, a chance to move up in the world of sports media, use a little more of my degree than I was as an on-air reporter.

Going home would have been the easiest thing to do at the time. And it would have kept me closer to dad. But, he convinced me to stay where I was. *Keep chipping away at that glass, Nell.*

So I stayed. I worked hard and found my way to a larger network where I was producing the eleven o'clock sports report and a weekly Saturday sports wrap up where we covered all the local and state sports news. I burned out fast. My work and productivity declined and everyone knew it. I was transferred again. And demoted.

When dad died, I was angry and fell into depression. I was a production assistant after two years of producing, and felt like my career was stalling out. I couldn't see a way up and out. I had applications and resumes crisscrossing the country and a strong desire to move back home to hide away for a while. And take care of mom, who was battling her own demons. Mom talked me into staying where I was. And when she lost her own fight with cancer a few months after dad, I had to work just to get out of the loneliness of my apartment each day. My work still suffered, but I slowly began to heal.

Two years ago, I got a call from American Sports Network. They'd seen my resume and thought I had potential. I was hired as a production assistant, which was a step back professionally but I got my foot in the door at the network and when the producer spot opened up for *On the Field,* I jumped at the chance and landed my dream job.

———

On the Field broadcasts live every weeknight from five to six pm and tonight was my last night with the show's current hosting duo, Jim McCann and Devon Wilson. These guys are consummate pros; both former broadcasters and pro baseball players before that. I grew up listening to Jim call games on the radio for Detroit before he moved to ASN. Devon did play-by-play in Los Angeles before ASN called him and offered him a hosting gig. Devon and Jim are fan favorites, and favorites of mine as well. It is an honor to work with your heroes, and I get to work with mine every day.

Jim reminds me of my dad, his quiet strength and gentle encouragement get me through some of my toughest days. And like dad, he loves baseball. Dad taught me the game and the history, and would love knowing that I'm producing his favorite show. He'd have loved to visit the studio with me. He'd have pushed me to go for the hosting gig.

I used to love being on the air.

I haven't been in front of a camera in years.

My own insecurity keeps me from doing it, and just the thought of being on camera again gives me hives and the early warning signs of a panic attack. So, these days I stick to behind the scenes work and besides, *On the Field* has the best hosting team in the business.

But tomorrow that changes.

"I haven't met the guy yet. Mike brought him in and interviewed him without me."

Mike Fletcher. My boss. And a thorn in my side since the day ASN hired me. At the mention of Mike Fletcher the mood of the call changes. I roll my eyes as Peter and Sofi have a sidebar to figure out how to approach the rest of this conversation.

I was there the day he gave the new guy a tour of *On the Field's* studio and offices, barely sparing a glance in my direction. *She's just a producer.* The new host stopped for a moment in my doorway and I did my level best not to look up and make eye contact with him. Mike ushered him along with a comment about the skirt I'd chosen that day...and subsequently haven't worn back to the office since.

Just one more thing to add to the Mike File; a file I've been mentally adding to since the harassment began. Peter tells me to be cautious, Sofia has offered her legal expertise should I ever need to "sue him for everything he's got and then some." She gives me a knowing look through the screen and I know that I'll likely get a call from her later tonight. I look forward to it.

"Remind me who the new host is?" Sofi asks.

"Jake Hutchinson."

Peter eyes me warily.

"You gonna be okay?"

Jake Hutchinson. Rookie of the Year in his first season in New York. Two-time Cy Young Award Winner, National League MVP, and two world championship rings. He's my age. When I was starting my career, he was starting his. And what a career he had. Until Tommy John surgery put him out for a year. Then, in what should have been his comeback year, he blew out his elbow during a game.

Doctors did their best to repair the damage, but he found himself on the way to an early retirement. For the last year or so, he's been off the radar until a few months ago when rumors started going around that he wanted to get into the game again. This time, as a member of the media.

Jake was dad's favorite baseball player. Hence, the reaction from my brother. We were not New York fans growing up, but Jake came from Dad's hometown. A small dot on a map in Northern Michigan. We were strict Detroit sports fans in our house until that fateful year that I took dad with me to Spring Training. Dad met Jake before a game and was impressed. Suddenly, we had to watch every start the guy made once he got called up to the majors.

When dad died, I'd inherited all of his Jake Hutchinson tee-shirts. They are tucked away in a drawer, except for the one that I sleep in. The one I am currently wearing. He can *never* know.

When I would go to chemo treatments to sit with dad, I'd always bring my tablet so we could stream New York games. Dad always got excited to watch Jake pitch, claiming he knew from the very beginning that Jake would be a star. And he ended up being one until his injury. The night Jake's second arm injury occurred was the night I lost my dad. We'd been watching him pitch...and the next thing I knew...dad was gone.

Strangely, Jake has been tied up in my memories of my dad. And now I have to work with him. But I'll be fine. At least that's what I tell Peter.

———

As my brother continues to discuss my show and our new host, I start on my dinner. Pulling a few pans out of my closet and the assortment of spices I'll need from my small spice drawer. That's the problem with a studio apartment. The lack of space and storage means my good cast iron pans are stored on the floor of my closet, the linen closet holds canned goods along with towels and sheets, and the small cabinets are stuffed to bursting with spices and dry goods. I am thankful however that this apartment isn't as small as a few that I'd looked at, at least in here I can move comfortably between spaces, and my bed has its own corner, separated from the rest of the studio by a blackout curtain hanging from a ceiling track.

I listen to Peter and Sofi while I start toasting my spices in the pan. Soon my space is filled with the smell of cumin, coriander, garlic, and ginger. When the seeds start to dance in the pan, I add my onions and sauté them until they're soft. I add chickpeas and tomatoes and cook the whole thing until it's reduced into a thick, stew-like consistency. Leaving the dish to simmer, I roll out small pieces of my dough and fry it in a dry pan, allowing it to bubble and char.

All the while, I listen to the sounds of my family.

Their voices fill the small space and I'm hit with a sense of loneliness that I can normally stave off. But tonight? Tonight it sits like a weight on my chest. I look forward to this call each week. I miss my family dearly and on Sunday nights we have a standing date for this video call. I look forward to our group text thread throughout the week, this sense of connection that I have with my family that reminds me I'm not alone.

I didn't know what to do when our parents died. But I do know that I wouldn't have made it through those days without my brother. As the youngest sibling, I was afraid that I'd be a burden to him. I was afraid to lean on him too heavily, so for a while I distanced myself from him. I'm still learning that I'm not a burden. I'm a work in progress. Someday I'll get over that feeling.

Listening to them laugh has taken my mind off of tomorrow's show. My family makes me laugh like no one else can. They know my heart better than anyone else; they know my fears and how to snap me out of my worst moods. They also know that I cook to decompress and don't take it personally when I cook or bake bread during our weekly calls.

When I sign off, silence blankets my apartment once more. I turn on the Sunday night baseball game and settle into my sofa with dinner. I have very little appetite tonight, even for one of my favorite meals. My mind won't stop racing and a sense of dread has my stomach twisted in knots. I eat a few bites before scraping my plate into a plastic container and snapping on the lid. I set aside one container for lunch tomorrow and dish the rest of the meal into a series of containers for meals later in the week.

The game goes off and I turn on music. A playlist that would make my parents proud -- full of jazz and show tunes and old standards sung by crooners. I sing along as I wash my dishes, not loud enough for neighbors to hear me (I hope), but loud enough to fill the silence of my studio. Once my dishes are washed and my kitchen is clean, I change into pajamas and a sweatshirt that I stole from Peter the last time I visited him and Sofi, and I step out onto my small balcony with my tablet in hand.

The storm has blown over, leaving a slight chill in the air. I dry off my table and chairs, and sink into one of the chairs, propping my feet on the railing in front of me. I watch lights glimmer across the Hudson as the sun finishes her descent past the horizon. I sit in the cool spring air and allow the city to wrap her arms around me. New York City has an electricity, an energy, like no other city I've lived in. It was a bit of a culture shock when I first moved here, but now I wouldn't trade this place for the world.

I open up my tablet and pull up my notepad app, finding the document I've been working on for the last year. I have an idea for a show I want to pitch to the network, a special episode of *On the Field*. So far, I haven't worked up the courage to do anything with it. As I do most nights, I read through what I have so far and end up more discouraged than I was before.

With a frustrated sigh, I close my tablet and head back into my apartment, pulling the balcony door shut behind me. I turn on a late ballgame and then set about making sure that everything is cleaned up for the night, which means taking out the trash. I walk everything down to the garbage shoot, and on my way back, I find a note stuck to my door, from my neighbor across the hall.

Hi neighbor,
Whatever you cooked tonight smelled amazing.
Signed,
Hungry in 10C

Finally.

Something to do. Someone to take care of. A need that I can meet. I have enough leftovers to last me a week, the least I can do is share them with my neighbor across the hall. I remove the note from my door and step back into my apartment to gather the food and get ready to take it across the hall. I load up a tote bag with containers of rice and Chana, wrap up a few pieces of flatbread, and even add a bottle of my favorite ginger ale.

As I step across the hall, part of me hopes that no one is home and I can leave the bag and run back but, before I lose my nerve, I knock on the door.

And Jake Hutchinson answers.

Shirtless.

He stands in front of me with all his broad shouldered, long torso-ed, chiseled and handsome...maleness. A dusting of dark hair on his chest, arms that spent years throwing fastballs at ninety miles an hour, toned but not grotesquely muscular. I remember watching him pitch and thinking he was cute back then...and I have to say, these last few years have been good to him. Very, very good to him.

I stand on the other side of his door for way too long without saying anything...

And then my brain decides to go rogue.

2

NEIGHBORS
JAKE

I need to get out of here.

I need to go for a run or something. But a storm is raging outside and the last thing I need is an injury. Or to get sick the night before I start a television hosting gig. But I have to work off these nerves. My gut is twisted in knots, my mind won't stop racing, and all I can think about is the fact that my first foray back into the world is going to be on a national network broadcast. Five nights a week.

I change into shorts and a tee shirt, lace up my running shoes, and get ready to head to the fitness center here in the apartment. It's better than nothing. I step into the hallway and pull my door shut behind me. I'm hit with the smell of something cooking in a neighboring apartment; it smells warm and savory and slightly spicy.

My neighbor is cooking again.

I've lived here for all of a month, and in that month I've learned that my neighbor across the hall likes to cook, and based on smell alone? They are very good at it. We are both in the units at the end of our hall, and while I can't always get a whiff of what they are cooking, when I do it always makes my mouth water. And my stomach rumbles. A reminder that I haven't eaten in a while and probably should. The problem is, I have very little appetite tonight thanks to my nerves.

I take the elevator down to the ground floor and run a few miles on a treadmill. With music and my pulse pounding in my ears I run. I run and I try to shake out my nerves before tomorrow morning. I run like I used to before starting a game. The trainers were always a little worried that I'd hurt myself. Turns out, it wasn't my running they should have been worried about.

I'd had arm issues before the surgery. Long before the night that my tendon blew out. I thought for sure that I'd come back to the game and get right back to business, but those first few starts were rough. My arm felt like someone had restrung a bow incorrectly, like a rubber band pulled too tight. Bending my elbow hurt, releasing the ball made my eyes sting with tears. Then something snapped. The ball flew wide to the left, and I dropped to the mound as fiery pain engulfed my right arm.

I didn't know when I walked off the field that day that I would never be going back.

I'm glad to be back in the baseball world. When the network approached me about joining the *On the Field* team I was hesitant, but my agent convinced me to put myself out there and join the team. And it doesn't hurt that I'll be sitting next to my childhood idols while I talk about the game that I once devoted my life to.

After a quick cool down, I head back up to the tenth floor and can barely think to unlock my deadbolt. My senses are consumed by the aroma coming from across the hall…and once again my stomach reminds me that I've still not eaten yet. The spices and warmth that fill the hallway drive me to do something crazy. Something stupid. Something I absolutely shouldn't do:

I step into my apartment and scribble out a quick note to my neighbor.

Hi neighbor,

Whatever you cooked tonight smelled amazing.

Signed,

Hungry in 10C

I stick the note to my neighbor's door and linger in the hallway a moment longer. A smoky alto drifts through the door from the other side. My neighbor is singing along to an old jazz standard. She's good too. Really good. I stand and listen to the end of the song before stepping back into my own apartment for a quick shower.

I turn on a ball game and settle into my couch, too nervous over tomorrow to actually eat anything, even though I know I probably should. I stand in front of my open, empty, refrigerator before deciding I'd be better off just ordering takeout. A knock on my door sounds just as I'm opening the delivery app on my phone.

I answer the door to find a wide-eyed young woman standing on the other side of the door. I've never seen her in the building before, if I had I don't think I would have forgotten her. We stand not quite eye-level, she's short enough that if I hugged her, I could rest my chin on the top of her head. Her dark hair is pulled into a bun, adding a little to her height, and clearly the NYC humidity is not her friend; little wisps and curls stick out all over and she tries to smooth back as much as she can under the scrutiny of my gaze. She's hiding curves under an oversized tee shirt, a pair of leggings hugging the rest of her.

There's something strangely familiar about her, about the purple framed glasses perched on her nose, as if I've seen her somewhere before. She's gorgeous, with her flushed cheeks and bright eyes. I'd remember having seen her before…

I have to chuckle at the fact that she's wearing a Jake Hutchinson tee shirt. It's not often that I have encounters with fans who recognize me, but this one is certainly memorable, her gaze travels from my eyes to the floor and back again, the blush in her cheeks deepening.

"Abs…" she shakes her head, eyes wide, clapping a hand over her mouth, and all I can do is laugh. I am not usually in the habit of answering my door while shirtless, but I'm kind of glad I did tonight if only for this encounter to help me take my mind off of tomorrow. It takes her a minute to gather her composure and courage to speak.

"I'm 10D," she says, gesturing to the open door behind her. "I got your note and had leftovers so I thought I'd share."

She thrusts a bag into my hands and hightails it back across the hall before I have a chance to say thank you.

I shake my head with a laugh, and turn back inside, emptying the contents of the bag onto my small dining table. There's several containers in this bag, plus a bottle of ginger ale, and something wrapped in foil. She even took the time to write out reheating instructions...which I attempt to follow. Soon my apartment is filled with the same smell that had my stomach rumbling before my run tonight.

And now I'm so glad I wrote her that note. I've never tasted anything like this.

My mom is a great cook. She made lots of wonderful food for my siblings and I while we were growing up, and my sister Jenna has learned most of the recipes. Jax – the oldest of us – has picked up a few too; James and I are the only ones of the four of us who are hopeless in the kitchen. I've been here a month and have missed mom's home cooking. This meal, home cooked by a very gracious neighbor, is exactly what I've been missing since I moved here. Takeout just isn't as good as food cooked from the heart.

I wrap a bit of the onion and bean mixture into the flatbread and take a bite, closing my eyes and savoring the mingling of spices and textures. I devour the rest of the food and wash out the containers, repacking the bag to return across the hall. It's not too late, so I step into the hallway once more and knock on my neighbor's door, making sure to throw on a tee shirt before I do.

The door opens to reveal the same young woman, though seemingly less flustered than earlier. Her dark hair is no longer piled in a knot on top of her head, her curls fall just to her shoulders, and it's all I can do to keep myself from slipping a few wayward strands behind her ears. But I just met her. That would be weird. I hear the sounds of a baseball game coming from her television, and between that and my name and number on her back, she has my attention.

That enticing blush creeps into her cheeks and she gives me a small, tentative smile. I peer behind her into her apartment, wanting to soak up as much information about this beautiful, generous stranger as I possibly can.

"I brought your containers back," I give her the bag and half expect her to slam the door in my face. Instead, she walks away. I take a tentative step through her doorway as she starts putting the containers away in her cabinet. "What was all of that anyway? I don't know that I've ever had anything like it."

"Chana. It's an Indian bean and tomato stew. I'm still trying to perfect the recipe. Was the bread okay? It's the first time I've made it on my own?"

Was it okay?!

That was the best flatbread I've ever had. It was soft and light, airy, and toasty without being burnt...and I know a thing or two about burnt food.

"It was fantastic. All of it was." It's pretty hard to miss the look of pride that briefly flashes across her features. She throws me a small, sheepish smile and my mother's voice in my head reminds me of my manners.

"I'm Jake, by the way," I have no doubt she already knows who I am, but I hold out my hand for a handshake anyway as she drifts back toward the door. She grasps my hand in hers and meets my gaze. She has striking brown eyes that seem to bore into me. Brown eyes flecked with bits of gold; bright and engaging. Eyes that crinkle at the corners when she smiles.

"Penelope. Penelope Nichols."

"Nice to meet you Penelope."

"You too, Jake."

Awkward silence settles between us, punctuated by the sound of the ballgame. Her eyes look everywhere but at me, and when I can't take it anymore, I say the first thing that comes to mind.

"So, you're a baseball fan?"

Her cheeks turn the slightest shade of pink as she crosses her arms over the logo on the tee shirt she's wearing, eyes drifting to the television.

"I am," she's far away all of a sudden, her eyes trained on the game before turning back to me. "Would you like to stay and watch an inning or two?"

I end up watching the rest of the game with Penelope, the two of us on either end of her sofa, chatting easily as we watch the game. She's a very expressive baseball fan, groaning when easy plays are missed, arguing out loud with the umpires, knowing full well that they are calling everything right. "That *was* a strike," I mutter under my breath while she rails against the umpire for being inconsistent with the strike zone. I honestly didn't think she heard me, but her eyes meet mine and she tries to scowl at me, all the while one corner of her mouth is tipping up in a smirk that she can't hide.

"You're only saying that because you were a pitcher." She crosses her arms over her chest and settles back against the arm of the sofa, gaze trained on me instead of the game as if issuing me a silent challenge.

"You're right," her smile turns smug, until I continue. "I was a pitcher. But even someone who didn't spend their career on the mound should have been able to see that that pitch was a strike."

"You're as blind as the ump, Hutchinson." Penelope grumbles around a smile.

"And you're as stubborn as a manager arguing balls and strikes."

She laughs at that, and tries to stifle a yawn. It's getting awfully late and I should let her get some rest.

"I should be going," I stand and make my way toward the door. "Thank you for tonight. I haven't had this much fun watching a game in a long time."

"Me too," she offers a small smile, tinged with sudden sadness. "Goodnight Jake."

"Night, Penelope."

I walk back into my apartment suddenly feeling a bit better about tomorrow.

3
OPENING DAY
JAKE

I wake up early. Too early.

I spent about four hours last night lying awake in bed, staring up at the ceiling in the semi-darkness of my studio apartment. I should invest in blackout curtains for the balcony door. That's the one thing I remember from my playing days – the days before I moved out of the city – New York never *truly* goes dark at night. Usually the glow of the city and the lights on the various appliances and electronics in my space don't bother me, but on nights that I just can't sleep, there may as well be floodlights on in my apartment.

Last night was one of those nights.

So this morning I run another two miles on the treadmill before returning to my apartment for coffee and a much needed shower. Then it's time for work.

There's a production meeting at ten AM, I have a meeting scheduled with Jim McCann and Devon Wilson immediately following the production meeting, meetings with HR and the network owner, and then we are on the air at five o'clock.

I pack my work bag, network issued tech, and a few things for my new office before my short walk to the building. I pick up a coffee from the shop around the corner from the ASN building, and then make my way up to the office and dressing room space waiting for me on the fifteenth floor. Devon and Jim are waiting for me when I arrive. They greet me as if they've known me for years, and I do my best not to introduce myself with stars in my eyes.

Jim and Devon show me around the office, taking me down to meet the producer, but she's not in her office. They assure me that I'll meet her in the production meeting later this morning.

Mike Fletcher comes out of his office and shouts across the common area full of cubicles and people trying to work. He welcomes me and reminds me that we're having lunch together today. I couldn't forget it if I tried.

I can't quite put my finger on why, but Mike Fletcher rubs me the wrong way. There's just something about the guy that sets off warning bells in my head. Our first meeting left a lot to be desired; he was vulgar, rude, and disrespectful to the other people around him but put on a great show for me. I have to remind myself that I don't work for him. He does not own the network or my contract. I don't have to like the guy or be his friend.

"Anybody seen Lucky Penny this morning?" He shouts. No one responds to him but I see a young woman emerge from down a hallway, dark hair pulled back in a severe bun so unlike the mess of curls I saw last night, purple glasses that she pushes up the bridge of her nose with a knuckle, a computer and notepad in one hand and cup of coffee in the other. She takes one look at Mike and turns on her heel, heading back down the hallway.

Penelope.

Penelope Nichols. My generous and adorable neighbor.

This is a surprise.

I follow Penelope down the hall to the conference room and step inside to find her setting up for the meeting.

"So is it Penelope? Or Penny?" she turns to me and there's unease in her gaze, her brows furrow as she regards me closely.

"It's Penelope. Please don't call me Penny," she says softly, her eyes darting around as if looking for someone who may walk in on us. She watches me for a moment, a small smile tugging at the corner of her mouth. "Nice to see you found a shirt for work today."

For a brief moment, humor flashes in her eyes, replacing her uncertainty, and I get a glimpse of the woman I met last night. Eyes a rich chocolate brown. Eyes that hold my gaze, and crinkle at their corners when she smiles. Eyes so bright and beautiful that I can't string a sentence together.

"Anything I can help you with?" I ask, stopping her in her tracks. She must not be used to offers of help. She'll have to get used to it with me. She hands me a stack of papers and tells me to pass them out to each place at the table.

I finish dropping a packet at each seat as she sinks into the chair at the head of the table, readying herself for the meeting. Her eyes grow intense, almost darkening as she reads from her computer screen. She shrugs off her charcoal gray blazer and drapes it over the arm of the chair, exposing the tailored burgundy silk blouse underneath, with a bow tied at the neck. I find myself thinking that the color suits her; the rich red compliments her hair and coloring.

I take a seat close to her and study the notes she handed out; a rundown of the day's show. I try to strike up a conversation with her while we wait for the morning meeting, but she's quiet and withdrawn, nothing like the woman I met last night; gone is the shy smile and look of pride when I complimented her cooking. The only thing that's changed is that we are no longer alone in the conference room; her assistant is nearby, and Mike Fletcher has claimed a seat not far from us. He scrolls through something on his phone, a smirk on his face as he clearly listens in on our conversation.

Every now and then Penelope's gaze shifts to Mike, she is obviously uncomfortable with his close proximity to her. Morgan Donaldson, Penelope's associate producer and editor, enters the room and inserts herself between Penelope and Mike. The change in

Penelope is subtle, but her shoulders sag with relief and the crease between her brows smooths out. She smiles at something Morgan says and I can't tear my eyes away from her.

―――

Penelope Nichols is a study in contradictions. The soft curls of her hair and the whimsy of her bright purple glasses, the burgundy canvas sneakers on her feet that match her blouse, our interaction last night…all led me to believe that she'd be vibrant and outgoing. But you know what they say about judging a book by its cover?

She's quiet and guarded. Even that flash of humor from just a minute ago is gone. The vulnerability from last night locked behind a wall. She seems uneasy, unsure of herself and her place at this table. She shrinks away from Mike Fletcher, her eyes darkening, her confidence slipping away. When Devon and Jim enter the room, it seems to bolster her, she flashes them a smile, and watches as the three of us begin to acquaint ourselves, tossing a smile and raising an eyebrow in my direction.

Jim asks if she caught the game last night. *Which* game? Doesn't matter. When she starts talking about baseball, the air in the room changes. She speaks with authority, with a depth of knowledge on the game and everything that happened overnight, predictions about today's games, and all I can do is sit and marvel at her. I think I could ask her about a game from a week, a year, even a decade ago and she could give me an expert analysis of it.

"Jim," she exclaims, voice laced with exasperation, "if he can't hit his weight, why not send him to Triple A for a while and see what happens? Bring him back when he's ready to play in the big leagues." She's impassioned. There's fire in her eyes. She's laughing and carrying on with Jim and Devon.

Mike is annoyed. He rolls his eyes and a scowl slowly emerges. I can't tell if his annoyance is at Penelope or the fact that he's not being included in the conversation. A few times, it looks like he's going to jump in, but Morgan keeps diverting his attention.

"Jake, what do you think?" Penelope turns to me with a serious look and a sparkle in her eyes. And I have not been paying attention to the conversation. I've been paying attention to *her*. They're talking about someone who isn't hitting and that's all I know, so I say the one thing that comes to my mind:

"Penelope is right."

Her eyebrow lifts and a smirk tugs at her lips as she glances away from me, trying to hide a laugh. Devon leans toward me with a conspiratorial grin, "you didn't hear a word she just said, did you?"

He leaves me no chance to answer. But he's not wrong. I was paying more attention to the way she laughed. The way she spoke with so much authority. And when she turned her attention to me, I froze. Her eyes met mine, and my mind went blank.

I'm in trouble.

———

As soon as everyone is gathered in the conference room, Penelope kicks the meeting off by going over a rundown of the day's show; since I'm new, I don't have much to offer outside of my official introduction and whatever conversation arises with Jim and Devon prior to the night's litany of games.

"Try to keep your intro short, we have a full show today," Penelope tells me, her voice softer than before, the ghost of a smile on her lips as she looks at me over the rims of her glasses. Something in her mood has shifted since our initial meeting; she's in professional mode. She seems... lighter somehow. In her element. And then Mike opens his mouth.

"Penny," Mike interrupts and she flinches, shrinking back in her chair, and she starts to tap out a rhythm on the floor with her foot. It's subtle, but I can see it through the glass top of the conference table. She's on edge. The light in her eyes dims, her smile changes and suddenly her walls go right back up. "This is *Jake Hutchinson*! He can have the whole hour to himself if he wants it. Lay off."

Like storm clouds obscuring the sun, those few words from Mike cause a change in Penelope. The light in her eyes is gone, her lips slip into a tight, inauthentic smile when she looks up from the rundown in her hands. If I hadn't been watching her since the beginning of the meeting, I wouldn't have noticed, but I have been and I did. She's magnetic, I'm drawn to her in a way I can't explain. She lights up a room until someone has the nerve to dim her light. She had a commanding presence and was running the meeting just fine until Mike jumped in and shut her down.

If there's one thing I've learned from my sister Jenna, it's that women in male dominated spaces are often defensive. Jenna is a brilliant scientist and researcher, she teaches, she mentors, she's published in all kinds of magazines and journals, and yet I know from her texts to the siblings' group chat lamenting her interactions with men in academia that she still doesn't get the respect that she deserves. I'm not about to be one of *those* guys for Penelope. I don't want to step on her toes, but I also won't just sit by and watch as someone steamrolls her.

"I can do a thirty second intro if you need me to..." Penelope's eyes meet mine and the ghost of a smile plays across her lips. She nods and jots something down on her notepad. I notice a tremor in her hands, and a quiver in voice when she speaks again.

"The show is pretty well locked down unless something comes up in the afternoon games today," she doesn't address Mike directly, but rather the room as a whole. The edge in her voice is clearly meant for the man sitting closest to her. "Jake, I've already allotted you time until the first commercial for your introduction."

"That's great. Thanks, Penelope."

Mike scoffs and leans forward into her space, throwing an arm across her shoulders, his hand slipping dangerously south of Penelope's collarbone. Something like anger twists in my gut when Penelope's eyes widen in shock and she very pointedly shrugs Mike's hand away. I glance around the room to see if anyone else noticed. If they have, they aren't saying anything.

"Mike, ever hear of personal space?" I ask, trying my best to keep my tone light. Penelope's gaze meets mine, her eyes wide as saucers, a blush creeping into her cheeks. Mike, narrows his eyes at me and makes a show of scooting his chair away from Penelope. But he's clearly not happy about it.

The rest of the meeting is uneventful. Penelope gives us notes from last Friday's show, a rundown of the games that will be taking place today and the news that broke between Friday's show and now. She then opens the floor to Devon and Jim, in case there is anything that they'd like to add to the show tonight. I'm given the opportunity as well, but would be more comfortable getting a show or two under my belt first. At least, that was the plan.

"What about you, Hutchinson?" Mike's voice fills the small room. "Any ideas for tonight's show? Penny would be happy to accommodate you."

I really don't like the way he looks at her. The way he speaks to her, what he says about her. I remember the day he hired me, when he took me around the offices and stopped in front of her door. He downplayed her importance to the staff, *that's Penny, she's just a producer. You don't need to meet her. But if you see her later...* He was so focused that day on her appearance rather than what she contributes to the show.

I was intrigued by her, even from that fleeting moment. She was working hard at something on her computer, bare toes curled into the rug beneath her feet, a pen sticking out of the hair piled on top of her head. I wanted to know more, but Mike hurried me right away from her door.

I know now why I didn't recognize her the night she showed up at my door. Here in the office, she's guarded, even her appearance is more severe and armor-like than she was that night. The only thing recognizable was her glasses. She adjourns the meeting and slips past me, pausing for just a moment.

"Thank you," she whispers. "But I can fight my own battles."

Yep. Should have seen that coming.

4
INVASIVE SPECIES
JAKE

After tonight's show, I climb in my car and make my way out of the city. I have an hour or so drive to James's place, which means I have plenty of time for my mind to overthink every mistake I made today. The show was fine, it was a dream come true to work alongside Jim McCann and Devon Wilson, but I can't figure Penelope out.

I can't think about that tonight. Tonight, I'm having dinner with my siblings to celebrate my first day on the show. My sister Jenna came down from Ithaca, Jax left his daughters with our parents and drove down from Saratoga, and we're meeting at James' house in Newburgh.

After a stop at the Thai restaurant in town to pick up the order Jax phoned in, I find myself sitting in the driveway, staring at the house -- the house that the four of us own together, though my name is technically the one on the deed. James had, *has*, grand plans of fixing this place up and flipping it. So far, he's done an incredible job restoring the outside of the house and updating the inside. The only problem is the kitchen.

His kitchen and dining room are gutted. James claims that he's "not inspired" and can't figure out how to finish those rooms. So tonight, we humor him, sitting on the couches and floor and eating straight from the takeout containers that I deliver right to the coffee table.

"How are things going with the producer," Jax asks before shoving a forkful of noodles in his mouth. I may have texted the family that the neighbor who fed me is my producer.

"I honestly have no idea," I answer, reaching for a spring roll. "I can't figure her out. It's frustrating, you know? When we're outside the office, she's...different. She's warm and funny and easy to talk to. In the office she's a different person. She's guarded and cold. When I stood up for her in a meeting she basically said...thanks but no thanks."

I'm met with a collective groan from my brothers and a *very* pointed look from my sister.

"Tell me exactly what happened in that interaction," James says. "I need to know where you screwed up."

I can't believe he's assuming that *I* am the one at fault in that circumstance. I start at the beginning -- officially meeting her on my first day, the conversation before the start of the meeting, her obvious discomfort, and my comment about personal space...and this is where things apparently went off the rails.

"And on the way out she said, 'thanks...but I can fight my own battles.'"

Our sister Jenna, who I thought wasn't paying attention, hangs her head before slapping me across the back of mine. She's ticked. James is shaking his head at me and Jax just sits there, staring.

"Dude." James intones. "You can't do that."

"He's right," Jax points his spring roll at James, and annoyingly offers no other explanation.

"Someone explain to me why." I am truly at a loss for why I shouldn't have stepped in that day, and why that should be affecting our working relationship now.

"Because," Jenna says on the sigh of a long suffering sister and a woman who has dealt with similar situations, "you made her look weak. In that moment, you took away her power. Her voice. You made it appear that she can't stick up for herself, and the man abusing his power in that situation will do it again. And he'll likely do it when you aren't around to say anything about it. So you not only took away her power in that situation, but made her more vulnerable in the future."

Crap.

She's right. And I don't need to ask to know that she is speaking from experience.

"So. What should I do?"

"Right now, you're an invasive species," Jenna says, pushing her glasses up her nose. James and Jax give her the same blank-faced stare I do.

"Explain," James asks for the three of us.

"He's an invasive species. An invasive species that has disrupted her ecosystem - the office, and the power dynamic therein. She may feel threatened by you. What you viewed as helpful, she saw as an attempt to disrupt the balance."

I love my sister. I really do. I don't always love that she's the smartest of the four of us. She has her doctorate in environmental science, and spends her time teaching and researching at a nearby university. She's brilliant. Most of the time at our expense.

"Hold on, I'm not trying to throw things out of balance!" Am I a little indignant? A bit offended? Yeah. I'm at ASN because I was asked to co-host *On the Field*, not because I want to disrupt an ecosystem. "And don't invasive species get destroyed?"

"Only if they can't adapt." Jenna takes off the top bundle of papers of the stack and moves it to a pile on the floor before starting on the next one. The three of us stare at her blankly...again. "Oh for the love...do I need to spell this out for you?"

"Yes," the three of us answer in exasperated unison.

"Prove to her that you can adapt. That you belong within the office ecosystem. You're not there to destroy her. Adapt. Adjust. If she's cold, warm her up. If she's thorny, wear gloves."

"Or," James looks at me with a glint in his eye and a waggle of his brows, "maybe she just needs to...get biological."

Jax whacks James across the back of the head, Jenna throws a spring roll at him, and I glare at him. That's not the approach I've ever taken with women, and she deserves better than some kind of fling. It's James, and I can tell that he's joking, but something about it sets my blood boiling. His comment reminds me too much of Mike Fletcher and all the things I know about him.

"She's better than that," my voice is steely and cold, an angry whisper. "She *deserves* better than that. Did you not hear a word that I just said?"

James grins, that gleam in his eye is downright sparkling now, and I'd like nothing more than to wipe the grin off his face. "So, you like her."

It's not a question. No. He says it as a statement of fact. *You like her.* As if this is obvious. He shares a glance with Jax and Jenna who have equally smug looks on their faces. I can't deny it, there is an attraction there but she's kind of my boss.

"No. I don't. She's my neighbor. And my producer. And sure, she cooks better than anyone I know - don't you dare tell mom I said that - but that can only take you so far. I don't like her..." I'm not convincing them. I'm not even convincing *myself.*

"Sure, sure." They all look so smug. It's obnoxious.

I thump my head on the edge of the coffee table, "I think you're right."

"We know he's right," I look up to find Jenna setting aside the papers she's been grading and removing her glasses to look intently at me. "Now the question is: what are you going to do about it?"

I groan and drop my head to the coffee table again. I don't know what I'm going to do. But tomorrow starts my new approach to Penelope: convince her I'm not an invasive species bent on destroying her ecosystem.

5
THE FILE
PENELOPE

What a week.

Jake is a natural in front of the camera and has already developed a great rapport with Devon and Jim. While Jake and I got off to a bit of a rocky start, he's more than made up for it by not screwing up my show. His introduction was fantastic, he endeared himself to our audience when he admitted to being star struck by his co-hosts. One look at our social media feeds tells me that hiring him was a fantastic choice.

"Penny!" Mike bellows across the office bullpen, the poor editors and writers between us are so used to his volume that not a single one flinches or breaks their concentration. Too bad I can't kick Mike in the shins until he stops calling me "Lucky Penny". Not that I think it would make much difference. He doesn't take no for an answer. Ever.

"Ease up on the new guy next week," Mike laughs as he crosses the floor toward me.

Like a lioness catching the scent of her prey, Morgan turns away from the kitchen where she was chatting with one of our staff writers, and makes a beeline toward my door.

"Sorry Mike! Urgent business with Penelope. We need to discuss tomorrow's show." Morgan all but shoves Mike out of her way before ushering me into my office and shutting the door. "You okay?"

"Nope." I know I can be honest with her. I know that she saw what happened in the production meeting and she stood by my side through the entire broadcast. Morgan is the only person outside of my family who knows my history with Mike Fletcher. She knows what his gaze, his voice, and his touch do to me. She knows that he has no boundaries where I'm concerned. No one else in the office knows, or if they do, they turn a blind eye. "But as long as you're the only one who knows that, I *will* be okay."

After a few minutes, Morgan heads back to her desk and Mike darkens my door again. If he comes inside, we'll have a problem. He doesn't always, not when people are around anyway.

"Let him do his job…and I'll let you keep doing yours."

I watch Mike stalk back to his office, wishing I could say something, wishing I could stand up for myself, talk back to him the way I would to any other person who dared threaten me in my own office. But I can't. He still has this shadowy control over me. He still turns me into a ball of nerves whenever I'm around him. He acts as though he's won some twisted, unspoken game between us, that he can wield some kind of power over me.

The feeling of my fingernails digging into the palm of my hand snaps me out of my distant memory. I flex my fingers, opening my hands wide, over and over again in an attempt to calm myself.

I need to get out of here.

"Morgan?" I call into the outer office area.

"What's up, Nell?" Her eyebrows furrow in concern. "Are you ready to go?"

Bless her.

Most nights, Mo sticks around with me, waiting to walk me home. She knows that I don't like being alone later in the evening, certainly not when most everyone else from our floor has cleared out after the show. Mo and I have been friends since college and one of the draws of hiring into ASN was getting to work with my best friend. She knows me better than anyone who isn't family. And knows how to talk me through my anxiety attacks when I need the help.

I look across the way and see the lights on in Mike's office, his shadowy form visible through the drawn shades on his windows. The movement behind the shades sends a shiver down my spine. Because of my complicated history, working for him is not the easiest thing in the world, and while I've always had anxiety issues, spending prolonged periods of time with the man who causes them makes my life a nightmare.

That's why having Morgan around has been a literal lifesaver for me.

"Yeah, let's get out of here."

We walk a few short blocks to our buildings, across the street from each other, and part ways with a hug on the sidewalk before splitting up and heading home. I grab my mail and skim through it while I wait for the elevator; a postcard from an old college friend, a late birthday card from Peter and Sofi, and a cooking magazine. I shove the cards and letters down into my bag and open the magazine to peruse on my way to my floor, making note of all the recipes that I want to try soon.

I step into my cozy home, dropping my work bag by the door, kicking off my shoes, and turning on some music. In the kitchen I start grabbing things from the fridge and pantry. Tonight, I'm working out my aggression while I cook. I couldn't decide what I wanted this morning, but now I want to pound something. Chicken Milanese is just the thing.

I start by pounding out chicken breasts until they are roughly a quarter inch thick. After today, it feels good to hit something. Repeatedly. And with a lot of force. Except that I pound so much I tear one of the chicken breasts. Oh well. They're all getting cooked anyway.

Once the chicken is pounded flat, I set up my breading station with flour, eggs, and seasoned breadcrumbs. I dredge and bread my chicken and then shallow fry it until it is golden brown and crispy. The smell of fried chicken mingles with the city smell drifting in from my open balcony door. When the chicken is cool enough to touch, I start to plate.

I lay a chicken cutlet on the plate and top it with an arugula salad. Salad is a generous word for what it really is: baby arugula tossed with olive oil, balsamic vinegar, salt, and fresh ground pepper. I have so much left over, that I decide to share with Jake. Why not?

Grabbing a plate from the cabinet, I begin to arrange the chicken and salad the same way I did for myself, but on his plate I add a second piece of chicken. The guy was a baseball player, and I'm not blind. He's built. I'm sure he'll eat everything I give him.

I step across the hall and knock on his door. He left before I did tonight, so I assume he's home. But that doesn't stop my surprise when he opens the door. He stands in front of me, still in his dress shirt and slacks, sleeves unbuttoned and rolled to his elbows. *Oh boy. Those arms.* Toned and tanned and lightly dusted with dark hair. All corded muscle and strength. *Don't let the arms distract you!*

"I got a little carried away and made too much food. If you've eaten already, I'll box it up, but if you'd like to come in and eat with me that would be fine." *Fine? Really Nell? You couldn't come up with anything better than fine?*

"Thanks," he steps into the hallway, closing his door and following me into my own apartment. "I haven't eaten yet. I was going to order out. But...this is even better."

I don't usually know what to do with compliments so, I let that go. Jake sits down and I hand him the already prepared plate and some silverware. Pouring two glasses of iced tea and grabbing napkins, I watch Jake waiting patiently for me to join him. He looks like that and has good manners too? That's a lethal combination.

"I wanted to congratulate you. You've done a pretty okay job," I glance up and see a lopsided smile tugging at one side of his mouth.

"Thank you, I think." We share a laugh and a pang of loneliness settles in my chest. I've missed having people to cook for, to laugh with, to just...be around. I have Morgan nearby but I always feel like the single third wheel when I'm with her and Dan. But this, right here with Jake, this is nice. He's easy to talk to, easy to laugh with. I can be myself around him without fear of being too loud or too brash. He lets me be me.

As we eat, a video call comes in from Peter and Sofi, and Jake insists that I take the call while he steps into my kitchen and starts washing my dishes, which...is unexpected.

"Great show tonight, Nellie!" This earns me a sideways glance from Jake. Peter smiles and suddenly the stress and tension in my shoulders releases. Peter has dad's eyes. When he looks at me like that, with so much pride beaming from his face, I have to choke back my tears. "The new guy was good, too! Took him a bit to get into the swing of things, but he seems like a good fit for the show."

Jake silently fist pumps and it's all I can do to stifle a laugh at the sight. Peter's right, he is a great fit for the show. Everyone on set loved him. Everyone has *always* loved him, from his first pitch to his last. Mike – though it pains me to admit it – was right when he hired Jake to co-host the show. He's charming, handsome, and fits right into the dynamic that Jim and Devon had already established.

"Yeah...he's doing a great job," I concede. "Turns out, he's my new neighbor. He's actually here right now...I invited him over for dinner tonight."

I'm met with blank stares and total silence. Sofi gives Peter a look and Peter's face splits into a grin as I turn the camera toward Jake -- Jake, with a dish towel slung over his shoulder and arms elbow deep in sudsy water. He waves with one soap covered hand and thanks Peter for the compliment.

After a few minutes, Sofi interrupts and sends Peter into the other room, unfortunately I don't have that kind of luxury in my studio apartment, so I step out onto my balcony. She asks me about the stuff that no one sees on television; about my day and the meetings I ran, and whether or not we're adding anything to the Mike File today. I know that I can be honest with her. So I tell her about the morning meeting and Mike's wandering hands. I tell her about our encounter at the end of the day, too.

"Penelope...what if you walked away?"

I have that thought at least once a week.

I *could* walk away. I've wanted to a few times. But this show is my dream. I should be able to put up with seeing Mike for a few hours a day in order to fulfill my dream, right? Maybe I've overblown all of our encounters in my head. Maybe things aren't as bad as they appear. I can put up with nicknames and rude comments in meetings right? Or the way he tries to insert himself in my work, little things he does to try and control the show.

The only people who know those details are my siblings and Mike. He made me sign an NDA when I was hired, and the thing is, I didn't think anything of it. And it makes me wonder how many more women in our office experience similar things.

"I can't Sof. I don't want to walk away. This show is my dream job. I can put up with him for a few hours a day if it means putting *On the Field* out into the world.

"But you shouldn't *have* to put up with it, Nell," her smile softens as she watches me through the screen. Then, her courtroom intensity returns. "Anytime you want to break that contract, you let me know. We'll take him on."

Sofi always knows how to break my moods. We laugh and I can feel the clouds lifting in my head. I stay on with her a few minutes longer, and when we disconnect, the silence in my apartment is overwhelming. Even with the sounds of the city floating in through the open balcony door.

A part of me longs for connection with people I care about. Someone who will let me nurture and take care of them. But I'm afraid to get too close. My grief over mom and dad nearly severed the relationship I had with my brother, we are still healing from that. As much as I hate the silence and loneliness, I'm afraid to get close to someone, only to end up hurting them.

I turn and lean against the railing, my gaze traveling inside my apartment to the man doing my dishes. The man who reminds me so much of some of the darkest days of my life, but who was willing to speak up for me this week – even if I couldn't appreciate it at the time. A man who after knowing me for barely a week took me up on the offer to join me for dinner.

Jake looks up from the sink, as if he can sense me watching him, his eyes meeting mine. It's like the universe dropped him right in my lap...or, right across the hall.

A friend.

An ally.

I'm determined not to screw this up.

6

A COMMON BOND

JAKE

That was entirely unexpected.

When Penelope knocked on my door tonight, I never would have imagined I'd get a dinner invitation out of it. Or that the company would end up being so good. She was quiet, sure, but she wasn't nearly as guarded as she is in the office. I still get the sense that she's nervous when I'm around, but tonight was a step in the right direction. I think I managed to show her tonight that I'm not an invasive species. Jenna would be proud.

And the food was fantastic. Not that I'm surprised.

What I am surprised by is the conversation with her sister in law. She took the end of the call out on her balcony, but it's not like the door or walls are soundproof.

What if you walked away?

If she walked away there would be other Mike's. Other men who didn't respect or take her seriously. And if she walked away she wouldn't be working on her dream show.

This show is my dream, Sof.

There was so much sadness in her voice, I could hear it even through the glass of the sliding door. I finished up the dishes and pretended like I couldn't hear the end of her conversation and when she walked back inside, she took the towel from me and thanked me for the company and the help with her dishes. I insisted that it was the very least I could do to thank her for the food.

"I like to feed people. Consider this an open invitation to dinner any time I'm home."

"You really mean that, don't you?" I ask, making my way toward the door. Her brow furrows as she watches me.

"Yes," she replies, rather emphatically, "I really do. I would do it for any neighbor."

I believe she really would do this for any neighbor that knocked on her door. She strikes me as a nurturer. The kind of person who will go out of their way to take care of strangers and neighbors and friends.

"Speaking of neighbors," a blush creeps into her cheeks and she pauses, as if debating how best to continue. "Can I ask…how did you end up in this building? It's not exactly…"

"Luxury?"

"Yeah," she chuckles.

"It's close to the office. And to be honest, I'm on my own. I don't know what I'd do with a bigger space. It would just be more for me to clean."

Penelope furrows her brow, head tilting to the side as if she wants to ask me another question but decides not to. I wish I knew what was going on inside her head, but for tonight I let it go.

―――

In the silence of my apartment, I settle in to watch some baseball, take notes for tomorrow and call my folks, and then do my best not to think of Penelope as I fall asleep. I try not to think about seeing her at work tomorrow, being near her. I close my eyes and don't think about the silky, mahogany curls that skim her shoulders, or the way her blouse hugged her curves. Or the rosy blush of her cheeks when she stood at my door and invited me to dinner.

Or the look on her face as she watched me from the balcony after ending the call with her family. I think I've finally found a friend here in the city, in the most unexpected place.

When I played ball, I had a team full of guys to hang out with. Our days were spent in training, then we'd play, we'd go out to eat, we'd travel. I spent every waking minute of the season surrounded by teammates. As a single man, there wasn't much else to keep me occupied. I trained. I ran. I'd read a book every now and then.

After I was injured and began recovering from my first surgery, I spent more time with my brothers than I had during the entire five years I was in the league. I moved home with my parents, and had my brothers nearby. After my second surgery, James and Jax were working full time but Jenna was back home. She kept me company. She kept me from despairing over my circumstances. And then I moved back to the city to do the show and left my family behind. The teammates I'd had before have mostly all moved on to other teams or left the league entirely.

I was alone again.

And then I met Penelope, an invitation to dinner turned into a standing invitation to dine with her each night after the show. I have to come up with a way to repay Penelope's kindness. I can't cook, so cooking dinner for her is *way* out of the question. But there must be something I can do. I wrack my brain to come up with ideas to do something for Penelope, something to repay her for nearly a week's worth of meals plus whatever meal I join her for in the future...which isn't even a question.

Just as I'm getting ready to crawl into bed, my phone chimes with an incoming text—it's from Penelope to the group of hosts. She's talking about one of the games that's in progress. I turn it on to see what she's talking about.

I'm watching. I type and send the message, and soon three little dots appear. Someone is replying.

If you just turned it on, you missed the play of the game. I've never seen anything like it. And I've seen a lot of baseball in my lifetime.

I have a couple of options here. I could look up the play and watch it for myself, or…I could walk across the hall, knock on the door, and see if she can run the play back. It's a terrible idea, but so was writing that note and look at how that turned out. I throw on a shirt, though after our first meeting, I'm sure it isn't necessary, and head across the hall.

I knock and after a bit, I hear the bolt disengage and a chain slide away. The door opens to Penelope in pajamas, hair piled on top of her head like that first night we met. She looks surprised at first, but then opens the door a bit wider and ushers me inside. I sit down on the couch and she sits cross legged on the floor in front of me, grabbing the remote nearby and running the stream back to the play that brought me here in the first place.

She was right, it's wild. I've never seen a play like this before; it's a comedy of errors—cutoff men are missed, the ball is thrown over the head of an infielder then thrown back into the outfield. Errors, wild pitches, and missteps galore. Penelope pauses the stream and then turns around to face me, still seated on the floor.

"So?" she watches me expectantly.

"We absolutely have to talk about that tomorrow. Between the three of us, in our combined years in the game, I'm sure nothing like this has been seen before."

"Right?! And all he had to do was tag the bag for goodness' sake!"

I love it when she gets excited about baseball. It reminds me of my nieces and their unbridled enthusiasm for…everything. There's a sparkle in her eyes and her smile is so genuine, so wide that it crinkles the corners of her eyes, and reveals a hidden dimple that I've never seen before. She resumes the game and leans back against the couch, seeming to settle in for the rest of the night. She turns to me, almost startled to see me still on her couch, "you can stay and watch the rest if you'd like. Baseball is more fun when it's shared."

She's right about that. It is more fun when it's shared.

"How do you feel about popcorn?" She asks during a commercial. I love popcorn, and when I tell her as much, she steps into the kitchen and starts popping some on the stove and before long we're both on the floor in front of the couch, a bowl of popcorn between us as we watch the end of the ball game.

When the game is over, I stand and make my way toward the door, unsure of what to say but knowing I don't want to leave. I turn to Penelope just before reaching for the door, "any time you want to watch a game, feel free to knock on my door."

"I will," she smiles, and the slightest hint of a blush creeps into her cheeks. "Goodnight, Jake."

"Goodnight, Penelope." I head back across the hall and crawl into bed, where I fall asleep dreaming about baseball and popcorn and curly haired producers with enticingly pink cheeks, who drive me all kinds of crazy.

7
THE POWER OF PASTRY
JAKE

I wake early, hoping to get to the office before Penelope for once. I stop at a bakery near the office and pick up two croissants and two coffees. No one I know can resist a chocolate filled pastry. Except for my sister. But she's a self-described scientific anomaly. Penelope's office is dark when I arrive, her door slightly ajar. Morgan stops me on my way toward the door and asks what I'm up to. I wordlessly raise the pastry box, and with a sly smile Morgan waves me forward, allowing me to leave it on Penelope's desk. I duck out quickly, with a word of thanks to Morgan and head to my office.

I see Penelope walk into her office and sit at her desk. The bakery box sits in front of her and her brow wrinkles in confusion, her glasses slipping down her nose. When she opens the little box in front of her, I see her face transform from confusion to absolute joy. She picks up the croissant and takes a bite, closing her eyes and enjoying the flaky pastry and rich dark chocolate filling.

No one can resist a chocolate filled pastry.

On our way to the production meeting, she falls into step beside me, coffee in hand along with her usual stack of electronics, papers, and notebook.

"Thanks for the croissant," she sounds unsure of herself but continues on. "Those are my favorite. And thank you for the company last night, I haven't had anyone to watch games with in... too long."

There's a sadness in her voice that I can't quite name. She's looking at me, but it feels like she's looking through me, like there's something in the room that she can't quite see. She's...far away. She shakes herself out of it as if it never happened and then we're on our way into the production meeting.

My mind wanders during the meeting. I find myself thinking about popcorn and late night baseball games. Of sharing coffee and pastries together, maybe spending a weekend exploring the city together...

"Jake," Penelope's voice slices through my daydream. "Did you hear me?"

Her face betrays no emotion, but her tone of voice says: *hey moron, get your head in the game.*

"Sorry," I swallow back a snarky retort and meet her hardened gaze. Those gorgeous brown eyes of hers bore into me and I find myself getting lost in their deep golden brown. "I spaced out for a minute."

"No problem," she says, shuffling her notes around on the table in front of her before shooting me a sly smile. "You must have been up late watching that crazy game."

If I'm not mistaken, I think Penelope might be flirting with me. And I won't lie, I kind of hope she is.

"I was. It sure was something." We share a laugh and I notice James and Devon eyeing us, and Penelope must see it too because she quickly gets back to the topic at hand.

"I asked if you'd be willing to talk about your experience with Tommy John surgery, considering we're opening the show tonight talking about the reigning Cy Young winner being out for the rest of the year with an elbow injury requiring the surgery."

Crap.

It's not that I don't want to talk about my experiences. I will, if I don't have a choice. But talking about the end of my career? To an audience who thinks they know everything there is to know about it? No thank you.

"What am I supposed to say? I heard the sound of a rubber band snapping and felt like I'd been shot in the elbow? That I was so disoriented from falling to the mound that I could barely stand under my own power? Or that in my first rehab start my command was totally gone and it felt like my arm was put back together the wrong way? How about the night I punched a locker in the clubhouse because I got pulled from my last start in the third inning? Though, at the time, I didn't realize it was my last start."

Penelope scribbles something on her notepad, pain etched in the lines of her face. I scrub a hand across the back of my neck as Jim claps me on the shoulder, and Devon shoots me a small, pitying smile. That was an inappropriate, and entirely out of character response. I shouldn't have snapped. But I don't willingly discuss the end of my pitching career. It's too painful. It signaled the end of everything for me. I lost my passion, my livelihood, my life's purpose all in one fell swoop...and she wants to exploit that. For what? A *unique perspective*.

She looks wounded, and I can't say I blame her. I shouldn't have lashed out at her. But there's something else in her gaze too. Something more.

There's sadness.

Pity.

I don't need that from her.

"I'm sorry..."

"I didn't mean..."

I shake my head and motion for her to continue.

"I'm sorry," she continues to write something in her notes before looking up and meeting my gaze, the usual coffee brown of her eyes has turned stormy and dark. "That was my mistake. I wasn't thinking about it like that; I was only thinking about the perspective you could bring to the conversation. You don't have to discuss it if you're not comfortable with it."

"I didn't mean to snap at you like that. It's still a pretty raw subject for me. It's not the easiest thing to lose everything so suddenly...and then have to talk about it."

Something shifts in her gaze as tears glisten at the corners of her eyes. "I know a thing or two about *losing everything*."

She shuts her notebook with a sharp *thwack* before standing and breezing out of her office and down the hall. I can't say I didn't deserve that reaction, because I did. My sharp words deserved an even sharper reaction than that, but there were tears glimmering in her eyes when she stood and left. I've seen a lot of things in my time at this network. I've seen worse interactions than that between her and Mike and never once has she left in tears because of *him*. But me? I've made a mess of things. I look to Jim and Devon who seem to be having a silent conversation of their own. Devon eventually leans forward, hands clasped together, elbows on his knees.

"She lost both her parents, Jake. Within a month or so of each other."

"So when I said 'I lost everything'..."

Devon shakes his head. "It's not your fault, Jake. You couldn't have known."

I run a frustrated hand through my hair before standing to follow after her. Which isn't easy to do with both feet in my mouth. I find her in the control room, bent over a computer screen, watching a highlight reel for tonight's show over Morgan's shoulder. She stops the reel and makes some notes, pointing out something to Morgan and they collaborate to tweak the editing a bit. She stands tall when I enter the room, regarding me with a quirked brow and a hand on her hip. Morgan glances between us before grabbing her empty coffee cup and mumbling something about needing a refill as she scoots out the door.

"I spoke out of turn back there."

"Don't worry about it," her voice is thick with emotion as she pulls out the chair Morgan just vacated and sits down, restarting the highlight reel for tonight from the beginning.

"See, the thing is, I think I said something that bothered you. And I *am* worried about that."

She pulls out the chair beside her and points to it. "You wanna talk? Talk. But I have work to do."

"When I said I *lost everything*, I don't mean *everything*. I lost my dreams and my career. But I recognize that others have lost much more than me, and I don't ever want to act as though my pain compares to that."

She pauses the video and turns to me, head tipped to the side as she watches me, conflicting emotions in her eyes and face, a sad smile tugging at the corner of her mouth.

"Pain isn't a competition, Jake. Your loss is still loss. *My loss* is still loss. We grieve, we walk through the pain, and then we heal and move forward. If you stub your toe and I have a migraine, my pain doesn't negate yours. I'm not going to tell you that your grief is insignificant because our experiences are different."

"Devon told me…about your parents."

"I figured one of them did," she shakes her head and gives me a lopsided smile, "but I also have a feeling you'd be in here even if they hadn't."

"You've got me there."

"We're fine, Jake. Don't worry about me."

That's the thing, I have a feeling I won't be able to stop worrying about her now. I nod, though I'm sure she misses it as she turns back to the screen in front of her. I stand and head back to my office; I have just enough time between now and the pre-production meeting to figure a few things out.

The show tonight is even better than last night's. I can tell by the smile on Penelope's face as she approaches the desk after the cameras are done rolling. I unhook myself from my mic and for just a moment Penelope smiles at me. "Good show tonight, Jake."

I'll take it.

I head back to my office and get ready to go home for the night. I pass Penelope's office on my way to the elevator and knock softly on her door. She looks up, pushing her glasses up the bridge of her nose, brow furrowing when she sees me standing there.

"What can I do for you?" She asks. Her voice has a hard edge to it and she watches me with a bit of wariness in her gaze.

"Nothing, I just wanted to say goodnight before heading out…and see if maybe you wanted to walk home together."

"Oh," a look of surprise flashes across her features for just a moment. "Sure. Give me just a minute to finish this. You can sit if you'd like."

She gives me the opening and I take it.

Stepping into her office, I sit down across from her and watch as she bends her head down again, getting back to work on whatever is in front of her. She switches between the notes on her desk and something on her tablet screen, a baseball game on the television across from her that she doesn't pay attention to. A crease forms between her eyebrows as she pinches something on her tablet screen, shutting her tablet with a sharp hand.

"Have dinner with me tonight," I say, as she rises from her desk and starts to pack her bag, frustration clear on her face. She glances at me, her brow wrinkled as she stops what she was doing. "I can't cook, but I order some mean take out."

This makes her laugh. And it's a beautiful sound.

"You don't have to do that Jake." She sounds tired. And I can't say I blame her. She always seems to be working. Even on the nights I eat dinner with her, she's taking notes for the show, typing furiously into her tablet. She deserves a night off from everything else.

"Please. You've been feeding me all week. Let me do this for you. What's your favorite food to order out?"

She doesn't hesitate. "Cheeseburger and french fries. Extra

crispy. Olives on the burger." I like a woman who knows what she wants. File that one under: today I learned something new about Penelope Nichols. I hold out my hand for her bag, and when she protests, I gently take it from her and sling it over my own shoulder as we walk to the elevators.

"I'm sorry again for what I said today. I feel like a Class A Jerk."

"I appreciate that. Not that you felt like a jerk, in fact I'm sorry if I made you feel that way."

"You didn't. Thank you though, for trusting me with that small piece of your story. I hope someday I'm deserving of more of it."

I keep walking, but Penelope remains behind, a stunned look on her face. I turn and watch as she shakes her head, almost imperceptibly and joins me in the waiting elevator.

I place our order as we walk toward our building. Penelope starts to veer off toward Riverside Park and we pass through the gardens on our way home. She stops every now and then to admire the flowers and I follow along, observing. Maybe making a mental note or two about which flowers she pays the most attention to.

By the time we make it to the building, our food arrives, delivered by a young woman on a bike who knows me by name because I'm a frequent food order-er. Or, I was until Penelope came along.

"Good to see you again, Mr. Hutchinson," she says. "I was starting to worry something was wrong when you stopped ordering."

Heat floods my cheeks as the girl rides away, and I glance over to Penelope trying - but not trying hard enough - to keep from laughing out loud.

"Shut up," I mutter as I open the door and hold it for her.

"I didn't say a word," laughing, she holds her hands up in surrender. She doesn't have to say a word as long as she keeps laughing like that.

———

We eat in my apartment tonight. I find a movie on television instead of a ball game and for the first time, we talk about things other than work. She tells me a little bit more about her parents and her brother. I tell her about my siblings and nieces. It's companionable and fun. The most fun I've had in a very long time. She smiles when I ask if I can walk her home.

"Don't forget, we have a breakfast meeting on Monday," Penelope stops just before her door, "everyone usually brings something...and I usually bring too much, so don't feel like you need to cook. You're still new."

In other words, you order takeout and pour cereal...don't try to cook.

I know a challenge when I hear one. When I return to my apartment, I pull up a recipe mom sent back when there was still hope for me, and pray that my hopeless kitchen skills improve over the weekend.

8

A BARGAIN

JAKE

Monday morning comes early. Penelope has called the hosts in for a breakfast meeting today, some kind of pitch meeting before she meets with the big guys upstairs at the end of the month. We have an hour or so to discuss and pitch stories for the month of June. This is my first pitch meeting; it's more laid back than I thought it would be. Just the four of us bouncing ideas around and collaborating with each other.

Everyone contributes to the breakfast offerings; Devon and Jim brought food their wives made, Penelope made some kind of breakfast casserole with potatoes and sausage, and basically all the things that breakfast dreams are made of. And I tried my hand at baking last night.

Years ago, mom sent me a recipe that she told me was "idiot proof", so we'll see. It came out of the pan, so I'm off to a good start. Until Penelope slices off a piece. It's…completely raw in the middle. The bread is oozing. Devon and Jim do their best to contain their laughter, and Penelope, being the woman that she is, picks off as much baked bread as she can and pops it in her mouth.

She barely chokes it down.

"You do not have to eat that." I am apparently the idiot that is the exception to mom's recipe. This bread is awful. I break off a piece that is mostly baked and...clearly something went horribly wrong. It's somehow both burnt on the outside and raw on the inside. And it tastes like a saltlick.

This is why I don't cook. This is why mom doesn't give me recipes. This is why dad kicks me out of the kitchen at every family gathering.

"Penelope, seriously. Don't eat it."

"No, it's," she chews for a minute. I haven't seen her swallow yet, which means I have time to convince her to spit it out. Too late. She swallows it. And looks pained. "It's...different."

Terrible.

"The parts that were baked had good texture..."

Burnt.

"And I could tell that it was supposed to be lemon bread..."

Banana. It was supposed to be banana bread.

Without a word, I pick up the plate that I brought it in on, carry it out of the conference room and scrape the whole loaf into the kitchen trash can. Penelope, one of the best cooks I know, thought my banana bread was *lemon* bread. That's the last time I try to impress anyone with my cooking skills.

I return to the conference room to find Penelope and the team waiting for me. I put the empty plate on the table and Jim claps me on the back, shaking his head with a pitying smile. Penelope pushes her plate away and graciously starts the meeting.

We talk about the games coming up this week, the season ahead, and our plans as things progress from this point. Jim and Devon both throw out some ideas and near the end of the meeting an awkward silence fills the room as they begin a conversation consisting of head tilts and quirked eyebrows.

"Penelope," Jim hedges, his face softening while one glance at hers tells me she knows what's coming. "What about the show you've been working on?"

"No. It's not ready yet. I still have some fine-tuning to do."

Jim and Devon share a glance, and I'm suddenly on the outside looking in on a conversation that they've had several times. Penelope glances down at the notes in front of her and my curiosity takes over.

"What show?" I ask, innocently enough. Devon gives me a look that says it's your funeral and Penelope shoots her eyes up to meet mine.

"Nothing. It's...nothing." She ducks her head and scribbles something on the notepad in front of her.

Jim reaches out a hand and places it on her shoulder, her gaze meeting his and her shoulders sagging just a little bit. "Penelope, you say that every month. You've been saying that every month since you started here," he chastises her, not unkindly.

"I know," her voice is tight, barely above a whisper. "It's been shot down before, Jim."

"What's it about?" I ask, meeting her gaze. She looks at me for a long, tense moment. I can only hope that over the past few weeks I've earned enough of her trust that she'll answer me. And when she does, I'm immediately on board and willing to do whatever I can to make sure her show gets on the air.

Penelope explains that she's writing a show about women and their involvement in baseball -- coaches, front office staff, executives, and media members -- and we are on board immediately. Jim even offers to let Penelope host the segment. She balks at the idea, but after a lot of persuasion from the three of us, she eventually tells us she'll think about finally pitching it to the network.

After the broadcast tonight, on my way toward the elevator, I stop at Penelope's door. I gently knock and she looks up from her computer screen, offering me a small smile. "For what it's worth...I loved your idea. I think you should try to pitch it again."

"Really?" She looks surprised, her smile grows. "Do you think..." she stops. Measuring her words, gathering her thoughts. She pushes her glasses up her nose and sits back to look at me.

"Do you think you might be willing to look over what I have so far?"

"Sure. If you'll help me with something in return."

She looks skeptical. And honestly, I don't blame her.

"Okay...?"

"Do you think you could teach me to cook?"

9
THE WAY TO A MAN'S HEART
PENELOPE

I stand in Jake's kitchen and take stock of my surroundings. I told him I want to see what he's working with and go from there. The kitchen feels familiar, it's the same size and layout as mine across the hall, the main difference is...mine is stocked. I open Jake's cabinet doors, rifle through drawers, and stand in front of the open refrigerator as if I can will food to appear inside by the power of positive thinking. And when that doesn't happen, I shut the door and turn to him.

"So..." how do I ask this without offending him? "What *can* you cook?"

He thinks for a moment, watching me.

"Cereal, toast, and takeout."

I've got my work cut out for me.

"And I tried my hand at banana bread," he smirks.

"That was *banana* bread?!" I clap my hand over my mouth to keep myself from laughing. Could've fooled me, I thought for sure it was lemon. "Let's start with something easy. Versatile. Hang tight."

I walk across the hall into my own apartment where I allow myself a moment to laugh. That "banana" bread was horrendous. I don't know what he did to it, but it was an abomination. I ate what I could to humor him, and I was still tasting it after lunch. He tried to contribute to the breakfast meeting and I can't fault him for that. I can, however, fault him for simultaneously over and under-baking it.

Grabbing a pan and spatula, butter and jam from my fridge, I decide I'm going to start him with eggs. Eggs are easy. You learn how to cook them correctly, and the possibilities are endless. You can't possibly screw up cooking eggs.

Jake found a way to screw up scrambled eggs.

This is going to be harder than I thought.

I stood right beside him and walked him through the steps; I made sure his burner wasn't too hot, there was plenty of butter in the pan, there's no way that he should have completely overcooked the eggs…but he did. I got a bit of shell in mine too. At least the toast is good, with plenty of butter and jam slathered on.

We sit at Jake's table, a ballgame in the background, and I pass him my tablet as I pick at his attempted scrambled eggs. He reads my rough outline of *Shattered Glass*. I watch him, nervously, as he reads my passion project. He hands it back and tells me it looks good. He thinks I should pitch it at the next meeting. Which makes me even more nervous than I was while he was reading it.

"It just needs a little polish, that's all."

"So do your cooking skills," I blurt before I can stop myself. "I'm so sorry!"

"No," he laughs, a bold, throaty laugh that seems to echo in his apartment. "You're absolutely right. What's this?"

He opens another note on my tablet, the one labeled *NYC Bucket List*.

It's exactly what the label would lead you to believe: a list of things that I want to do in New York City. I've lived here for two years and haven't gone south of Chelsea Market. There's a whole world in Midtown and Lower Manhattan that I just haven't taken the time to visit.

"That's… not important…" I brush off his inquiry. I need help with *Shattered Glass*, and Jake needs help with...all of his cooking skills. I don't need to play tourist any time soon. I can help him learn basic cooking skills and he can help me polish my *Shattered Glass* pitch before the meeting at the end of the month. I think it's time to make him an offer.

"How about another lesson in exchange for some polishing of the pitch outline?"

"Sure," he grins. "I like the sound of that."

"How's Saturday, my place?"

"Works for me."

Works for me too.

I think I could get used to spending time with Jake outside of the office. He's a handsome man; tall and muscular, but toned and trim. His dark brown hair has a slight curl to it, and when he's frustrated he runs a hand through it, leaving tendrils sticking out every which way. There's a woodsy, spicy smell to his apartment, which must be his cologne or something because that intoxicating smell follows him around the office most days. And not only that, but he's kind. And funny. He isn't turned off when I rant about baseball, in fact he encourages it.

I have to get out of this apartment before I drive myself mad.

Neighbors. That's all we are.

And coworkers.

And friends. Just friends. There can be nothing more.

We make a plan to meet up Saturday morning for a trip to Chelsea Market. I assure him that I will come up with a simple meal for him to cook, one that I will walk him through, and one that he should be able to replicate on his own afterward, and then I head home for the night.

It's gotten easier to be around Jake. I don't feel those twinges of grief quite as much anymore. But there are times... he'll crack a joke, or flash me that lopsided smile, or talk about his playing days...and it triggers a memory in the back of my head of a spring training my dad spent with me in Florida. Or the night I spent in the hospital with dad. The night he...

I have to snap myself out of this.

I head out to my balcony with my tablet and work on *Shattered Glass* a little while longer. I edit my draft until my eyes grow too tired and I have to drag myself off to bed. I have a show to worry about. A show that exists. I put *Shattered Glass* to bed for the night too. I can't do my best work for *On the Field* if I'm focused on something else.

I lay in bed and scan highlights of tonight's games, making notes for the show tomorrow night. I fall asleep to the sound of baseball. There's no better lullaby than the roar of a crowd, the sound of a bat connecting with a ball, or the *thwack* of a ball flying into the catcher's mitt. It makes me feel safe.

Comforted.

Reminds me of home.

10
SUPERSTITION
JAKE

I've survived another week and I finally feel like I belong at the desk with Devon and Jim. I've had dinner with Penelope every night this week - sometimes she cooks, sometimes I order take out. She hasn't said anything, but I can tell that there are nights when she isn't quite herself, and has mentioned that she doesn't feel like cooking, so we eat take out or bowls of cereal for dinner at my place. Getting to know her has been an experience, but I have the feeling there are things that she still isn't telling me. In time, I'm sure she'll trust me with those parts of her story.

What I *do* know about Penelope is that she is hilarious. And brilliant. She routinely leaves me speechless. Her approach to the game —and the show – is nuanced and her analysis is stunning. It's no wonder the network trusts her with *On the Field*.

Today, our prep for the show is pretty laid back. Our usual pre-show meeting takes place about twenty minutes before the show, just to go over the afternoon games and any news that broke between the morning rundown and airtime. Today however, Jim, Devon, and I are crowded around my tablet on the desk in my office, watching a game in progress.

It's a good one too.

So far, the pitcher hasn't allowed a single runner to get on base. There's just a few innings left, and I'm feeling hopeful. We watch with bated breath as a long fly ball is caught on the warning track, as the third baseman turns an incredible play to get the runner out at first base, and as the third batter strikes out looking at a nasty pitch.

Morgan gives us a five minute warning and the three of us scramble into our ties and jackets before heading down to the studio. I pass through the control room and Penelope hands me a notecard and tells me that I'll be opening the show. As the only former pitcher at the desk, she wants me to open, and we'll be starting with the game in progress.

"Good evening and welcome to *On the Field*! We have an exciting show for you tonight, as we join the Detroit and Houston game in progress. Detroit has taken a perfect game through eight in Houston..." Devon and Jim turn to me with horrified looks on their faces. I look through the control room where Penelope's team stands in stunned silence, and she stares at me from her post, slack jawed. The monitors show that our broadcast has moved to the last inning and a half of the game. And then Penelope starts to pace.

My attention is drawn from the game to Penelope. I see her shed her blazer and ditch the heels on her feet. She's now barefoot and pacing the control room. At one point, she steps into the studio, drawing Jim and Devon's attention, but then she turns and re-enters the control room. Morgan looks concerned and I wonder if I should be too.

I leave the desk for a moment and enter the control room, casting a worried glance at Morgan. "Is she okay?"

"Nope," Morgan's answers as if I just offered to fetch her a refreshment. Meanwhile Penelope continues to pace. And the game continues on. There's an inning left to play. Penelope passes me in one of her laps up and down the control room.

And...she's taken to muttering to herself. I faintly make out the words "that's not what my note said" as she passes me again.

And then it dawns on me.

She's superstitious.

She thinks I jinxed this game.

And I'll be darned if this isn't the most endearing thing I've learned about this woman since I've worked here. I've taken my siblings' advice and have been spending the last few weeks trying to get to know Penelope on her terms and on her turf. But this? This is something else.

She has a brilliant analytical mind. She speaks with such authority and has the ability to recall statistics and names of players, she could tell you who was in the 1928 world championship and that New York swept St. Louis in four games. She blows me away each day with her analysis and the way she uses the show to write a love letter to baseball.

For all of her logic, all of her knowledge, the woman is superstitious. And I get it! I was a baseball player, I was immersed in that world for a long time. Baseball players are an odd bunch, we all have quirks and superstitions, but Penelope?! This comes as a surprise, but a welcome one.

The bottom half of the inning rolls around and Detroit takes the field once more. I know better than to stop someone in the middle of a routine, or in the middle of trying to ward off a jinx as the case may be. So I throw a smile at Morgan, chuckling as I head back to the desk.

"You better hope this lasts," Devon says as I take my seat.

I glance between the monitor showing the game, and Penelope now standing ramrod straight, her attention fully on the game. The first out is recorded and rather than looking relieved, Penelope looks more tense than ever. I'm one out away from calling a paramedic to make sure she doesn't stroke out. I watch her as the pitcher enters his windup.

And then I hear it. The sound I always hated when I was on the mound. Solid contact. It just sounds different when a guy connects with the ball and you know, somewhere deep in your heart…it's a homerun. I don't even have to watch the monitor. I watch Penelope, her shoulders slump, she slips her shoes back on and scribbles something on a notecard which is delivered to me by a production assistant.

Jim reaches over and whacks me across the back of the head as Devon dissolves into a fit of uproarious laughter. My eyes scan the notecard and I look up to find Penelope...smirking.

She's smirking *at me.*

"I have a correction," I say, trying my best not to laugh as I see Penelope dissolving into giggles. I peer down at the notecard in front of me, her handwritten note making it even harder to contain my laughter. "I was supposed to say 'there is *something special* happening in Houston', and now that I've jinxed things, we are going to start the show. At the end of the night, Penelope Nichols is going to send me back to school so that I can learn how to read her notes for the next show."

Devon and Jim sit next to me cracking up. Morgan can no longer contain her laughter, and Penelope actually wipes away tears from her eyes. As we wind down for the night and preview the games ahead for the weekend. At the end of the show I laugh with Jim and Devon as we get ready to head out of the studio, "Somebody fill me in on the superstition."

"Ask her yourself," Devon gives me a knowing smile and tilts his head in the direction of the control room. One look that way tells me that she's on her way back to her office.

Just outside Penelope's door, Mike intercepts me, a scowl on his face.

"I'm sorry about her," he all but growls. "That was entirely inappropriate. She should know better than to treat the hosts that way."

"We were having a little fun, Mike. It's not a big deal." I wave him away, assuring him that I wasn't offended by Penelope's antics with the notecard. If anything, it helped me learn a little bit more about her. She can be a lot of fun. Tonight proved that.

Mike walks away muttering under his breath with language that would have the FCC breathing down our necks if he said any of it on the air. I pack up and head toward Penelope's door, eager to talk to her after what happened during the show today and to make sure that Mike didn't reprimand her for it.

I stand outside her door until I'm sure that Mike is shut away in his office once more. As I stand there, I hear music drifting out from her office, I knock on the slightly open door, and she calls for me to come in, turning down the music as I enter. There's a sadness in her eyes as she watches me sit down across from her.

"I never took you for the superstitious type," I lean back in the arm chair across from her desk, a smile tugging at one side of my mouth.

"Sorry about that..."

I wave away her apology. Assuring her that I enjoyed the playfulness of our banter and the notes she passed me. "Don't be sorry. That's the most fun I've had on this show since I got here."

Her eyes sparkle when she looks at me again, any trace of sadness that I thought I saw earlier is gone.

"I'm not usually superstitious. Only when it comes to baseball. Thanks to my dad."

She leans back in her chair and reaches behind her, pulling a picture frame and spiral bound book off of the shelf behind her desk. She hands me the picture frame. I lean forward to grab it, my fingers brushing hers and sending a tingle up my arm. I take the frame and sink back into the chair. In the picture, I see Penelope as a child, maybe ten years old. There's no mistaking that it's her in the picture, the hair, eyes, and smile are the same despite the younger features. Seated next to her is, I assume, her dad. They are at the stadium in Detroit. I've been there a thousand times with my own dad.

Penelope and her mom and dad wear matching caps and sweatshirts, she's bent over something in her lap, and her dad is pointing to something on the field, their heads close together, a smile spread across her face.

"What are you doing? In the picture?" I gently hand the frame back to her as she absentmindedly flips open the spiral bound book in front of her.

"Learning to keep score." She closes her eyes, silently sinking into the memory. When she smiles, it softens her whole face, smoothing out the wrinkle that sometimes settles between her eyebrows, and crinkling the corners of her eyes. She opens her eyes and meets my gaze again, her stare is so intense I almost have to turn away. For just a moment, she tilts her head to the side as if deciding on something and with an almost imperceptible nod to herself, she hands me the notebook that was on the shelf with the picture.

I hold it in my hands, running my thumb over the faded ballpoint ink on the front cover; "2006 Season" is scrawled across the front of the book, and inside are handwritten scores that she kept for each game that she attended that year. I flip through and read the dates, times, the teams that played, each set of pages tells a story. Holds a memory.

I remember when I learned to keep score. I was probably the same age as she was. Seeing the boxes filled with her flowy, feminine, pre-teen handwriting brings back memories of my own—less neatly written—score cards and the way that I bonded with my dad and siblings over learning this aspect of the game.

"That was a great season," I hand back the scorebook and ask her to elaborate on the superstition. The reason for our conversation.

"If a no-hitter was going on, from the time I was a little girl, my dad would always say 'there's something special happening.' Always. Even when I was grown and lived away from home, covering sports professionally, if there was a no-hitter he'd call or text: *Nellie girl, something special is happening.* It was his only superstition. So it became mine too. If you say no-hitter or perfect game around me when it's happening and it gets broken up, I'll blame you. I instituted it on my first day in the studio, and Jim and Devon loved it."

We had the same superstition in the dugout and clubhouse. It's one of many superstitions in baseball. Baseball is a world filled with superstition; I played with guys who would bring sheets to hotels with them so that they could have their lucky sheets. There were guys who'd eat the same meal each night before a game, or listen to the same playlist.

During my last season, I had a no-hitter of my own going through eight innings. It was interleague play and we were on the road, so I didn't have to bat. Every time the nine spot rolled around, I'd go into the batting cage and take a swing. I started it early on, and kept doing it throughout the start. Because if we'd been home, I'd have been hitting. The guys let me do it. You don't break routine in the middle of a no-hitter.

All that to say, I understand the superstition.

I also appreciate this private glimpse into her world, this little piece of her heart, and her trust that she is giving me. This goes beyond the meals we've shared, the surface level pieces of our history that we've given away. It helps me make more sense of her brain, and the way that she focuses when it's time for the show to start. Or the way that she drifts off to another place when the guys and I start talking about our families. In talking about her father, she gets a faraway look in her eye.

I hand back her scorebook and watch as she replaces it and the picture on the shelf behind her, a tear slipping down her cheek. I turn away before she notices that I saw. Pushing myself out of the chair, I sling my bag back over my shoulder and catch her eye as she turns back around.

I realize now that I have a problem. Something stirs in my chest. Something like affection. I haven't felt this way about anyone in a long time.

I'm in even more trouble than I thought.

11
ADVENTURE
JAKE

On Saturday morning, I wake up early and go for a run before showering and getting ready for my day with Penelope. I'm excited to spend time with her away from the office. Away from the pressure. I want her to have a chance to be herself, to be the Penelope I see when she's trying to teach me to cook, or the Penelope whose personality shines through in the group chat. I want to get to know her without her feeling the need to be 'on' all the time. Her turf. Her terms.

I step into the hallway to find Penelope already waiting for me. She's in jeans, canvas tennis shoes, and a sweatshirt from her alma mater. Her hair is piled in a knot on top of her head, a few loose curls poking out here and there. There's something endearing and vulnerable about seeing her out of her professional armor. She's always polished at work; pressed slacks, sleek blouses, hair pulled back in a severe bun. But today she's casual, loose.

Seeing her like this is like receiving a gift – something you've always wanted, and you're finally able to unwrap it; sure, the wrapping is beautiful, but the gift underneath is even better.

"Morning!" She pockets her phone and we set off toward the

elevator bank. All the while, I can't help but think of the bucket list I spied on her tablet the other night. To have lived in New York as long as she has and not seen the sights yet? I want to shake things up a bit today, I just hope she's on board with it.

"So," we step on the elevator and I hit the button for the ground floor, taking a moment to enjoy my proximity to Penelope. "What would you say to a change of plans today?"

She gives me a wary glance and suddenly office-Penelope is back. She's skeptical, and I don't blame her. She tried to brush off the list the other night, but there are things that you *have* to see if you're in New York! At least once!

"That depends..."

It's not a no!

"I was thinking about your bucket list that I not-so-accidentally snooped on, and thought I could help you with that...*and then* help you with *Shattered Glass* tonight."

She thinks about it as we ride the rest of the way to our building's lobby. And as we walk out onto the sidewalk, she glances across the street, watching sunlight glitter across the Hudson. People pass us as she deliberates. And finally...

"Sure," she hands me her phone, open to the note with her NYC list and I start to peruse, figuring out what we can do today and what we should save for another time. "But we save Chelsea Market for the last stop. That way we take the groceries back to the apartment quicker. And...I get to pick where we have breakfast."

"Then I get to pick lunch."

"Deal."

I follow her to the nearest subway station, close to the ASN building, and she stops at a street vendor where she doesn't order. She walks up to the open window and the grizzled, gruff, grey-haired cook stops barking orders and grins when he sees her.

"The usual?" He asks.

"Two," she points over her shoulder at me and I lift a hand in greeting. He winks at Penelope and hands her two coffees. We step aside and wait for our food, and I stand beside Penelope as she chats with the cooks through the windows and door of the truck; she asks about their kids and family and I stand there in amazement. Away from the office she is a vibrant, outgoing person. And I can't get enough of it.

After a few minutes, our food is handed to us out the window, and we walk toward a small ledge to sit and eat. I unwrap the foil packet that she hands me and sink my teeth into what looks like your standard issue breakfast burrito. And it is anything but standard. The eggs are light and fluffy and mixed with onions, peppers, and chunks of steak. This is incredible.

We eat in silence and when we've destroyed our burritos, Penelope looks at me expectantly. "Well...what did you think?"

"Are they here every morning?" I ask, glancing back toward the truck. I can't recall if I've ever seen them here when I've walked to work.

"Saturdays and Sundays."

"And are *you* here every Saturday and Sunday?"

"Most Saturdays," she chuckles. "Sometimes I'll even hit them up for lunch too."

"I can see why. That was amazing."

"I've tried to recreate it at home, but nothing compares. I think Alejandro, he's the one who took our order, has his own secret spice blend and I haven't convinced him to share it yet."

―――

Penelope cleans up our trash and stands before me on the New York City sidewalk, arms crossed, sunglasses pulled from the top of her head and now shielding her eyes. "I'm all yours now. I'm trusting you with the rest of the day."

There's a lot of pressure on me to get things right today. I have a plan. And I know where I want to take her; some items are on her list, and others are places that I think she'll enjoy. I'm taking a gamble on this entire outing, and I'm hoping it pays off.

I take her phone, insisting that I want to document the day for her. I'll hold onto it and take pictures as we trek around the city, and I'm surprised when she relinquishes it to me. She strikes me as the kind of woman who likes to have control, and I've taken every shred of control that she would have had over the day. It speaks to the trust that we've developed. I hope to build on that the rest of the day.

We start by hopping on the Subway and heading southeast, toward Times Square. I found a bus tour that will take us to a few of the places on her list and give us time to get on and off as we please. I did this once before when I first moved to the city, my parents and siblings were with me, and we had a fantastic time. I think it will give Penelope a chance to relax and enjoy crossing a few things off her list.

We get off the subway at a station near Times Square and I take her right to 45th and 7th so that she can see all there is to see in Times Square. She stands for a moment, speechless, making a slow turn and taking it all in. It's overwhelming, even early in the morning, with all the lights and people around. I take her phone from my pocket and snap a picture -- her head is tilted back as she looks up toward the tops of the buildings that surround us, a smile on her face as she looks around.

I take her hand and pull her out of the middle of the sidewalk, beckoning her to follow me to the corner where we'll board our tour bus. We stand in line behind older folks in matching tee shirts and fanny packs, families with young children who already look bored, and Penelope is almost giddy beside me.

"Top or bottom?" I ask as the double decker bus pulls up to the curb.

"Top of course," she looks offended that I'd even ask.

We head up and take our seats near the middle of the upper deck of the bus, and across the aisle is one of the older couples with their matching shirts and fanny packs. The woman leans across the aisle with her hand extended toward me.

"I'm Diane," she says, "and this is my husband Bob. We were watching you two cuties in line and I knew I just had to meet you. We honeymooned here too, almost fifty years ago. Where are you from? How long have you two been married?"

Married?! They think we're....*married*?!

12

NEW YORK STATE OF MIND
PENELOPE

M*arried!?*

Heat creeps into my cheeks and if I had to guess, I'd say I'm turning as red as the big red bus I'm sitting on right now. Jake squeezes my shoulder and laughs good-naturedly with the couple across the aisle, giving me a moment to compose myself before leaning forward and smiling at our companions.

"We're from Michigan," the words tumble out of his mouth and I have to actively stop myself from refuting him.

I mean...it's *technically* the truth. We *are* both from Michigan. I notice he's not touching that honeymoon comment. "We've both been to the city before but have never properly explored it. We thought it would be a fun way to celebrate our relationship."

Again with the technical truth. I should be concerned that he is so skilled at dancing around the *actual* truth. But, I also don't mind letting them think that I'm Jake's wife. He turns and makes eye contact with me, a gleeful, mischievous glint in his eyes as he smiles that dimple popping grin of his.

It's going to be a long day.

"We're Diane and Bob. We're up from Florida."

"Nice to meet you," Jake releases my shoulder and shakes hands with Diane and Bob, "I'm Jake and this is Penelope."

I give a small wave and lean forward to greet our new friends, Bob and Diane.

"What else do you want to do while you're in the city?" Diane asks, her eyes bright with genuine interest.

"Penelope has a list," Jake says. I bristle for just a moment before I realize he's not mocking the list. "What else is on the list, Sunshine?"

Something squeezes in my chest when he calls me Sunshine. I don't know what it is about the nickname but it fills me with warmth and...something like affection. Jake and I have been spending a lot of time together over the past few weeks, and I've let him into my heart more than I ever have with anyone else; I've shared parts of myself with him, and I know there is a lot more that he should know. The more I get to know him, the more I trust him, and for some reason this moment makes me want to give him *every* piece of my heart.

"It's on my phone..." Jake puts my phone in my hands and they shake a bit as I pull up the note with my NYC adventure list. He rests a hand on my thigh and gives a gentle squeeze. I meet his gaze before leaning across his lap and speaking to Diane.

"This tour knocks off a lot of my list, but I also want to see the Statue of Liberty, the Freedom Tower, the memorial and the museum at ground zero, Trinity Church...and that's just the stuff south of Central Park. I'm hoping we can do Central Park at some point, the Plaza...even if it's just the lobby, and as many of the museums as we can."

"That's quite a list," Diane's eyes sparkle as she laughs. "Bob and I did a lot of that on our first honeymoon. Make sure you leave some time for the two of you..." her eyebrows waggle and I glance at Jake to find his cheeks turning bright red, and panicked eyes staring back at me.

"Don't worry. We're making plenty of time for each other," I laugh and pat Jake on the arm. He buries his face in my neck, his body shaking with laughter, and it's all I can do to keep myself from laughing along with him. I breathe in the clean, slightly spicy, masculine scent of him and it goes straight to my head. Which is the only explanation for my response to him and the fact that I really wouldn't mind what Diane is suggesting. I swat him on the arm, "not *here*, sweetheart!"

His eyes meet mine and they are wide as saucers, as if he can't believe I just said that. *I* can't believe I just said that! This sets off another burst of laughter from Jake and I can't keep it in anymore. I bury my face in my hands in an attempt to muffle my laughter and cover it with a cough that sounds like sudden onset asthma. Jake thumps on my back with his hand and when I sit back up I find him watching me. He takes my phone from my hands and pulls me in for a selfie. And for the first time in a long time, I don't recoil or try to avoid having my picture taken. I trust him with this part of me.

Our first stop on this tour is the Empire State Building; our tour bus ticket includes admission to the observation deck so Jake and I happily disembark the bus with a few other groups – including our new friends Diane and Bob...who stick with us for the trip into the Empire State Building. I grab a pamphlet and start reading up on the history of the building. Jake guides me along with a hand on my back, my nose still buried in my reading. He steers me away from an obstacle in my path and eventually plucks the pamphlet from my hand.

"You're going to want to pay attention now," his eyes dance with joy while he watches me take in our surroundings. We're waiting for the elevator to the observation deck and are in a museum of sorts. Jake and Bob discuss the things on the plaques all around us, and Diane strikes up a conversation with me.

"So...how'd you two meet?"

"At work, actually." It's the truth, isn't it? We did *technically* meet at work.

"Ooh, workplace romance. That's risky." Diane laughs as she loops her arm through mine. "But what's life without a little risk?"

She's right.

What's life without a little risk?

For too long I've been avoiding risk.

I've been avoiding opening my heart to anyone, even the people closest to me. I don't want to risk being hurt, or hurting someone I care about. I don't want to risk my own heart, which is why I haven't taken the time before now to *really* get to know Jake. I'm grateful he took a chance on me. Now I need to take a little risk myself.

The times we've spent together outside of work have been fun. He still can't cook. But his scrambled eggs are improving. And his company is even better. It's nice to have someone to walk to work with in the mornings, or walk home with at night when we're done with the show. He's not the kind of neighbor you can borrow a cup of sugar from, but he is the kind of neighbor who doesn't mind if you march across the hall at eleven o'clock at night to complain about the officiating of a baseball game that you both happen to be watching. Not that I would ever do that…or did that just last night.

I was set on avoiding him. Having a strictly professional relationship with him. But then he had to go and leave that note on my door. And I had to go and give him my leftovers. And invite him for dinner, which turned into a standing invitation and dinners shared nearly every night for the past month. Nights spent watching baseball and movies and the occasional soccer game. And now I'm standing on the top of the Empire State Building with him as part of a tour of New York City.

So much for avoiding him.

We finally make it to the elevators and get in for the short ride to the observation deck. When we step outside, there's a crush of people, but Jake expertly navigates the crowd, leading me – and Bob and Diane – to the edge of the deck. It's a perfectly clear day. You can see for miles. Jake gets my attention and just as I turn to him, he snaps another picture. Diane sees, and insists that Jake stand with me for a picture.

We stand shoulder to shoulder and Diane raises the phone and stops short. She waves her hand, gesturing us to get closer to each other. Jake smooshes in, our arms touching. We smile, and still Diane is waving us closer.

"For goodness' sake you two! Act like you like each other!"

Jake looks to me for approval, a move I appreciate. And respect. I give him a small nod and his arm drapes over my shoulders. My arm slips around his waist, and he pulls me close to his side, overwhelming my senses with the warmth of his arm around me, and the spicy, warm scent of his cologne.

"Much better." Diane is pleased. And a thousand butterflies have just taken flight in my stomach. And heart. Everything feels fluttery.

I take a picture of Bob and Diane together before Jake and I head back down to the bus stop. Our new friends decide to stay a little while longer, opting to catch the next bus. We hug them both and wish them well on the rest of their trip. We ride the elevator in silence and board the waiting tour bus once we're back to street level.

"They were fun," Jake comments, stretching his feet out into the aisle as we wait for more tourists to re-board the bus. "I'm surprised at you."

I turn to face him, there's a smirk tugging at the corner of his mouth and I can't help but smile when I think of our introduction to our companions.

"*I* was a surprise? You let them go on believing we're on our honeymoon!"

"I'll remind you, Sunshine, you went along with it too."

"I did...I'm sorry."

"No, no," he puts a hand on my arm and turns to fully face me. "I'm not upset about that! I had fun! It was fun to laugh and joke with you. You surprised me. That's all."

I surprised him.

What he's saying is, I'm not usually this fun. And I suppose he's right. At work, I wear a kind of armor. To keep myself protected, to keep from getting hurt or letting anyone's snide remarks get to me. It comes with the territory. But outside of the office, when I can be myself? I like to think that I'm a lot of fun. It was nice to let loose today.

We opt to stay on the bus for a few of the next stops, choosing to ride and listen to the tour guide as he tells us stories about the buildings and streets that we pass. We come to the next stop on the tour: Chinatown and Little Italy. Jake tells me we're getting off here, and I follow him off the bus...right into Little Italy.

13
TO MARKET
PENELOPE

This was a terrible idea.

I can't be falling for Jake Hutchinson. I can't. We are friends and nothing more.

I've tried to control the parts of my heart that I share with him in an effort to get close but not *too* close. But then he endears himself to me even more and does it all while being incredibly, annoyingly, handsome. Especially today, with a bit of stubble on his cheeks, and hair that seems to have a mind of its own, and those obscenely toned and tanned forearms of his, with his sleeves rolled up as if he just *knows* I'm a sucker for those arms. I've tried so hard not to get close to him.

Ugh.

This was a terrible idea.

He quoted my favorite movie to me. On the way from the Empire State Building to Little Italy, he started quoting one of my favorite romantic comedies and endeared himself to me even more than he already had. Now, he's steering me into every market on the street, insisting that if I find anything that catches my eye he'd be willing to cut our tour short to get things back to the apartment.

Everything about him should point to something different than the man that I've found him to be. He's gentle and kind. He's empathetic and good humored. And I've been an absolute nightmare to him because I'm afraid to take a risk. But if there's one thing to be learned from today, it's that life needs a little risk.

Even now we're wandering a market, Jake stays right next to me, a grin on his face as I add things to my basket. Every now and then he'll ask what something is, or how to use something I've chosen, and I find that I don't mind answering him. I love talking about food and I love having someone to share it with. Morgan doesn't share my enthusiasm for food and cooking, so while I'm sure she'd have been happy to come with me, she wouldn't have enjoyed it nearly as much as Jake seems to be.

"I hope I'm not boring you," I turn to him as I browse a case of gourmet, aged cheeses. "You'd tell me right? If you were bored out of your mind and wanted to ditch me?"

"Sunshine, you couldn't bore me if you tried. I'm really enjoying this. I love the way your eyes light up when you find something new, or something you've always wanted to try. And there's a wistfulness in your voice when you answer my questions that makes me think cooking is more than just a hobby for you..."

Sunshine. There it is again.

I can't explain what that term of endearment does to me. It breaks open something inside of me, something that I'd been trying to hold back from him. It breaks down the wall that I tried to put up between us. I like it. And part of me hopes he never uses my name ever again.

The wall that I've kept up all this time is starting to crumble. I have to give this piece of myself to him.

"It's a stress reliever. Anxiety too. When I'm in the kitchen, I feel like I have control of the situation; chopping, prepping, plating. I'm in control. There are too many areas of my life that I can't control" *Dad's cancer. Mom's cancer. Their deaths.* "At the end of the day, I can walk into my apartment and step into that kitchen, and have complete control of the situation."

Tears prick the back of my eyes, because it's so much more than that.

"It's also how I connected with my mom. Everything I know - every recipe and technique - I learned from her. Mom's love language was cooking and feeding people, and I picked it up from watching her example. I still feel connected to her when I'm in the kitchen, even now."

I watch him for a moment. Looking for his flight response to kick in. I sound like a control freak. And in some ways, I am. I also sound a little crazy. And in some ways, I'm that too. But he doesn't drop my basket and run. No, the lines on his face smooth out and he gives me a lopsided smile.

"I understand the feeling of not being in control," he chuckles. "When my arm went out, I had no control over anything. I spiraled. I moved home, spent a year cooped up in mom and dad's house, watching every movie I could, eating crappy food because I could, and shutting out all the people who cared about me."

―――

The baseball world was devastated when Jake's arm went out the second time. There was hope that the surgery had repaired it, but the second injury was beyond repair. His career was over before it had ever really begun.

"It took my agent coming to the house and knocking sense into me to get me out into the world again. So believe me when I tell you, I understand the need to have control. Especially when other people won't let you have it."

He gives me a knowing look. He says more with that look than words could ever say. This look tells me he knows, he sees what goes on in the office.

"Maybe I've said too much..."

"No," I reach out and touch his arm, the electric tingle in my fingers startles me. So does the twisting in my gut when he looks at me with those mesmerizing, deep blue eyes of his. "You've said just enough. It's nice to know someone in the office understands."

He puts an arm around my shoulder, a friendly gesture. But a shock runs down my spine as he pulls me close to his side, the smell of his soap -- fresh and masculine and slightly spicy -- makes me wish this could be a regular thing. "I see how Morgan steps in without you needing to ask. Let me do that for you, too. I think Mike wants to impress me, and is maybe a little afraid of me. I won't say anything if you tell me not to. But I'm not afraid to stand next to you and look...brooding."

The laugh that bubbles out of my chest is so unexpected that I startle myself, Jake, and the moms wearing expensive yoga gear with perfect ponytails who eye me from nearby, and clearly ogle Jake. Can't say I blame them.

"First of all, I can't imagine you "brooding", but I'll take your closest approximation. Second of all...thank you. Morgan does her best, and mostly I think she just annoys him. But, he doesn't always get the message. I think if you stared him down like he's a batter with a full count and the bases loaded, he'd likely back down."

He squeezes me closer, and we walk together through the rest of the store, one arm slung around my shoulders, the other carrying my basket. After making my purchases, we stop at a restaurant for pizza. Jake tells me it's the best pizza in the city. He pulls me close for a selfie on the street, showcasing all of Little Italy behind us.

He shows me the screen and I pull a face. I know I do.

I hate pictures of myself. I always have. Even the few years that I was on the air as a sports reporter, I couldn't watch myself. Or read social media comments.

For some people, one of the telltale signs of Polycystic Ovarian Syndrome is an excess of body hair. For me, that means facial hair. I shave every morning. And it works, but there's still a shadow. And by the end of the day, there's sometimes stubble. Not to mention the cramps and pain when I eventually have a period. And a cycle that I can't predict. But no one *sees* those things. What they see is what I see. And even as an adult, there are still days that I hate what I see. Though, I'm getting better about it.

I'm not as bad as I used to be; these days, I'll stand for pictures, I don't hide behind scarves or wear my hair long to hide anymore. But there are days I wish I could just crawl in a hole and hide.

Today, I woke up in one of those moods, so I can't explain what compelled me to accept Jake's invitation for a walking tour of the city, now with pictures of us together. I look again at the screen, and in my head I scrutinize my appearance; my hair is frizzy, the shadow on my chin is all I can see. But then I look at Jake, whose eyes aren't on the camera...his eyes are turned down, trained on me. He's grinning as he sees me taking in the view from atop the Empire State Building.

On closer inspection...I don't hate this picture. I don't exactly love it, but I don't mind it. I've never had anyone look at me like that. Like they're looking beyond what they can see. What I can see. I tuck this moment away in my heart as one that I don't want to forget. As we walk to our next stop, Jake carries the conversation and I listen to him absentmindedly, all the while thinking about our interactions since the day we met; I've never felt as though he's judged my appearance. I take care to make myself presentable, sure, but there are days that I avoid mirrors because my brain is a jerk sometimes.

People don't always see what I see, the things that I hate about myself, and the things that I think about at night when my insomnia keeps me awake. Or when I lay in bed with a migraine that makes me want to puke, and play over in my head all the ways that people respond when they meet me.

But Jake. He sees me, and doesn't seem the least bit phased about what he sees. He sees deeper than the surface, which is going to take some time to get used to. Because while my brain may be a jerk sometimes (and my last serious boyfriend was an even bigger jerk), Jake isn't. And I don't know what to do with that.

Jake orders for us -- a Margherita Pizza and basket of the most heavenly smelling garlic knots. We sit outside talking and enjoying each other's company. We continue our conversation about our favorite books and movies. He's not at all surprised when I tell him what some of my favorites are. But, he continues to surprise me just the same.

"I will take this secret to my grave," he says, "but given the choice between an action film and a romantic comedy, I choose the romantic comedy every time. I love the meet-cutes, the tropes, the happily ever after. There's something comforting in those stories."

I wholeheartedly agree with him. There is something incredibly comforting in knowing that everything works out at the end of those movies. In a world so filled with uncertainty, the certainty of those movies is good for the soul.

"So," I wait until he has a mouthful of pizza before asking the question that has been lingering in the back of my mind since the market this morning. "Where did the nickname Sunshine come from?"

"You don't mind it, do you?" He's cute when he's worried. He draws his eyebrows together and a wrinkle appears between them, disappearing when I tell him that no, I don't mind. "I come from the world of baseball where everyone has a nickname..."

His cheeks redden as he takes a sip of his drink and avoids my gaze. But then he continues and knocks the wind right out of me.

"You bring a ray of sunshine with you everywhere you go, you make rooms brighter just by being in them. And sometimes, just like the sun, something comes along and blocks you out, dims your light, but never for long. And sometimes that something is an idiot who can't see how brilliant and capable you are."

Well.

Okay then. I wish I knew how to respond to that with something more than the incoherent sounds that pinball around in my brain.

"Thank you," my voice is almost a whisper as I try to hold back the tears stinging my eyes.

"My turn to ask a question," he wipes his hands on a napkin before crossing his arms across his chest and leaning back a bit in his chair. His brow furrows as he regards me from across the table. "You were on television for a while, as a sports reporter right? Is that why you don't like having your picture taken? I've noticed the face you make when you check out the pictures after I take them…you don't have to answer if you're uncomfortable. I know we're not quite to that point yet…"

And just like that, another wall comes crashing down.

Well, we've come this far right? I think I finally trust him enough with this part of myself, but even as I get ready to answer him, my jerk brain starts telling me all the ways this could go wrong. Almost reflexively, I lean an elbow on the table in front of me, and use my hand to hide my chin. An old defense mechanism from my high school and college days. A way of hiding my face without fully hiding my face.

"I tend to not like having my picture taken," I tell him. He tilts his head to the side, as if waiting for me to elaborate. There's no teasing or judgment or rebuke in his gaze, so I continue despite my subconscious screaming at me not to do it. "I have PCOS – Polycystic Ovarian Syndrome – and for many women, for me, it causes facial hair. And even though I take care of it, it's still the first thing I notice in pictures or when I look at myself in the mirror. Or when I used to watch myself on television."

"Believe it or not," he leans forward, reaching across the table and gently takes my hand away from my face. His touch sends a spark up my arm and down my spine. My cheeks flood with warmth as he holds my hand in his and his eyes lock with mine before roaming my face. "I'm familiar with PCOS, at least insomuch as my brother is a doctor and has a few journal articles published about it."

He continues to hold my hand and watch me from across the table. Normally, I'd be clambering to cover my face again, to hide myself from his scrutiny. But there's something about him, a softness in his gaze that tells me I'm safe with him. That my heart, my trauma, my story is safe with him.

"When I look at you, I see a brilliant and capable woman. A woman whose baseball knowledge could give me a run for my money. A woman who has been hurt before, who hides away to keep from being hurt again."

He's right.

I have been hurt.

That's why I keep so much to myself. Why I don't have a lot of friends that I trust, and the few friends that I do have, I often hold at arm's length. But when I look at him, I see someone that I trust. I also see someone whose very presence in my life dredges up old, buried memories, grief that I haven't confronted, grief that I've longed to leave buried. The last of the walls between us.

"Penelope...," he takes a deep breath and releases my hand. I move it back to my face before self-consciousness butts in and I end up folding my hands in my lap instead and shifting my gaze away from Jake. "I hope I'm not out of bounds in saying this; you're a beautiful woman, and I'm not just saying that or saying it to be nice..."

He has somehow anticipated my reflexive responses to being told that I'm beautiful. My brain is incapable of accepting compliments; too often I find myself doubting their sincerity and whether or not the person offering them truly means it or if they're "just being nice."

But in Jake's eyes, there is not an ounce of malice. And for the first time in my adult life, I believe those words. Or, a small part of me does.

"Thank you," I whisper, wiping away the tears forming at the corners of my eyes. I shake my head. There's nothing else to say besides thank you. I can't think of how to express what his words mean to me. Sure, I've heard them before from other men, from friends and family. But up until a few weeks ago, Jake was a stranger. And somehow that makes his words land a little differently than if we'd have known each other for years. Will this completely change the way I see myself? No. But it's a start. "Thank you."

He nods, empathy and understanding in his eyes as he watches me fidget under his gaze. I clean up the table while Jake pays for our lunch, and then we make our way toward the nearest subway stop. Jake insists that he doesn't mind cutting the tour short, and I won't argue with him. He takes the bags from my hands and carries them the short distance to the subway, and stands in front of me, almost protectively, for our ride back uptown.

"What am I going to learn to cook tonight," he asks, almost nervously.

"Pasta primavera, but that was before I realized we'd be having lunch in Little Italy."

I picked a dish that can't really be screwed up. All it is, is pasta and vegetables. Sometimes cheese. Not even Human Kitchen Disaster Jake Hutchinson can screw up pasta primavera.

I hope.

14

SUNSHINE AND STORMCLOUD

JAKE

We walk back to our building and ride the elevator to her apartment in silence. As she opens her door, I am hit with the smell of warm spices almost immediately—cinnamon with a hint of vanilla; it smells like my mom's house at Christmas. I take a seat at her small dining room table and look around at her cozy apartment.

Unlike mine, her apartment looks lived in. It looks like a home. It's starting to feel like a home away from home. Throw pillows and blankets, pictures on the walls, bookshelves on either side of her wall mounted television filled to bursting with books of all kinds. Baseball memorabilia on the shelves in front of the books. As she continues to put away her market haul, I walk around and look at all the pictures on the walls.

All the time I've spent here, I've never taken a close look at the pictures surrounding her space. It always felt like an intrusion, but after our discussion at lunch today, I've been entrusted with another piece of who she is and want to know more about her.

There are pictures in every available space. There's a collage of photos from her days as on-air talent—on baseball diamonds, in dugouts, and clubhouses. Pictures of her with, I assume, her parents. These are hung close to the curtain that hangs from a ceiling track, dividing her space. The frames disappear to the other side of the curtain, and although my curiosity is screaming at me to take a peek behind the curtain, I make my way back to the pictures of her at various baseball fields.

"Have you always covered baseball?" I ask as I study the pictures, seeing some fields that I recognize, and that smile of hers. The one that outshines the sun when you get her talking baseball. Of all the things we've talked about, we tend to avoid shop talk.

"No," she snorts out a laugh and it's adorable. "I started at small stations covering everything from high school football to senior center horseshoe leagues."

"That has to be a joke," I turn to face her and she is regarding me with a stony expression. I keep waiting for the facade to crack and her smile to shine through, or for her to chuckle and confirm that she's kidding.

"Nope," she steps close to me and it's all I can do not to reach out and touch her. She lifts her hair away from her temple and points to the faint line of a scar just past her hairline. I lightly run my fingers over it, and notice her shiver beneath my touch. "Got beaned with a stray horseshoe at the championship tournament. Even got the stitches and scar to prove it...there might also be video footage. It happened live on the air."

"No!"

"Oh, that's not even the worst of it."

As we step into the kitchen, she tells me all kinds of stories. From little league baseball tournaments with kids running into her, or having to jump out of the way of foul balls. To local equestrian competitions where her manager expected her to sit horseback and report the story.

"My favorite," she leans against the counter, bracing herself with her hands on the counter and crossing her ankles, the picture of casual, "was the time they wanted me to take batting practice with the local college baseball team. The station manager and lead sports anchor thought it would make great b-roll to have me out on the field with the guys. This was when I had a camera guy with me and didn't have to film everything myself. Kid steps on the mound and throws to me underhand."

She stops and nails me with a pointed look. And honestly, I'm offended on her behalf.

"I wish I still had the footage somewhere. I tried to look intimidating - adjusting my stance, hiking up my pant legs, the whole deal. I tell the kid on the mound not to hold back. He looked from me to his coach, and the coach just shrugged. At that point all I wanted was to prove them all wrong; my boss, the lead anchor, and every man standing around me on that field."

There's fire in her eyes as she recalls the memory and I can almost picture her in the batter's box, that intensity in her eyes as she fights to prove herself to the men around her that are looking for a cheap laugh at her expense. To prove herself to those who would believe she can't do something.

"I crushed that ball. You could hear it when I made contact with the bat—my dad would have called it a 'no-doubter', solid contact. The pitcher turned and watched it sail over the fence. It was batting practice, but I still took a victory lap around the bases. Kyle, my camera guy, got the whole thing on camera."

"Yes!" I pump my fist in the air, "that's my girl!" *Where did that come from?!.* Shock registers briefly on her face, and is quickly replaced with a sad smile.

"My first thought was to call my dad. By then he'd been gone a few months, mom too. I sat in my car in the parking lot and cried. I hadn't really cried up until that point. I tried to hold things together for my brother during the funerals and wanted him to be able to grieve the way he needed to. I didn't realize until it was too late that I hadn't taken the time to grieve. So I had a good cry that night. Not your usual home run celebration."

I don't know what to say. So I stand there like an idiot, watching as she collects herself. I feel like I need to say something, but don't know *what*. I can tell that there's a lot she's not saying, but already today she has trusted me with *so much*.

"Anyway..." she smiles and wipes her eyes before tossing me an apron and handing me a small knife. I'm kind of insulted that she doesn't give me a bigger knife or trust me with anything other than chopping vegetables, but she assures me she trusts me and insists that I'll work my way up to bigger knives.

Penelope gives me instructions and sets an assortment of vegetables in front of me, demonstrating with her own – much bigger, scarier looking – knife how to cut each type of vegetable. I ask a lot of questions, and she patiently answers every single one of them. While I chop the bowl full of veggies she placed in front of me, Penelope boils the pasta, puts homemade garlic bread in the oven, makes salad *and* dressing, and then tells me step by step how to cook and season the vegetables before adding the noodles to the pan. She then hands me a block of cheese and a wood rasp that she insists is some kind of cheese grater and turns me loose.

"Voila," she exclaims with a literal chef's kiss, "you've just made pasta primavera!"

She plates it, and I take a bite before we even sit down, and I can't believe that I made this. Me. Jake "Cereal, Toast, and Takeout" Hutchinson. It's delicious. And I could probably make it again if I had to.

"Why sports media?" I ask as we clean up. We've already broken the no shop talk rule, so why not go all in.

"It was something I shared with my dad. Dad was a lawyer, and Peter followed in his footsteps. I wanted to blaze my own trail; I didn't want to go to law school. I had no desire to practice law, and my dad always told me to do something that I loved. So, I picked a school with a sports broadcasting program. When I graduated I got hired at a small affiliate station for a national network. I hopped around for a while, hoping to work my way up to a job on the other side of the camera. Ten years later...here I am."

"You ever think of getting in front of the camera again? You're brilliant. You're more knowledgeable about the game than half the guys I played with. And I really do love your *Shattered Glass* idea. I'd love to see you host it."

She'd be an incredible host. She talks about baseball with a passion unmatched by most of the men I've worked with. I'd watch her. I'd host with her if she asked. Just listening to her running commentary through the game we are watching together makes me wonder what must have happened – beyond her PCOS and self-consciousness – to make her hate being in front of the camera. I hope someday she trusts me enough with her whole story.

"I have a complicated history with hosting," she turns and looks at me, a sadness in her eyes. "I'd have to work through some things before I could get in front of the camera again. But, you'll be happy to know I will be pitching my story to the network next week."

It's a step in the right direction. Which reminds me.

"Let's have a look at it." I hold out my hand and she hands me her tablet. I sit and read through her proposal for *Shattered Glass*, and she gives me the liberty to make a few notes and suggestions wherever I see fit. While I read, she cleans up the kitchen, insisting that since I "cooked" she'll take care of the clean-up. She even packages up the leftovers for me in her neat little containers, complete with reheating instructions.

What she has is a great start. It just needs...a punch. Something emotional to get the viewers hooked and keep them tuned in. She sits down across from me at the table, her brows furrowed as she worries her bottom lip between her teeth.

"I like it. But don't just tell their stories. Tell yours too."

She takes her tablet from my hand and disappears behind the curtain. When she comes back and heads toward the door, I take it as my cue to head out. At the door, I open my arms...and she steps into the hug. Add that to the list of surprises today.

"Goodnight, Sunshine."

"Goodnight, Stormcloud."

I quirk a brow and she smirks, as she closes the door, she says "figure it out."

Sunshine and Stormcloud. I like it.

Back in my own apartment, just across the hall from a place so vibrant and full of life, I'm overwhelmed by the silence. Silence that is quickly broken by the sound of my phone dinging with text notifications. I glance at the screen and see that Penelope is sending me all of the pictures we took today. I flip through them and notice her smile in each of them; nothing like the tight smiles she gave me in my first few days as the network. I love her smile. I love the way her eyes stray to my face in almost all of these pictures.

I think about it while I get ready for bed, but can't figure out the nickname. Feeling defeated, I fire off a text.

You're going to have to help me out...

Three bouncing dots appear. And they stick around for a while. Finally...

Sometimes the Sunshine needs a break. It can be exhausting to try and be sunshine all the time. Sometimes, Sunshine needs a Stormcloud to come in and give her some cover. And even though we've only known each other for a few months, you somehow already know when that is.

Thanks for being my Stormcloud.

Stormcloud doesn't know what to say.

Stormcloud wants to march across the hall, take Sunshine in his arms and kiss her. Stormcloud also knows that would be wildly inappropriate for a number of reasons...but it doesn't make me want it any less.

I respond:

I'll always be your Stormcloud, Sunshine.

Three dots appear and then disappear. And then there's a knock at my door. I know it's her. There's no doubt. I open it and she seems nervous. She silently steps into my apartment and walks past me, planting herself in the middle of the space. Hands wringing, a slight blush in her cheeks. And then the dam bursts.

"You know how hard it is for me to trust people. Which means you know how hard it was for me to tell you all of those things today..." she takes a deep breath and then finally, *finally*, her eyes meet mine. "Jake, I need to know what this is between us. And I need you to know that...I'd very much like to date you. If that's something that you would be interested in."

And then....she walks out.

She steps out of my apartment, shutting the door behind her and presumably walking into her own apartment and shutting that door too. As far as I know. I'm still stunned by her admission and the way in which she just...left.

I'd like to date her too! And I would have told her as much if she'd have given me a chance. Good grief. This woman drives me crazy...in all the best ways.

15
THE WINDUP AND THE PITCH!
PENELOPE

Once a month, the American Sports Network gathers in the executive floor conference room for a network-wide pitch meeting. Producers, programming managers, network directors, we all gather for an afternoon to pitch ideas for our shows, special programming, and play-off coverage for the sports we cover.

Once a month, I am reminded that sports media is still a boys club.

I'm the only woman in the room. As the producer for *On the Field*, it's my job to pitch our special broadcast ideas, stories and segments that go beyond our usual nightly broadcast. Each night, during the regular season, we recap the day's games, interview players, managers, or coaches, and cover any breaking injury news, trade rumors, and whatever comes up at the last minute. During the off-season we cover trade rumors, drafts, and winter ball in Central America.

We like to try and do one special broadcast a month – a Hall of Fame tribute, anniversary shows, Jackie Robinson Day – and this meeting is usually the one that is most discouraging for me. I usually come away from this meeting and head right home to bake something. Usually bread. The kneading is a good stress reliever.

I walk into the executive conference room and take a seat as close to the door as I can. In *On the Field* meetings, I have Jake and Morgan with me, but not in these meetings. In network meetings, I'm on my own, and I never feel that more than when Mike Fletcher stares me down for the length of the meeting.

I've come in today with a pitch. One that I'm proud of. I've got a presentation with research and statistics, ratings information; I've gone above and beyond for this pitch meeting, but I want them to take me seriously. I *need* them to take me seriously. For once.

I listen to all the pitches, all the backslapping, and praise for the last month of shows and ratings and finally, the executives turn their attention to me. I pass out the materials I brought with me and open my tablet to my proposal, and on the inside cover is the note Jake wrote to me the night we met, before he knew who I was. It gives me a strange little confidence boost as I prepare to pitch my idea.

Shattered Glass: A Conversation about Women in Baseball.

I've been working on this idea for a long time. I've put in countless hours of research, I have a tablet full of graphics I've designed to accompany whatever stories I decide to tell. I've brainstormed talking to the few female executives in the game right now, a handful of the women who cover baseball in print, television, and on the radio. And even a conversation with female baseball fans.

I remember hearing comments when I was a kid and dad and I would attend games together, insinuating that I must have been an only child with no brothers at home to go to games with dad. Or, as I got older and went to games with Peter, men assumed that I must be attending games to impress a boyfriend. Or they'd scoff when I sat down with my scorebook and pencil.

I didn't go to a game again until I was covering them. And by then it was a lot of high school and college ball. I had to force myself not to read the comments on my social media feeds or those of the places I worked. There were a lot of people that didn't like to get their sports report from a woman, and they made their opinions known. Eventually, I deactivated most of my accounts or made them completely private when I could.

It's never been easy to be a woman in the male dominated world of professional baseball, no matter what aspect of the game you are involved in. My hope is that *Shattered Glass* would help us start the conversation and begin to make change.

I present the executives with the ratings and statistics on our audience demographic, particularly for *On the Field*. Of all the shows on American Sports Network, *On the Field* has the largest female audience by far, part of that can be attributed to Jake's presence on the show, but our numbers were high even before he was hired. More and more women are in prominent positions in major league organizations, in the media, and even on coaching staffs.

"Would this be a special broadcast? Or part of *On the Field*?" the network's programming manager asks, folding his hands in front of him, and staring me down from his perch at the end of the table.

"I thought we could do it as a special episode of *On the Field* since we already have the time-slot."

Mike watches me from across the table and I try not to squirm under his intense gaze. Once again, Mike has the power and he knows it. Leaving it open to being an episode of *On the Field* means Mike can veto, and I'm sure he will.

"Who would be hosting?"

"I would," I try to project confidence into my voice, and pray that no one hears it wavering. "I have on-air experience, as I'm sure you all remember. I was a sports anchor and reporter before stepping out from in front of the camera."

"I just don't think it would be a good fit for the network..." I take this opportunity to pass my research around the table. Showing them all the demographic breakdown of our audience, not just *On the Field's* audience, but the rating information for every game we've aired this season. Mike continues his rant.

"Men don't tune in to *On the Field* to hear a bunch of broads talking about something they know nothing about," he balls up the research I spent hours on, and tosses it in the garbage bin. "This is meaningless. Women don't watch baseball, they watch the baseball players. They don't care about the game, or the history. Tell me, Penny, when was the pitcher's mound lowered? Or the designated hitter introduced?"

What a tool. He thinks he's caught me in a trap? He'll have to try harder than that.

"In 1969 the pitcher's mound was lowered by five inches. And on April 6, 1973 Ron Bloomberg became the first ever designated hitter. He walked. On a full count."

"Once again," Mike's voice is tinged with annoyance. I've flustered him. He didn't expect that I'd answer his question. I not only answered, I'd bested him. And his red faced, spluttering response is the best victory. "The answer is no. But, I'm sure we'll hear about it again next month."

The victory was short-lived. But, I think I won a few of those old guys over to my side. And Mike was right about one thing, they will hear about this again. As soon as we're dismissed, I walk to my office, pack up, and tell Morgan I'm heading out for a long lunch but that I'll be back later to get the show on the air.

After a day like today, I want nothing more than to go home and bake. Take out my frustration on a ball of bread dough. Kneading it and slapping it against the counter, working up the gluten in the bread and working out my frustration. I want to sink my fingers into a bowl of shaggy biscuit dough, and feel it all come together in my hands. I want to focus on something other than my emotional state, so, like always, I tamp it down. I push aside the anger and frustration and unpleasantness, and brainstorm what to bake as I walk home from the office.

Last night, my nerves and insomnia had me baking batches of

cookies, enough to put several dozen in the office kitchen. The dejection I'm feeling after the pitch meeting today makes me want to do something more labor intensive, something that I have to pay attention to and focus my time and energy on, so I stop into the closest bodega and grab a can of sweetened condensed milk, a pound of butter, and a jar of cookie butter.

As soon as I get home, I change into comfortable clothes and get myself organized to make my version of Millionaire Shortbread Bars. The caramel filling is exactly the kind of thing I need to make today. It's slow, requires my complete focus, and when done right, it's exactly the kind of decadence that improves a crappy mood.

The shortbread base is the kind of soft, delicate dough that I need to focus on right now. The sugar, butter, and flour base is easy enough to make, but if you overwork it, it won't come together correctly. With just the tips of my fingers, I crumble the butter and flour and sugar together until the mixture looks and feels sandy. Then I press it into a prepared baking sheet. By all accounts, this dough shouldn't work. It shouldn't hold together and bake into the perfect, melt in your mouth, buttery, slightly sweet shortbread. But it does.

Just like the network acts like *Shattered Glass* won't work. I'm sure it will. I'm sure that it will appeal to our audience, and even *grow* our audience, if they would just give it a chance. If they would just give *me* a chance, I could prove to them that, like this shortbread base, *Shattered Glass* will hold up.

So much for not focusing on the pitch meeting.

I'm also focusing on the fact that I haven't seen Jake today. Or spoken to him since last night.

I don't know what got into me last night. I've never done anything like that before. I don't know if it was nerves over today's meeting, or Diane from Florida's voice in my head about taking risks. Or, more likely, the overwhelming feeling that something in my relationship with Jake has shifted...and I don't know what to do about it.

I shove the shortbread in the oven and get started on a caramel filling that starts with a tablespoon of cookie butter mixed with brown sugar, sweetened condensed milk, and a splash of vanilla. As I wait for the sugar to dissolve and the mixture to heat up, I stir with one hand...and eat cookie butter by the spoonful with the other. It's been that kind of day.

16

CONTROL

JAKE

I camp out near Morgan's desk, waiting for Penelope to walk back to her office. But when Morgan returns without Penelope, a nervous feeling tangles up in my gut. I know Penelope had her concerns going into the meeting today, and I want to be here for her if she needs support. Morgan comes back to her desk and tells me that Penelope headed out early. Apparently things didn't go as well as she'd hoped in the executive pitch meeting; Morgan doesn't give me details just that Penelope headed home, with plans to return tonight for the broadcast.

Penelope never leaves early. She's usually the first in the office and likes to work late. More often than not, I have to drag her from her chair and walk her home. The fact that she left the meeting and went straight home doesn't bode well for how things went today. We've worked hard to perfect her pitch - *she's* worked hard to perfect her pitch. I've made a few suggestions here and there, and learned how to cook a few basic dishes in return. I'm worried about what this means for Penelope, and for *Shattered Glass*. And for whatever it is she might be wallowing in right now.

I tell Morgan that I'm going to head out for a bit, to run a few errands, and I duck out. After a quick stop at the market on the corner, I grab a loaf of Penelope's favorite crusty bread and melty cheese, a four pack of her favorite extra spicy ginger ale, and before I know it, I'm knocking on her door before I let myself in.

Pushing open the door, I find her bent over the stove, stirring some kind of concoction in a pot, her hair falling out of a ponytail, sleeves of a too big sweatshirt pushed up above her elbows, the smell of butter and sugar hanging in the air. Little wisps and tendrils of hair curl at her temples at the nape of her neck, her brow is furrowed in concentration, eyes glued to the amber mixture in the pot.

I press a soft kiss to her temple, before putting the ginger ale in the fridge to chill and leaving the cheese on the counter to come to room temperature. Among the kitchen skills Penelope has taught me, she's also taught me about bread and cheese and that *good cheese* as she calls it, is better at room temperature. I watch her for a moment. She is tense. I can see it in her shoulders, in the way she furiously stirs whatever it is she has in that pot.

"Stir this for me," she steps aside and puts the spatula in my hand "just for a minute. I need to check the shortbread."

I stir and step to the side just enough for her to open the oven and check on the shortbread. As soon as the door opens, I'm hit with the warm smell of butter and sugar mingled together in a perfect shortbread. I assume it's perfect anyway, based on the quick glimpse I get before Penelope whisks it away and sets it on the dining table in front of the open balcony door.

She steps back over to me, and takes the spatula, resuming the stirring, and nudging me to take a seat at the table where she can still see me.

"How'd the meeting go?" I broach the subject gently, part of me already knowing the answer.

"Not great," she exhales a sharp breath and pushes a rogue chunk of hair behind her ear. "They don't think that there is a market for anything about women in baseball. We don't have a wide enough audience. Which, I know is wrong because I gave them ratings and demographic breakdowns."

She turns the burner off with a swift flick of her wrist, pulling the pot off and stepping toward the table. After rearranging her hair in an attempt to contain it all, she begins to pour the gooey mixture over top of the slab of shortbread. She spreads it evenly with the spatula and steps over to the sink where she begins to scrub at the pot furiously.

"I gave them anecdotal evidence, empirical data, and made a case for myself as the host of the show. Ultimately, it came down to Mike's approval. And he shot it down. So."

I join Penelope at the sink, gently taking the scouring pad out of her hand and nudging her out of the way with my hip before rolling up my sleeves and taking over washing her dishes. She takes a bottle of water out of the fridge and sits down at the table, finally taking a much needed break. I can see the tension melt out of her shoulders as she sits back and closes her eyes.

"What if we do it anyway?" I ask, pausing my scrubbing to rinse the pot in my hand. "Use my connections and yours, host and produce the piece and at the next network pitch meeting, you pitch them a fully produced show."

Her eyes spring open and she watches me for a moment, as if waiting for the other shoe to drop. But there's no catch. I love her idea, I loved it when she pitched it in our meeting the other day. Jim and Devon were on board as well, and I'm sure we could get them to help. She wants this. She *deserves* this. And I'll do anything I can to help her make it happen.

"You can host, conduct interviews, tell your story and the stories of other women in baseball. We probably can't use network equipment, but I'm sure we can find a way to make it happen."

"I want you to know what you're getting into if you take this on with me," her gaze darkens, her tone growing serious. "If Mike catches wind of this, he *will* fire me, and probably anyone he suspects of working with me. I don't want you to risk your job for me Jake."

"It's a risk I'm willing to take," I turn to her, meeting her intense gaze. "It's worth it...*you're* worth it."

Penelope picks up a towel and dries the dishes as I finish washing them. She's silent for a long time, just drying dishes and putting them away. Finally she stops, and leans with her back against the counter, facing away from me. I cut a glance in her direction and see tears slipping down her cheeks.

"Woah. Hey," I grab the towel from her hands and gently dab at her cheeks, "what's wrong Sunshine?"

"Have you ever wanted something so badly, but been terrified to put yourself out there and go for it? Because that's where I'm at and I feel like I'm letting my fear, among other things, hold me back. I used to love being a reporter. And now I'm afraid that if I don't do this, I'll be stuck producing for the rest of my life. But if I do it...if I put myself out there and I'm a failure...then what?"

I take her hand and lead her over the couch, sitting down with my arm around her shoulders. She leans her head on my shoulder and places a hand on my chest. It throws me for just a minute, but I pull myself together.

"I understand that longing, and the fear of failure. I wanted to be a pitcher since I could throw a ball. I worked hard for it. All through high school and college, I worked and worked. I studied hard to stay on the varsity team and to keep my financial aid eligibility. I worked hard in the minors to get called up. Rookie of the Year, two Cy Young awards, and two rings. All that work for a handful of years of pro-ball before my arm gave up on me. I felt like a failure."

"You weren't a failure!" She's indignant on my behalf. A wrinkle appears between her brows and I want nothing more than to smooth it over with a kiss. "You were a number one over-all draft pick out of college, called up to the big league club after one year in the minors and deserved all of those awards and then some. You were part of a back-to-back world championship run. 2.55 career ERA, a win-loss record in those few years that some guys would kill for. You're not a failure because your arm went out. That was out of your control."

I give her a "do you hear yourself?" quirk of my eyebrow, and can see the realization dawning in her eyes as she turns her face away from me..

"You put in the work. Do your best. I'll be right beside you, and if both of our arms go...that's out of our control. And for the record? I'd very much like to date you, too."

Penelope grins at me, wrapping her arms around me and kissing me softly on the cheek before setting the table for dinner. I step into her kitchen and she puts me to work. We cook together, side-by-side, and sit down to eat with a ballgame playing in the background. Listening to her talk about baseball is like a high that I want to chase. I want to keep her talking; she's got stories like the grizzled old guys in the league, and stats and figures like the commentators using all the new models and data analysis. She scribbles out a few notes on the pad of paper she keeps on her table and tucks them into her work bag to fit into the show as the game continues on.

Tonight's show is one of my best so far. The only problem was, I had to do it without Penelope in the control room. She called in midway through dinner, asking if Morgan would cover for her. As we were eating, she started to recognize the signs of a migraine and decided to try and head it off at the pass, so she called out and sent me back to do the show. And it went fine. But I prefer Penelope's voice in my ear.

After a quick debrief with Morgan and the guys, I rush home to change and check on Penelope. I find a plate outside my door, laden with whatever that shortbread was that she was making. I pick up the plate and unlock my door. When my hands are free of cookies and keys, I pull out my phone and text Penelope a quick thank you.

Her response? *Best enjoyed with a cup of tea. If you don't have any, stop over.*

I don't have any tea. I'm not a tea kind of guy. What I do have is the desperate urge to see her again. To be close to her. To smell the sweet fragrance that follows her around, to hear her laugh, to sit beside her on the couch and feel her warmth. So, I grab a coffee mug from my own cabinet and step across the hall to knock on her door.

Something tells me she doesn't want to be alone tonight and this is her way of saying it.

But she must know, I would have come over anyway.

17

TEA FOR TWO
PENELOPE

There's a knock at my door…and I'm tempted to stay here, stretched out on my couch, and ignore it.

I'm rather comfortable, or at least as comfortable as I can be with a heating pad across my abdomen and wrapping around to my lower back, and an ice pack draped across my eyes.

A migraine started to set in about halfway through dinner with Jake. I'm not usually sensitive to sound, but light is a killer, and studio lights are even worse. Between the pain in my head, the nausea, and the kind of cramps that sometimes lay me out for a couple of days…I'm in rough shape tonight. Add to that, the crushing blow from today's pitch meeting? I'm in no mood to play hostess, but he's technically my boyfriend now, I think, so it comes with the territory. Right?

But, I did tell Jake to stop by for tea. What I didn't expect is that he'd take me up on it. This is a man who likes his coffee roasted extra dark, brewed with double the recommended amount of ground beans, and all without any cream or sugar to cut through the absolute sludge that fills his coffee pot. Which is why I don't drink the coffee he brings me if I know he made it himself.

The last thing I wanted to do tonight was ask him to come over, but I really don't want to be alone with my thoughts tonight. Alone with the imposter syndrome that creeps in after those stupid executive meetings. I'm glad he took me up on the offer, but I really don't want to get up off this sofa.

I lay aside my heating pad and ice pack, do my best to clean up the coffee table and hide the evidence of my less than stellar evening, and straighten myself up. I smooth out my clothes, re-tie my hair, and make myself look mostly human before opening the door.

Jake stands there looking entirely too handsome for this time of night, in a snug tee shirt that hugs every muscle of his arms and chest, a pair of navy joggers that hang just right from his hips, and...corgi socks? Not just corgis but corgis in baseball caps with bats and balls in the mix. My hormone addled brain would marry him right now if he asked me.

He holds a coffee mug in his hand and smiles when he sees me.

Here's what I shouldn't have done.

I shouldn't have told him to come for tea. I shouldn't have assumed that he'd laugh it off as a joke. I shouldn't have thrown on baggy sweatpants and an old tee shirt when I got home from work tonight. I am suddenly very conscious of my slightly bedraggled appearance, and if that's not enough, every now and then I'm wracked with a wave of pain and nausea.

"You said you have tea?"

Lucky for him, I just put the kettle on.

"Water's in the kettle, and there's an assortment of teas in the second drawer by the fridge."

Easing myself back down onto the sofa, I replace the heating pad, then pull a blanket over it in an attempt to hide the obvious signs of my discomfort. I hear him in the kitchen; his mug meets the counter with a gentle *clink,* water pours into the mug, and the drawer opens.

Once the drawer is open...silence. I don't have to turn around to see what's happening.

Decision paralysis.

I wasn't kidding when I told him I had tea. I have a literal drawer full. Bagged and loose leaf. Black, green, and herbal.

"I'd suggest Earl Grey," I say from the comfort of the sofa. It offsets the chocolate."

In a matter of seconds I hear the rustle of a box, and the tearing of a wrapper. And then...he's setting his mug beside me and returning to the kitchen. My curiosity gets the better of me; I turn around to find him methodically opening each of my upper cabinets until he finds what he's looking for. He takes a mug, and two small plates, fills the mug with water and a tea bag, and plates two shortbread bars – handing one to me – before settling down beside me, and propping his feet on my coffee table.

I'm wracked with a wave of nausea, but take a sip of my tea anyway.

"If you're not going to use that ice pack," Jake remarks through a mouthful of cookie, "let me put it back in the freezer for you until I leave."

I open my eyes and give him a pointed look.

I don't understand how this man is able to see right through all of my defenses. I can't hide anything from him. It's time I stop trying. I sink further into the couch and lay my head back, draping the ice pack over my eyes once more.

"Sorry," I mumble, trying to adjust the heating pad on my lap at the same time. "I'm not great company tonight."

"You're always great company." I feel him get up from the couch, taking his plate and mine and setting them in the sink. "I can leave if you'd like..."

"You don't have to...but I'm not any fun to be around right now."

"That's not true. You're always fun to be around."

I hand him the television remote and explain that sound sensitivity isn't an issue with this headache, but he insists on keeping the television muted nevertheless. I lift the ice pack to find that he's found a romantic comedy to watch, an early nineties classic. He whispers the dialogue along with the movie and I can't help but smile.

I haven't told him this, but the movie he stopped on is my ultimate "bad day movie." If he hadn't stopped by and I wasn't in so much pain, I'd probably have chosen to watch this one on my own with a box of tissues in my lap because it always, without fail, makes me cry.

Today sucked.

Today was the kind of day that makes me want to curl up in bed and forget it even happened. And then Jake showed up at my door.

I spent a lot of time hiding my emotions, my pain, after losing mom and dad. I buried it all deep down inside in an attempt to get my life back to some kind of normal. I didn't want to burden my brother with my grief while he dealt with his own. That became a pattern of tamping down the big feelings, and letting them simmer under the surface.

I lay back and tears well up in my eyes and are absorbed by the ice pack that covers my eyes.

"Something tells me this is more than just a headache," Jake's voice is gentle beside me. Soft and kind. He's giving me an opening to share. I need to take it.

"I'd love to host something," I say quietly, removing the ice pack so I can look at him. "I'd love to host a special like *Shattered Glass*."

I see a smile tug at the corners of his mouth, so small, so quick that I almost think I dreamed it because when he turns to me, it's gone. His gaze has turned serious as he wipes his hands on a napkin and turns to more fully face me. "Tell me what's going on in your head, Sunshine. What is keeping you from getting in front of the camera?"

Other than the full body hives that break out just at the thought of it? Or the panic that wells up inside of me? This feels like a test.

Like some cosmic litmus test asking me to prove just how much I trust Jake Hutchinson.

I tell him everything.

I tell him about the social media comments. The posts and memes and pictures. No one wants a woman who looks like me reporting their sports. Even with hair removal, and all the options available to me, there's still a shadow. It's the curse of the PCOS and dark hair combination.

I promised myself I'd ignore the comments on social media. I ignored the notes and letters that came to the studio. But it all got to be too much. For my own mental health, I decided to move away from being on camera and shift my focus to production behind the scenes.

There's a storm brewing behind Jake's eyes as understanding settles in. This isn't a story I've ever shared outside of my family. Even Mo doesn't know all of the details. Jake watches me with sadness in his eyes, but not pity. I've seen enough pity from people over the years to know what it looks like. This is compassion. Empathy.

"Now, just the thought of being on camera again makes me break out in hives. Angry, red hives all over my arms and neck and chest. You've seen my anxiety manifest itself at work, in meetings, usually with Mike because of things he'll say…anyway" just thinking about it makes me scratch absentmindedly at my collarbone, drawing Jake's gaze away from my face as he gently reaches out and takes my hand in his with a soft squeeze. "It can get pretty bad at work, but behind the camera, I can control it. In front of the camera, I'd be lucky if I didn't have a full-on panic attack."

The pitch meeting was a bust anyway, so it doesn't really matter, but Jake's idea to produce the piece ourselves is still gnawing at the back of my brain. Maybe I could host it if I had him helping me. Just knowing that I have his support – and Jim, Devon, and Mo – is all that I need.

"What would it look like? If we do it ourselves?"

We'd need a studio.

Cameras, lighting, and sound equipment.

A set.

People willing to participate.

And I'd need to be on camera. Jake assures me that between us, and Morgan and her husband Dan, we can cobble together a crew and the rest will fall into place.

"It's a risk," I sigh and sink further into the couch, wishing it could just swallow me up. "We can't be guaranteed that the network would accept it, that any network would take it."

Diane's words from that day at the Empire State Building ring in my head, *what's life without a little risk?* I'm already risking my heart with him. I risk my career each time I pitch this idea, so why not try and do it ourselves. What's the worst that can happen?

"I'm okay with risk. In fact, I'm all for risk taking."

"Let's do it then. We can figure out the logistics of a crew, I'll see if Morgan wants to help with that."

"Let me take care of working with her on that while you put the finishing touches on what the show will look like...and take a little time to rest. You need it."

With anyone else, I would be wildly offended if I was told I needed to rest, but it only endears him to me further; that he recognizes I'm not at the top of my game and isn't afraid to call it out. Having a candid conversation about my pain and my insecurity...I've never had this before. I've never had anyone willing to listen and understand.

Getting to know Jake has exposed a longing that I didn't want to recognize until now. A longing for companionship.

For love.

I've been alone most of my life, as the youngest sibling, I was home with mom and dad when my brother went off to college. I was on my own for the first part of my career, moving around from place to place, never putting down roots long enough to get invested in friendships or relationships outside of the office. Except for Morgan, who has known me since our college days. But even then, I still feel lonely sometimes.

It's a curious thing. Living in such a large city, with a friend close by, contact with my family at my fingertips, yet still feeling lonely. Longing, yearning, for something deeper. For someone who will sit on my sofa at night after we've had dinner, watching baseball and letting me read, or write, or work on work that I should have finished at the office but didn't because I wanted to walk home with him through the park because the summer sun glistening off of the Hudson is magical.

Until I met Jake, I didn't recognize the loneliness, or if I did, I ignored it, shoved it down deep so that I didn't have to deal with it...and now I can't imagine not having Jake Hutchinson in my life.

"Thanks for the tea," he says, standing up from the sofa and heading toward the door.

I stand and step toward him, a few tears betraying my emotions in the moment. I wrap my arms around his waist and lean into him. His arms wrap around me and hold me close. He presses a soft kiss to my temple, a touch that leaves me hoping for more.

"Thanks for everything," I whisper into his chest before he releases me from his embrace.

"See you in the morning, Sunshine. Get some rest tonight."

18

PLANNING
PENELOPE

I get through the day with minimal pain, but still have a lingering headache right behind my eyes. I drop into my desk chair with a sigh of relief, and it's all I can do not to let my head drop right to the desk in front of me. I keep my office lights low, and hand write my post-show notes in an effort to avoid the lights from my computer and tablet screens.

Jake stops by my office, knocking lightly on the door, and I still have to pinch myself whenever I see him smiling at me. His jacket is off, his tie hangs loose around his neck, and his sleeves are rolled up revealing those arms that drive me crazy. My heart stutters and I have to tear my gaze away from his arms to meet his eyes.

"You have plans for the weekend?" he leans against my office door frame, his posture so casual and his smile so disarming that it barrels right through all of my usual defenses.

"I have a date with my couch, a heating pad, and a movie."

He nods and steps more fully into my office now, sitting down in the chair he laid claim to, and dropping his bag and jacket on the floor beside, a small smile on his face.

"You know Detroit is in town this weekend?"

"I saw that..."

"I was thinking about going to the game tomorrow. I wondered..." he looks a little nervous and it's kind of adorable. I do my best to hide the smile pulling at my lips. "Would you like to go see them with me? Only if you're feeling up to it. We could make it our first official date."

I haven't been to a baseball game in too long. Not for fun, anyway. For a long time, if I was at a game, I was working. And it's Detroit. Our hometown team. How can I say no to him?

"Yeah. I'd like that." Most of the pain from the last few days has subsided, and I've worked through a lot worse than what I'm experiencing today. I shouldn't put off the opportunity to spend the day with Jake.

"Awesome, it's a date! I'll stop by before the game and we can head to the Bronx together."

He stands and walks to the door, glancing out into the hallway. His gaze hardens. He turns back to me and shuts the door before sitting down again. "Let me walk you home. Work for as long as you need to, but let me walk you home."

I nod and begin packing up to head out. I don't need to work late tonight. I can work from home if I have to. Jake slings his bag and mine over his shoulder and we walk side by side to the elevator. Once inside, he hits the button for the ground floor, and before I know it, his hand is reaching for mine. Our fingers intertwine and something like an electric current races up my arm, hitting me right in the heart.

It's a gorgeous night in the city, and we walk hand-in-hand through Riverside Park on our way from the office to our building, the breeze off of the Hudson—and my proximity to Jake—sends a shiver through my body and raises goosebumps on my arms.

We have a routine now, Jake and I; in the mornings, he brings coffee and pastries, and in the evenings he holds my hand as we walk home, and then he stays for dinner. I've gotten so used to having Jake in my apartment that when he goes home at night, I miss having him around.

Some nights for dinner, I do new, complicated recipes, and others, I do old, familiar recipes. Tonight calls for comfort food. And tonight, I don't need a recipe. Finding a jar of homemade tomato sauce in the back of my fridge, I get it simmering on the stove, boil water for pasta, and prepare bread for homemade garlic bread.

We take our bowls of pasta out onto my balcony, settling into the chairs, ice cold bottles of ginger ale on the table between us as we eat and watch the sunset over the Hudson. I love that we are so comfortable with each other these days that not a word needs to be said. We move in sync with each other around my small apartment, I cook and he gets dishes and silverware. I fill bowls with pasta and he adds sauce and cheese. He carries the food to the balcony and I bring the drinks.

We start planning for *Shattered Glass*. We make lists of everything we'll need, our contacts -- in the media, in baseball, and in the city in general. We know that we'll need a studio. I want to get that nailed down before I contact anyone for interviews. Jake and I had lunch with Morgan and Dan today, and they are on board with whatever we end up doing.

Dan has offered us the use of his camera and lighting equipment, Morgan agreed to edit and work on graphics and music. Once Jake and I have a list together, I divide it into categories and send it out to the three people that I'm trusting with this piece of my heart. Now it will just be a matter of choosing women to interview. And figuring out how to tell my own story.

When the planning is done, Jake and I sit in silence for a while, watching the hustle and bustle below us.

The silence is comfortable. Familiar.

"This never gets old," he says in his rumbly baritone. "This view, or this company."

He turns to me with a grin, takes my empty dishes from my hands and I hear him start washing dishes. When I'm barely over the threshold into the apartment, he points back to the balcony with a disapproving (though very cute and not at all menacing) glare.

"You cooked," he insists. "I'm on dish duty."

"Jake, I always cook," I protest. "I'm all about equitable division of labor, but I feel like I'm taking advantage of your kindness."

He puts down the sponge and dries his hands with the dishrag slung over his shoulder before closing the distance between us and gently turning me to face the door. He nudges me, not forcefully, out the door and back onto the balcony where he plops me back in my chair and presses a soft kiss on my lips.

My heart speeds up and a warmth spreads from the top of my head to the tips of my toes as I settle back into my chair, my mind drifting back to that fleeting moment, leaving me fully without words.

He kissed me. That's new.

Even after he heads home for the night, I'm thinking about that simple gesture. There's something about it that screams "new territory ahead!!!" for our relationship. Of course my brain goes right into "overthink everything" mode, and even as I'm falling asleep, I'm thinking of that kiss. How natural, how *right*, it felt.

How warm it made me feel. And how I wouldn't be mad if he did it again sometime.

19
MEMORIES
PENELOPE

It's been too long since I've been in a baseball stadium as nothing more than a spectator. I think the last time I was at a baseball game and not working before, during, or after, was a family outing right before I started college. We were all together, Mom and dad got us box seats to celebrate my graduation and Peter getting his job at the US capitol. It was a huge, celebratory day, and one of my happiest memories.

Jake and I arrive at the stadium early. We take a lap around the concourse, scoping out all of our food options and figuring out what to eat. Jake stops at a small kiosk and purchases two scorecards, and grabs a few of the tiny pencils from the box. He hands me my scorecard and pencils with a knowing smile.

It's all I can do to keep from crying when I take it from him. As I hold that scorecard in my hand, I'm flooded with memories of games with my dad. I'm ten years old again, sitting beside him and learning how to keep score. Eating a slice of pizza as he tells me what's happening on the field. I'm thirteen again, and on my first trip to New York. Seeing our team on the road, sitting with my dad and Peter, enjoying hotdogs and cheering on our team surrounded by fans in pinstripes. I'm twenty, on a solo road trip to Atlanta. It was supposed to be my first game on my own, but dad flew down and surprised me, no skin in the game, no loyalty to either team, just a day in the ballpark with a hotdog, a soda, and a scorecard in my hands, and some long overdue time with my dad.

This is my first game – as a spectator, not a part of my job – that I've attended without my dad. My first time in a stadium without him. Without his laugh, his boisterous shouts, his joyous laugh. My first game without the man who is the very reason I'm in sports media in the first place. The man who taught me everything I know about the game.

I wander toward the edge of the concourse, standing behind the last row of seats and look out over the field. The visitors are out on the field taking batting practice. I close my eyes and listen; to the voices on the field and of the fans around us, to the sound of batting practice - the crack of the bat, the soft *thwack* as a gloved hand catches a fly ball. Children laughing and raising their excited voices.

A gentle hand rests at the small of my back, winding around to find purchase on my hip as Jake pulls me into his side and presses a soft kiss to my temple. With his free hand, he reaches over and wipes away my tears with his thumb.

I pick standard stadium fare for my lunch, choosing a simple hotdog with mustard, and Jake gets the most obscenely large order of loaded nachos that I've ever seen. I grab a handful of napkins, anticipating that at least one of us (mostly him) is going to need them.

We head to our seats and I take a minute to soak in the atmosphere. The grass, the dirt, the smell of popcorn and hotdogs and beer. The murmur of the crowd and crack of the bat as the home team takes batting practice. The late June sun shines down and I close my eyes and breathe deep the comfort and familiarity of the ballpark.

I eat my hotdog, and share Jake's nachos. We fill out our score-cards with the starting lineups for both teams, and as the game progresses, we compare notes on how we keep score. Each of us does it slightly differently. I keep score the way my dad taught me, and a few of my notations are different from Jake's, who scores the way *his dad* taught him. We chat about our favorite players while we were growing up. Jake's were mostly pitchers while I've always had a soft spot for the guys who couldn't hit but were monsters on the field.

When a foul ball comes our way, I let Jake snag it. He gives it to a little girl sitting nearby with her dad, and she runs back to her seat, a grin on her face for the rest of the game. A few people recognize Jake, and high five or fist bump him, but for the most part, with his ball cap and aviators, he's largely left alone. That, and the fact that we are both dressed to the nines in support of the visiting team. We certainly don't fit in with the crowd, but that's half the fun of being a fan of the road team. We get funny looks when we stand up and cheer for hard hit balls or well-turned plays.

Jake abandons his scorecard when things get messy in the late innings, with the home team batting around and running out of clean scorecard space, but I love the challenge. I watch each pitch and play intently, and I feel Jake's gaze as I note each move in the scorecard, his arm settling across the back of my seat, and eventually his hand finds its way to my shoulder. He pulls me in so that I'm leaning up against him, telling me it's so he can see my scorecard better. But the gleam in his eye tells me he has other motives. And I don't mind. Not at all.

We lose. Handily. But today was the most fun I've ever had while watching my team lose, and I tell Jake as much as we ride the subway back to Manhattan. We walk back to our building and make our way upstairs, turning on another ballgame while I work on throwing together a light dinner for us. As I'm working on dinner, a chime comes from my tablet where it rests, charging on my dining room table. Jake grabs it for me and opens it up.

"Want me to answer it?" he asks.

"Sure." I don't know who would be calling me on a Saturday night. Peter knew I'd be at the game with Jake today and...

I turn to Jake, and he sees the horrified expression on my face as I realize what's happening. Peter moved up our call. Because that conniving fox knew Jake would be here with me. I feel heat creep into my cheeks as Jake grins at me over the screen of my tablet before introducing himself to my brother and sister-in-law, explaining that I'm making dinner but he'd be more than happy to talk with them.

I set the table and show Jake how I usually set up the tablet so I can chat with my family and eat at the same time, and we both situate ourselves in the frame. It seems that my family and Jake have gotten very comfortable with each other, and I'm not mad about that. In fact, if anything, it only endears him to me even more.

"What was it like," Peter asks, "playing in the big leagues?"

"It was a dream come true," Jake patiently answers my brother, his eyes lighting up. "I got to play the game I loved and make a living out of it. What more can you ask for?"

"What about..." Peter grunts midway through his question and I notice that Sofi is trying to silently communicate something with him by using her elbow. His brows furrow as he turns to his wife, who sighs as he finishes his question. "What about your arm?"

"I mean...It certainly wasn't an ideal way to go out. You never want your career to be cut short, least of all by an injury. But I enjoyed the game while I played it, and now I get to spend my days talking about it with some of the most brilliant minds in baseball," he turns to me, lips curled into a small smile. Heat fills my cheeks as his gaze shifts back to Peter and Sofi, "what more could I ask for?"

We end the call and I thank him for being such a good sport with my family as we stand side by side, washing dishes together. "I'm sorry my brother brought up your injury."

"I'm not. It's something I have to learn to talk about more. I'm glad he asked." He nudges me with his elbow and laughs. "Besides, it was fun. I like your family. They remind me of mine."

Jake tells me more about his brothers and sister and their parents as we finish the dishes and settle onto the sofa for more baseball, his arm around my shoulder, my feet tucked under me as I lean into him and open a book. He watches the game and I read, and after a while we realize it's getting awfully late. He softly kisses my cheek before pulling himself off of the sofa and heading to the door.

I stand and follow him to the door. He stops and turns to me, a question in his eyes and in the tilt of his head.

"What is it?" I ask, my voice comes out sounding huskier than I'd like and I feel heat spreading across my cheeks and neck.

"Can I kiss you?" He asks as his own cheeks redden. "I didn't ask the other night, and I realized after the fact that I should have..."

No one has ever asked me that.

My first boyfriend in high school kissed me without warning, surprising me just before a band concert. It wasn't great. And we didn't last long, though not because of the kiss. My college boyfriend never asked for my consent, and was offended when I pointed it out to him.

My chest tightens with sudden emotion as he watches me and waits for my answer. Something as simple as asking for my consent shouldn't make me this emotional. But it's more than that. He's not only asking for my permission, but in doing so, he's acknowledging that it's important to him, that he respects me enough to allow me to choose.

I nod. But he doesn't move. "Words, Penelope. I need words." His voice is a rough whisper that sends a tingle up my spine.

"Yes," I whisper, and he closes the distance between us. One hand slides through my hair, cupping the back of my neck, and the other he settles on my hip. I wrap my arms around his neck and lean into his touch, inhaling the spicy scent of his cologne and my knees go wobbly as my senses are overwhelmed in the best way. That hand on my hip wraps around and presses into my lower back as he holds me up and deepens the kiss.

"For the record," I pull away and take a second to catch my breath. "You don't have to ask again."

Jake grins at me as he opens the door. "Goodnight, Sunshine," he leaves a soft kiss on my cheek before walking out into the hallway and closing the door behind him, leaving me...speechless.

"Goodnight Stormcloud," I whisper to my door as it closes for the night, my fingers tracing the lingering warmth on my lips. *I love you.* The thought startles me at first, but it's true. I'm in love with him.

This is *seriously* new territory.

20

SHATTERING THE GLASS
JAKE

Every night for the last two weeks, after the broadcast, Penelope and I set up shop at her dining room table and work on *Shattered Glass*. I've called in favors with people across the league who are more than happy to help us out; we've set up interviews, and rented a studio in Brooklyn for a weekend. Morgan has used her connections (and her husband Dan) to make sure that we have camera and audio equipment, lighting and set design, and a hair and makeup team, while I work out the logistics of the interviews, Penelope designs graphics to overlay with the video.

It's all coming together beautifully. And it doesn't hurt that I've gotten to spend all this time with her. Something in our relationship shifted, as evidenced by that kiss that I can't stop thinking about. That kiss in her apartment two weeks ago. It was a good kiss. I haven't kissed her again, but I've wanted to. Every time I stand next to her and wash dishes or learn a new skill in the kitchen, I think about taking her in my arms and kissing her senseless.

Sitting across from her right now at her kitchen table, I'm distracted. Her glasses slipping down her nose, her hair blowing in the slight breeze from the open balcony door...I sit back and take my own glasses off, rubbing the sting out of my eyes. She meets my gaze with a smile and a heavy ache settles in my chest, right near my heart.

I love this woman.

Simple as that. I love her. I don't know how it happened or when it started, but somewhere along the way we became more than friends. More than coworkers. I *love* this woman and want nothing more than to spend quiet nights like this together for as long as she'll have me.

Penelope's brow furrows as she looks at me, removing her own glasses and rubbing her temples. I can tell she's working through a migraine. I step into the kitchen and grab her ice pack from the freezer, handing it to her without a word. I hold out my hand and she softly twines her fingers with mine. I lead her over to her couch. She flashes a quick, grateful smile before tugging me down and pressing a soft kiss to my lips.

"Thanks, Jake."

"Get some rest, sweetheart. You've got a big day tomorrow."

I lay awake most of the night thinking of how and when to tell Penelope how I feel about her. I torture myself with the idea that she may not feel the same way, and eventually I fall asleep thinking of our tour of New York City and how...natural it felt to be her fake husband that day. After a rough night of sleep, I wake long before the sun and head down to the fitness center for a run. Then, I step into my kitchen.

Using all of the skills that Penelope has taught me over the last two months, I start chopping vegetables with the knife and cutting board she gave me, I cook them in a small pan that I bought so that I could practice at home without bothering Penelope, and soon I have eggs scrambled with peppers and onions, crumbled sausage, cheddar cheese, and a seasoning blend that cost me a handful of New York baseball tickets...turns out Alejandro isn't just a fan of mine, but was all too eager to share his blend when he knew it was going to Penelope.

I text Penelope to stop over for breakfast, and a few minutes later she's walking through the door of my apartment with a skeptical look on her face. A skeptical look that soon becomes a smile when she sees the mess on my counter, and no doubt smells the lingering scent of onion in the air.

She takes a seat at my small dining table, removing her blazer and draping it with my sport coat on the back of the sofa. Under her navy blazer she wears an ivory sheath dress that hugs her every curve. I'm a little worried about her wearing breakfast so I grab a sweatshirt from my closet for her to throw on over her dress. As she does so, I take tortillas from the fridge and begin to assemble breakfast burritos for the two of us.

I have to admit, I'm really proud of myself when she takes her first bite and closes her eyes, letting out a low moan of pleasure. No one has ever reacted like that to anything that I've cooked. She takes another bite and I watch her, not even bothering to eat my own burrito yet.

"Jake," she wipes her mouth with a napkin and takes a long look at me, "that was fantastic!"

The pride in her voice is unmistakable. Everything I did this morning is something that she taught me, so she has every right to be proud. But my heart swells when she tells me that she's proud of me. I've never been the kind of guy that wanted to impress women, but I'm enjoying impressing this woman.

And I'm proud of her, too.

"And *this* is for you," I hand her a small jar with its accompanying recipe card, "from Alejandro."

She beams, thanks me profusely, and pulls me in for a kiss before helping me clean up and get ready for the busy day ahead.

Penelope has spent a lot of long nights working on writing, organizing, and designing for the show. I'm so proud of the work that she has put into making her dream come true, and overwhelmed with gratitude that she trusts me to be a part of it. I know she's scared. I know that she hasn't done anything like this in a long time, but she's put together something special. And I look forward to watching it all come together for her. I also look forward to our relationship outside of the show and how we move forward from here.

With Morgan standing in to run the morning and pre-production meetings today, Penelope and I both call out and head over to Brooklyn to meet with Dan and his crew, and get ready to conduct the interviews. Penelope has arranged for the first female general manager in the league to join us, two women who paved the way for women in television and radio broadcasting, and a round table discussion with female fans of varying demographics, including my sister.

And I've arranged a surprise for her for later in the day.

We have a long day of filming ahead but I see an energy in her that I've never seen before; she's practically buzzing as we walk into the studio and see the set that we (she) designed. I see Jenna across the way in a makeup chair and my pulse races.

I don't know why I'm so nervous. It's just my sister. It's not like I'm introducing Penelope to the whole family...which I hope to do soon. But not yet. Today it's just Jenna. The thing is, I really want Jenna to like her. I'm so glad that Jenna agreed to be a part of the roundtable of fans for *Shattered Glass*; she was always one of my biggest supporters during my playing days, having her here is a support not just for me, but for Penelope.

We've just gotten to the studio and Penelope is busy with moving things around on the set while we wait for the ladies to get mic'd up for the roundtable. Jenna is the first one to the set, she sidles up to me and wraps me in a hug.

"Good to see you, Jakey!"

"You too, Jaybird!" I squeeze her tight, calling her by her old childhood nickname. "Thank you so much for doing this."

"Oh, I'm not doing this for you," she throws me a cheeky smile before glancing across the set and watching Penelope. "This is for her. This has nothing to do with you. So...when can I meet her?"

She's giddy. Turns out, introducing my sister to the woman I love is more nerve wracking than pitching in a world championship game.

"How about right now?"

I walk Jenna closer to the set and Penelope sees us coming, stopping what she's doing and giving me a nervous smile. I introduce them to each other and Jenna hugs Penelope...and for just a moment I worry about how this is going to go, until I see Penelope visibly relax in my sister's embrace.

Penelope begins to show Jenna around the set, taking out her tablet and showing her the outline for the show and what the plans are for the day. I take a step away and let them get to know each other, laughing and joking and acting like old friends. The rest of the women for this segment file onto the set and Penelope gets them situated around the table, with herself at the head. After a quick mic check, the cameras roll, and Penelope is on.

I stand off camera and watch, in awe of these women and their stories. And then Penelope throws a gut punch.

"Jenna, tell me about the night of your brother's injury. As a fan, I remember the devastation that I felt...you're more than just a fan though, you're a sister..."

Jenna casts her gaze on me before answering. Jenna and I have never talked about this before. Jax and I briefly discussed it in the hospital that night, and James was with me through my physical therapy. But Jenna? Jenna was in the stadium that night. Jenna was whisked away to the clubhouse when it happened. She rode in the ambulance with me. She was pale and shaky and didn't say a word for most of the night. We've *never* discussed this. But judging from the look on her face, Penelope prepared her for this line of questioning. I'm the one who got thrown a curveball.

"As a fan of the game, you never want to see a pitcher go down with an injury, especially not an elbow injury. Obviously a lot of guys have had Tommy John surgery and come back stronger. Jake had already had Tommy John, and that was supposed to be his comeback season; as his sister, I was hopeful. I'd seen him through his first surgery and rounds of physical therapy and I was excited to see him get back into the game..."

Jenna takes a deep breath and gathers her composure. Penelope puts a steadying hand on Jenna's arm; a friendly, reassuring touch to let her know that she's not alone. Just like I wasn't alone through my first surgery and months of therapy that followed. Jenna was with me. By my side through it all. Jax and James were in the middle of residencies and internships, and I don't blame them for not being around. I've never held that against them. Jenna was there, she wanted to be with me. It was a time of bonding for the two of us, I got to know my sister better in those few months than I did while we were kids. I also learned way more about biology and ecology than I ever wanted to know.

I wouldn't have made it through that first injury if it wasn't for Jenna.

"That night was my first time in the stadium for one of his starts that season. I was giddy. I got there early, bought my food and scorecard," the other ladies nod, each of them relating to this part of the story, as it sounds so much like their own. These are women who appreciate the game - not just their team, not just a single player (not that there is anything wrong with any of those things) - they appreciate the beauty of the game and its history. "I had perfect seats down the first baseline, just a few rows up from the dugout. When he went into his windup, I held my breath...I always do when he's pitching."

I didn't know that.

"It happened in slow motion for me: the stretch, the windup, the release. And then he was crumpled on the ground and my heart stopped. I jumped to my feet, my vision narrowed, and an ache settled in my chest and wouldn't go away..."

Tears prick the backs of my eyes, emotion welling up in my chest.

I can't interrupt the shot, but I really want to go hug my sister right now.

"I realized after the fact that I was having a panic attack for most of that night -- from the time he hit the mound to the time he was admitted to the hospital. I honestly don't remember much about that night after the initial injury. I was out of it..."

I had no idea. None. Sure, I knew that Jenna dealt with anxiety, but I never knew that she was in the middle of a panic attack the whole way to the hospital that night.

"Thank you Jenna," Penelope transitions into the closing portion of this segment, wrapping up with anecdotes from each of the women before closing things out. After a moment, she leans over and wraps my sister in a hug, holding on for a long time, tears glistening in her eyes, as Jenna openly cries in Penelope's arms. Eventually she lets Jenna go and then hugs each of the women in turn, thanking them for participating and promising to let them know if the special ever airs.

I walk onto set and take Jenna in my arms, pressing a kiss to the top of her head.

"I had no idea..."

"It's okay," she wraps her arms around my waist and leans into me, "you had other things on your mind that night."

"Yeah...but nothing more important than my sister. I really am sorry that I didn't realize what was going on."

"You've more than made up for it."

Penelope approaches us and stands a short distance away. Jenna disentangles herself from me and hugs Penelope again, tighter and longer than last time, and by the end both women are in tears. Penelope convinces Jenna to stick around for as long as she'd like. Jenna agrees to join us for lunch following the next interview.

After filming the segment with the fans, we clear the set and get ready for the one on one interviews with the general manager and the media personalities. When Amy Kim walks through the doors, she commands the room. Penelope invites her to sit down and after a shaky start to the interview, they settle into a comfortable conversation. They discuss breaking barriers and, appropriately enough, shattering glass ceilings. By the time Amy leaves, Penelope is shaking. I suggest we break for lunch; she needs a break from the cameras, I'm sure of it.

The fresh air outside of the studio seems to do her some good. We eat in a park that allows us a view of Manhattan, and I thank God for the time that we have together away from the office. She's in her element in front of the camera, she's relaxed and laid back away from Mike and the pressure cooker of the network offices. And more than that, she's supported.

No one here is shooting down her ideas or invalidating her experiences. She's got full creative freedom. Morgan's husband and his crew are accommodating and answer all of her questions with an enthusiasm that matches Penelope's. I find myself wanting this for her, wanting to find a way to give her a show, get her doing this on a regular basis.

After lunch, Penelope busies herself tweaking the set and rewriting her note cards to film the wrap up of her show. I watch from behind the bank of cameras, and get a feel for what it must be like for her on a nightly basis; watching us as we conduct our interviews and offer commentary, all the while she is doing the hard work of getting the show on the air. After a few hours on this side of things today, I have a new appreciation of the work that she and Morgan are doing on a nightly basis, along with the rest of the production team. It's thankless, and I wouldn't have a job without it.

This last filming session is the one that I pulled a few strings for. Penelope doesn't know it, but I'm bringing in the radio broadcaster that she looked up to as a young girl. Susan called games for my organization. I got to know her really well during my short major league career, and when I called her up, she was thrilled to come into the city and meet with us.

At the sound of the studio doors opening, I turn and see Susan striding toward me, arms outstretched for a hug.

"Jake!" Susan folds me into a hug and I feel a sense of calm. A sense of home.

"Susan, thank you so much for doing this."

"You're welcome kid. She must be pretty great if you're calling in the big guns." We share a laugh and Penelope turns to see what's going on. Her clipboard and pen clatter to the ground and she does her best to play it cool when she leans down to pick up her notes. I leave Susan and walk over to an obviously flustered Penelope.

"Sunshine." I walk over and put my hands on her shoulders to steady her. She looks panicked. It's adorable.

"Stormcloud."

"Everything okay?"

"That's Susan Walters," she points toward the door where I left Susan standing, as if I have no idea who my old friend is.

"Yes, it is."

"I know you did this. Somehow. I just... when I can put a coherent sentence together I'll say thank you but, for now..."

She stretches up and kisses me squarely on the lips. Her hands on either side of my face. And now I'm the one who can't put a sentence together. It's all I can do not to grab her and pull her closer to me, deepening the kiss, but not in front of Susan and all these cameras.

"Let me introduce you." I take her hand after we collect ourselves, and bring her over to where Susan stands, a satisfied smirk on her face after what she just saw.

"Mrs. Walters...it's an honor." I hear the quiver in Penelope's voice and am starting to worry that she's going to burst into tears.

"Please, call me Susan," she pulls Penelope into a hug and I think not only does the sunshine in the room grow brighter, but I think I see my Sunshine grow another two inches.

She's ecstatic.

21

TURNING TABLES
JAKE

One of the first phone calls I made when Penelope decided to go through with this project on her own, was to my old friend Susan Walters. Susan has been a part of the New York radio team for as long as I can remember. I got to know her while I was a part of the organization, and that friendship has lasted even in the day following my retirement.

Susan was one of the first women to do color commentary on the radio for a major league baseball team. And she's one of the best in the business.

"Role models," Penelope says, handing me a freshly rinsed dish to dry. We've just finished having dinner together in my apartment, and have been discussing plans for Shattered Glass, discussing questions to ask the women she'll be interviewing at the end of the week.

"Jim McCann", I don't even have to think about it. "Aside from the fact that he was a catcher, I wanted to be Jim when I grew up. He was one of the best guys - on and off the field. He led in hitting categories and was a great pitcher, but beyond that he was involved in his community, and was a real leader. And the fact that I get to work with him now is a dream come true."

She nods, scrubbing the pot in her hands when I catch her off guard and ask the same question. Without a moment's hesitation she answers.

"Susan Walters."

It doesn't surprise me. But I have to ask anyway. "Why Susan?"

Penelope freezes. Hands submerged in the sink filled with soapy water, her eyes fixed on the soap bubbles.

"Because she made it possible for me to believe that I could make a career out of talking about the game I love." Penelope takes a steadying breath and pulls her hands from the water, rinsing them in the stream from the tap and absentmindedly taking the towel I offer her. "She made me believe in myself again when I was at my lowest."

Penelope explains, with tears in her eyes, that listening to Susan call games on the radio is what helped her get through the first few months after walking away from being on television, and as she navigated the career change that eventually brought her to New York.

When the dishes are done, I hand Penelope a ginger ale and one of the cookies we made earlier, and point her toward the balcony. My balcony doesn't have a great view of the river like hers does, and the best I can offer her for seating is a couple of blankets spread out and the throw pillows my mom and sister insisted I have on my couch, but you can't beat any view of New York City and I really don't mind having her lean up against me while we're out here.

I place my phone between us on the blanket, the New York radio broadcast pulled up with the volume turned up as loud as it will go. As Susan's voice floats through the speakers Penelope closes her eyes and leans into my side, and I wrap an arm around her shoulders. We listen long after the sun has gone down and a chill laces the air, Penelope resting in my arms as the wheels in my head start to turn...

Penelope walks Susan over to the set, answering all of her questions about the project, and Penelope is quieter than she's been all day. I see the panic on her face as Dan starts to help Susan get mic'd up and she takes a seat on the set. Penelope paces a bit before coming to a stop next to me.

"What do I do?" she whispers. "I don't have anything prepared?"

"Just sit down and have a conversation with her, and go from there."

She gives a resolute nod before smoothing out her skirt, adjusting her own microphone, and taking a seat on the set across from her childhood hero. I step behind the camera and stand beside Dan, watching as Penelope kicks things off.

She gets off to a bit of a shaky start. Susan, sensing Penelope's nerves, lays a hand on her arm, stopping her line of questioning, and turning the tables.

"Penelope," Susan regards her with a glint in her eye, "what drew you to this profession?"

"You did," Penelope's answer is barely above a whisper. "Well, you and an eight year old boy who made me cry."

Susan laughs and asks her to elaborate, and Penelope's voice loses its quiver as she finds her confidence and tells her story.

"I was eight or nine, and I got into a fight on the playground with a boy that I liked. He told me that girls couldn't play baseball but that I could play in the lunchtime game if I proved that I knew the names of the current Detroit players. I rattled off the list and he told me that no girl should know more about baseball than the boys. When my dad asked me how my day was, I cried when I told him the story. That night, he told me about a woman who did color commentary on the radio. That she was brilliant, and knew all about the game of baseball. We listened to her together…"

Something softens in Susan's gaze as she realizes where this story is going, and I realize how we have to end the episode. We end it with this, this turning of the tables. We have to end *Shattered Glass* with Penelope being interviewed by her childhood hero.

"Every chance we got, my dad and I would listen to your games. It became comforting to me. After my first breakup in high school, I didn't turn on moody music, I put your games on the radio so that I could hear your voice and your stories. When I was splitting my time between mom and dad's chemo treatments, I would sit in my car and listen to you. It brought me so much comfort to hear your voice as you talked about the game that I love so much."

I told Susan a few things about Penelope and her career history that I thought would be useful. Things that Penelope has already shared with me. And Susan, sensing the direction of the conversation, and being a good interviewer herself, asks the question that I've been asking since I met Penelope.

"Do you think you'd go back to being on camera after this?"

Penelope pauses. She glances off camera at me, and I give her the signal that I see from her daily—keep going, we have time to fill. I see *the look* flash across her face, the wheels in her head are turning as she thinks about this question that I—and Devon and Jim—have been asking her.

"Honestly Susan," I'm amazed at how comfortable Penelope looks right now, how easily she's settled into this conversation. "I don't know. I do know that I've had a lot of fun working on this project. I'm thankful for the person who convinced me to take this on, and the opportunity that it has given me to shine a light on the places where women are often overlooked in the game. Whether that's in the front offices or the media or in the stadiums as fans."

The studio is silent.

Susan watches as Penelope takes a breath, pausing and collecting her thoughts. That's an answer, and it's a good one. But it's not an answer to the question that was asked of her. And she knows it. I know it. I know that Penelope enjoyed her time on television, and I know that she still suffers with self-consciousness some days. I consider it an honor that she's shared those struggles with me, that she trusts me enough to share those details of her life. Which is why I'm stunned when she answers.

"I think I'd like to be on television again, if given the opportunity. Some of the best days of my career were spent in and out of stadiums and arenas, covering everything from high school football to semi-pro baseball. I miss it. More than anything, I miss spending my days talking about the game I love, and I wish I hadn't let myself lose sight of why I chose this path in the first place. I shouldn't have let the voices in my head, and the voices of the critics, tell me that I wasn't good enough. It's hard to be a woman in the public eye, with social media and means of communication at our fingertips, there are comments on our appearance, our voices, the things we do and don't know...and I became overwhelmed by all of it."

Penelope pauses and Susan waits for her to continue. Every eye in this room is on her, riveted, waiting for her to continue.

"In the years since I changed paths, I've met a number of people who've helped to remind me why I love the game of baseball, but most importantly...they've reminded me that my worth isn't tied to my successes or failures."

Penelope's eyes glisten with unshed tears. The room seems to be holding its collective breath as both Susan and Penelope compose themselves. The rest of the hour *flies* by, and before I know it we're packing up. I help Dan tear down the set and the equipment as Penelope and Susan continue talking to each other off camera. Susan hands Penelope a card and wraps her in a hug before exiting the studio. When the door is shut, Penelope covers her mouth with her hand, shoulders shaking as tears stream down her cheeks. I'll be honest, I'm surprised she held it together this long.

I walk over to her and wrap my arms around her, her body trembling as I draw her close.

"Thank you," she whispers, leaning her head against my chest.

"It was my pleasure."

22

SAFE AT HOME
JAKE

Penelope is strangely quiet as we drive back to Manhattan. She looks tired, not that I'd say that to her, and I tell her to close her eyes and rest if she wants to as we head toward the studio. She nods and closes her eyes, letting her head fall against the headrest, a smile still on her face as we cross the Brooklyn Bridge.

I know this day took a lot out of her. She looks drained, and now she has to walk into our studio and offices and run the show tonight. I check in with her as we part ways to our own offices and she assures me that she's fine, she just has a headache. She gets lots of headaches, and I've been around for a few of them. Sometimes she's really good at hiding the pain, but since leaving Brooklyn, she seems to be doing worse.

I can't help but watch Penelope from my place at the desk as Jim and Devon join me to get ready for the show. I'm worried about her. She grins at her team, she counts down to the start of the show, laughs with Morgan, and cracks jokes to the hosts. She's in such a great mood, but underneath the smile and laughter, I can see the pain in her eyes. I can see that she's carrying herself differently. She's stiff and careful in her movements. There's a slight furrow in the space between her eyebrows and some primal part of me wants to drag her out of here and take her home to her ice packs and heating pads.

"You okay?" a faint voice asks through the headset. I look up and see a pained look on Penelope's face, she waves off whoever asked, and the show goes on. But that look stays. Her face looks stuck between a wince and a too casual smile. She's not okay, that much is clear.

I keep an eye on her throughout the rest of the show, trying not to get distracted, but as the broadcast progresses, she starts looking worse and worse. Even Jim and Devon notice, asking during commercial breaks if she's okay. She brushes us off too. But something is wrong. She was fine all morning and afternoon while we were filming, we split lunch so I know it's not food poisoning. She didn't seem like herself on the drive back from Brooklyn, and was oddly quiet throughout the pre-broadcast meeting tonight. And that look on her face? It makes me want to sweep her out of here and get her home.

When we cut, I watch her race to her office, and I take off after her, brushing off Mike on my way.

"Just stick her in a cab," I hear Mike's voice trailing behind me as I rush to follow her, "she'll find her way home."

I choose not to respond to Mike, knowing that it's not worth the trouble, but also not trusting myself not to punch him in the nose. He'd deserve it. I catch up with Penelope just as she stumbles into the chair in her office, her face pale and with a fine sheen of sweat across her forehead. She's pressing her hands to her abdomen and is clearly in a lot of pain, though she tries her best to hide it when she sees me.

"Hey…" I take a cautious step into her office, "let me get you home. Please? I'm worried about you, sweetheart."

She opens her mouth to protest and is clearly hit with another wave of pain that seems to knock a little sense into her stubborn head as she looks at me with defeat in her eyes and whispers a pained 'yes'. I help her gather up her belongings and tuck her into my side for the walk from her office to the elevator, where she leans on me for support, almost as if her knees will give out at any minute.

As soon as we reach the lobby, I scoop her into my arms despite her protests, and step out into the night. She shivers as I stand on the street corner and hail us a cab, I instinctively pull her closer to my chest. Her face is red and lined with pain, a sheen of sweat across her forehead and cheeks. While we wait for a cab, I dab her forehead with my wrist, wiping away as much as I can. Her brow crinkles and eyes squeeze shut as a particularly disgruntled driver lays on his horn while passing us. She's got a migraine. But there's more. I've been around for migraines and have never seen her like this.

A car pulls up and I gently deposit her in the seat before sliding in beside her. The cab driver shoots me a wary glance and I explain that she's sick and I'm responsible for taking her home, not the cause of her current condition. I give him the address to our building and ask Penelope for her keys, which she quickly hands over.

"Okay, sweetheart," I try to keep my voice down, "we're almost home."

She nods, keeping her eyes shut, pain still evident on her face. The elevator ride up to the tenth floor seems to take longer than normal. I hold her close, trying my best not to aggravate whatever is causing her pain. The elevator finally stops and I walk down the hall toward our doors, pausing in front of hers and setting her feet on the floor. She leans into me as I open her door and walk into her apartment. I leave the lights off and walk her toward her bed. She sits on the edge and finally opens her eyes.

"What's going on?" I ask, kneeling down in front of her and taking her hands in mine. "What can I do?"

Before she can speak, she lurches off the bed and stumbles into the bathroom. I hear her retching and I wince. I feel helpless. There has to be something I can do. The toilet flushes. I round the corner into the bathroom and she is laying on the floor, her cheek pressed against the cool tile. I scoop her up and help her sit. Finding a clean washcloth in her linen closet, I run cool water and gently wipe her face.

"You need to get comfortable. Where do you keep comfy clothes? This isn't going to be a rom-com cliché" I crack a smile, trying to lighten the mood. "I will not overstep my boundaries, but you stay here and I'll bring you something to change into, okay?"

The ghost of a smile tugs at her lips. We've talked several times about the rom-com trope of the hero changing the woman's clothes and then them sharing a bed. She hates the gimmick and so do I. And even if I didn't, I respect her too much to cross that boundary in this way.

"There's a sweatshirt and shorts folded up on my desk chair," her usually commanding voice is timid. I can hear the unspoken pain just below the surface. She closes her eyes again and leans forward over the toilet, her hair falling around her face.

"Hang on," I look around and find a hair tie in the basket on the counter and gently sweep her hair into a ponytail. She sighs, her shoulders slumping as she leans against the toilet again. I step out into the other room and find her small desk in the corner nearest her bed. I haven't been in this part of her apartment before, I tend to stay near the couch and the kitchen area.

I've *seen* this part of the apartment, I've been curious about it, but I've never ventured over here. She uses a curtain to divide up the space, separating her bedroom from the rest of the studio, usually the curtain is pulled close when I'm here, but the few times it hasn't been, I admit, I've paid closer attention to this corner, wanting to soak in every detail of her space that I can.

That's the thing about studios, you can see a person's entire space.

Where they eat, where they sleep, where they work. The other times I've been here, I've avoided this corner of the apartment, drawing an invisible line between her living space and her sleeping space. The balcony is the closest I've gotten. I pick up the pajama pants and sweatshirt from her desk chair and find myself observing her sleeping space now that the curtain is pulled back.

This space is...softer somehow, compared to the rest of the apartment. With the curtain closed, I imagine it blocks out most of the ambient light that is a part of city living. Her bedding is purple with a small floral pattern, the bedspread tucked in tight, matching pillows sitting atop the bed. She's a bed maker. Probably every day, I'd guess. There's a few pairs of shoes and some clothes on her floor, a laundry basket sits by her in-unit washer and dryer just past the kitchen. There's a stack of books on the table beside her bed, and even more stacked in neat piles against the wall. Family pictures are everywhere in this space -- whereas the rest of the apartment is an ode to her and her siblings, this space has pictures with her parents as well.

There's a vase of fresh flowers on her desk, daisies. Her favorite. The toilet flushes again, snapping me out of my observation. I take the clothes and step back into the bathroom to lay them on the counter. She's wiping her face with the wash cloth from before, and I sit down beside her again, taking the cloth and running it down her neck and the exposed skin of her chest. She is still flushed, and her face has gone pale.

"What else can I do?" I ask, as she closes her eyes and leans against the wall again.

"Nothing," she whispers. "It's a migraine. I haven't had one like this in a while, I just have to ride it out."

"It's more than that though, isn't it?" I can tell she hasn't told me everything. But I don't want to press her for more details if she isn't comfortable sharing. I've been here before when she's had pain and headaches, but this seems to be hitting harder than what she's experienced in a while. When she starts to cry, I start to worry. I've never seen her cry from her pain before. She's always composed, she grins and bears it, works through migraines and cramps and chronic pain.

Tears slip down her cheeks as she nods, and I know that her guard is down tonight. I sit down next to her on the tile floor and wrap my arms around her. She lays her head on my shoulder and I inhale the scent of strawberries and...mint? Her shampoo or something. It's intoxicating. She shudders and settles in closer to me, deeper into my arms.

"Hang tight," I whisper, softly kissing her temple and wiping her tears away with my thumb before I extract her from my arms. "Change your clothes. I'll be right back."

I turn down her bed, removing all the decorative pillows and stacking them in a corner. I pull the covers back to make a space for her to lay down, and find a towel spread out across the width of the bed, and pieces begin to fall into place. The migraine, the cramps, the nausea. When I return to the bathroom, she's rifling through the cabinet under the sink, her brow furrowed until she finds what she was looking for and moves it to the forefront.

She carefully walks to her bed and I notice the color in her cheeks as she arranges the towel. I let her get comfortable while I head into her kitchen to grab her ice pack from the freezer. I remember it from the night I showed up for tea. I gently lay the cold pack across her eyes and forehead and she visibly relaxes under the slight weight of the mask. Then I plug in her heating pad and she situates it the way she likes it.

"I'm sorry you have to see me like this," She says, turning her head away from me. She's embarrassed, and I never intended for that to happen.

"Don't be sorry," I kneel down, smoothing her hair away from her eyes. "This is your life Penelope, and if I'm going to share life with you, I want to share all of it - the good, the bad, and the messy. I want to know how to be here for you, how to help you through the pain. Tell me how I can take care of you."

"Just being here is enough."

Once she's tucked in and I'm sure she's asleep, I pull her curtain shut to block out as much light as possible, and make myself comfortable on her couch, choosing a book from her shelf that I've never read, and turn on a small table lamp.

After a while, her phone starts to ring. I can hear it coming from her briefcase where I dropped it beside the door. Not wanting her to wake up to the obnoxious ringtone, I quickly locate the phone and answer it.

"Hey Peter."

"Jake? Is my sister there?"

"She is, but she's sleeping. She's been sick most of the evening."

"Sick how?" Peter asks, and a hint of panic creeps into his voice.

"Uh..." I run through the symptoms in my head and relay them to Peter. "Migraine, abdominal pain, vomiting."

"And you're there with her?"

"Yeah. I'm here. I'm staying until I know she's okay."

"Thank you. I'm..." Peter's voice cracks, choking with emotion. "I'm glad she's not alone. Again."

Again.

There's a story there. I won't push. But there's a story there.

"I care about her, Peter. There's nowhere else I'd be right now."

"Thanks Jake. Sofi and I are going to drive up tomorrow. I want to be there with her, too."

"Okay. I'll see you tomorrow then."

It's hard to miss the emotion in Peter's voice as he hangs up the phone, presumably to hop in his car right now and drive up here from his home in Washington DC. As far as I know, Penelope's only living family is her brother. She briefly mentioned her parents and I've never worked up the nerve to ask her for more details, afraid that it may still be a sensitive subject. A quick search of her name led me to two different obituaries, a month apart from each other. Both parents, taken by cancer. Leaving behind Penelope and her brother.

I know more about Penelope now than I ever thought I would. We've spent the last few weekends exploring the city together, crossing off more of her NYC bucket list; museums and tourist traps, visiting all of the parks and historical sites, we even spent a Saturday on Liberty Island. It's been great getting to know her and even better having a friend here in the city.

I barely made it through the show tonight, seeing her looking so sick, it scared me. I wanted to get her out of there and get her home as quickly as I could to take care of her, to make sure she's okay.

If tonight has done anything for me, it's only confirmed my suspicions of Mike Fletcher. His "throw her in a cab" comment is still ringing in my head as I sit in the quiet waiting room. This is the most recent in a string of inappropriate or off-color remarks he's made to Penelope, dating back to my first meeting with him. That day he mentioned something about preferring her in skirts to pants. I was too stunned to respond. I was also too focused on her in that deep burgundy pantsuit, which I probably shouldn't admit in the same breath as condemning Mike for his inappropriate comment.

Penelope has worked hard to get to this point in her career and has faced a lot more adversity than anyone would know. I can't imagine what would drive a person to work through that kind of pain except for the misogynist that employs her. Mike would have probably made her work anyway, so rather than call out, she powered through it.

I sneak across the hall to my own apartment and swap my contacts for glasses, I lock up and step back into Penelope's apartment where I grab a blanket from the basket by her sofa, sink into her couch, and dial my brother.

"Hey Jake! Great show tonight!"

"Thanks Jax. Hey...can I pick your brain?"

"Sure. What's up?"

I explain everything. I start with what she told me weeks ago at the cafe about her PCOS, and then I list all of Penelope's symptoms tonight, telling him exactly what she told me...and what I suspect she *didn't*.

"How worried should I be? Should I be taking her to the hospital?"

"No. Just being there for her right now, is the best thing you can do. It sounds like Penelope is very aware of her body and how her symptoms present. Unfortunately, with Polycystic Ovarian Syndrome, it often goes undiagnosed and unrecognized. For years the symptoms that women presented with were often ignored, and their pain was written off as menstrual cramps and nothing more.

"My guess is...if she's in her thirties? This has been her reality for more than half of her life. She knows the signs and what to look out for. If something changes, she'll know. And if you're there, you can get her to the nearest ER. If for some reason that becomes necessary, I want you to call me. A lot of my patients have PCOS and in some cases they've called me in to speak for them when doctors won't listen. It sucks. But I'll do it for anyone who needs me."

"Thanks Jax. I knew it would pay off to have an OB/GYN in the family."

He laughs and I stay on the phone with him a while longer, catching up on how things are upstate, how my nieces are doing, and making plans for the family to get together upstate at mom and dad's next month.

"You should bring her with you," Jax says, and I can almost hear the sly smile in his voice. I know if I could see his face I'd probably want to punch it. "Let her meet the family."

I start to argue with him, insisting that we're not in that stage of our relationship where we meet each other's families...but I stop short. How many of her Sunday night video calls have I crashed? How many times have I received a call from one of my own siblings while I've been here, in her apartment? I spend more time in this small apartment with her than I do in my own place anymore. Our Saturdays spent in the park or watching movies and cooking together, our adventures in the city together...maybe, just maybe, I *could* bring her to meet the family.

"I'll think about it."

I'd love to see her at the house upstate with my family. I'd love to take her for a hike in the woods or up the foothills, spend a day on the lake with her, or go to bed at night knowing I'll wake up and see her there. I'd love to sit around a fire at night, with her in my arms.

"Hey," a raspy, sleepy, feminine voice calls from the other side of the room. "What are you still doing here?"

"Good to see you too, Sunshine." I can't help but smile as she pulls the curtain open and pads out into the living area, taking a seat next to me on the couch. Her sweatshirt sleeves are bunched in her hands, her hair sticks out at crazy angles, and I find myself wishing I could always be here when she wakes up.

"Seriously, Jake. What are you still doing here? It's late."

I end the call with my brother, promising to think about what he suggested, and it takes all my willpower not to ask her right now. Now is very much not the right time to ask her about a trip upstate with me for a long weekend. I should be taking care of her, making sure she's comfortable, and her pain is managed.

"I didn't want to leave you," my voice sounds foreign to my own ears, I'm choked with emotion as she looks at me, a softness in her eyes that not everyone is lucky enough to see. "I was worried about you. I wanted to be here to take care of you, to help if things got worse or if you needed anything. I'm sorry if I'm overstepping..."

She slides closer to me on the sofa, resting a hand on my knee. That small touch sends a jolt right through my body. Like a match being struck, I'm suddenly keenly aware of her presence.

"I'm glad you stayed," tears glisten in her eyes. I can't tell if it's pain from what she's been experiencing, or something deeper. "Sometimes I hate being alone..."

I'm glad she's not alone. Again.

Peter's voice echoes in my head as Penelope settles into the sofa cushions beside me. Her eyes meet mine, and as tears begin to slip down her cheeks, I take her hands in mine and slide closer to her.

"What is it? What can I do?"

She squeezes my hand and gives me a small smile as more tears fall.

"I'm okay. Just...surprised. Thankful," she gets a faraway look in her eyes, almost as if she's looking right through me. "No one should have to wake up alone when they're sick..."

"You sound like you're speaking from experience."

She meets my gaze again, leaning her head back against my chest as a sad smile tugs at the corners of her mouth. I don't expect her to answer. Whatever this is, I can see the pain in her eyes, and it's not appendix related. She squeezes her eyes shut as if conjuring a memory, as she does, I step into her kitchen and fix the two of us the few things I know how to cook: toast and eggs.

"I was with my dad. He'd just gone into emergency surgery, it was early evening, and I sent mom home with Peter...she'd had her own chemo that day and was exhausted. Dad didn't make it. I woke up in his room to a doctor giving me the news. And then I had to call my mom and brother and give them the news. The last thing I remember from that night was someone holding me on the floor of dad's room. I don't know who it was. I got off the phone with Peter and just...collapsed. At least when mom passed, we were all home, together. No one should have to be alone for that..."

What do you say to that? No one should have to be alone when their world shatters around them. I keep picturing her all alone in that room. In a heap on the floor, a stranger holding her as she cried. I can't imagine that kind of grief. That kind of pain.

No one should be alone when they lose the people they love.

"How old were you?" the only words my brain seems capable of forming, but I can sense that she wants to talk. *Needs* to talk. I sit down beside her again, and put the plate of scrambled eggs and buttered toast in her hands. The corner of her mouth tugs up in a smile as she looks from me to the plate and back again. She takes a bite of eggs and toast, washes it down with the tea I set beside her before sinking into the couch again.

She takes a deep breath, closing her eyes. Centering herself. I've seen Jenna do the same thing when she gets overwhelmed. When her anxiety creeps in on her. Penelope's breathing is controlled, measured. She's working through it all in her head. Finally, she responds.

"Twenty-four. I was home to help mom and dad, I had just started at a small station outside of Pittsburgh. Peter was managing a congressional campaign at the time. He came home as quickly as he could, but for a while it was just me and mom. Her condition deteriorated fast after dad died. A month after his funeral, we were planning hers."

"What were they like?"

She smiles. It's soft and small, but it's still a smile. Her eyes are open now, focused a little more clearly, and she shifts against me so that her face is turned up, watching me. Tears slip down her cheeks and I grab tissue from the table beside the couch, abandoning my plate and wrapping my arms tighter around her, shifting so that she is fully resting on me.

"Mom was a teacher. Kindergarten. I don't know how she did it. She had the patience of a saint, which I think comes from having two holy terrors at home. She was the sweetest woman you'd ever meet—loved everyone as if they were family, took care of everyone no matter what. A hard worker."

Sounds like Penelope.

You have to have the patience of a saint to be a woman in sports. To work in the same space as Mike Fletcher. To deal with the daily misogyny of the professional sports world. I've seen Penelope around the office, making sure that needs are met, anticipating people's needs, and doing everything within her power to take care of them. For goodness sake, she feeds me almost daily. She makes food and shares it with a stranger who was bold enough to leave her a note.

"My dad," she continues, "was quiet. Strong. Steadfast. He taught me everything I know about baseball. Everything. Took me to my first game, taught me how to keep score...some years, when I was assigned to spring training, I'd take him with me, and he'd go all around Florida to as many games as he could. He'd always tell me which prospects he thought would make it big. He almost always got it right."

Her eyes close again, as if she can see those memories in her mind's eye. She takes another measured breath, and I do for her what I used to do for my sister: placing my hand between her shoulder blades, I apply gentle pressure. She arches into my hand at the contact, the tension in her shoulders slowly releasing.

I see the tears slip down her cheeks as she remembers that spring with her dad. All of those pictures I saw on her walls, the fire in her eyes as she spent all day yesterday talking about this game that she loves...the game that her dad taught her. I think of my own dad, and make a mental note to call him tomorrow morning. If anything, this conversation has pointed out the ways in which I've taken him and mom for granted. And I'm not going to do that again.

"You were his favorite player. He'd be so excited to know that I work in the same building as you, producing your show. He'd also be really disappointed in me. Mom would be too..."

What?! Anyone who would be disappointed in all that Penelope has accomplished in her career would be crazy.

"Penelope...I don't think that's possible, from what you've told me about them, I know they would be proud of everything you've done for *On the Field*."

"That's true, but they'd be terribly disappointed that I don't stand up for myself. That I continue to let him control me..."

Mike. She means Mike. There's more to the story, I know there is. But I'm afraid that if I push her, she'll shut down. I'm also afraid that if she tells me, our relationship will cross into new territory, and I don't know if I'm ready for that.

"Why do you put up with him?"

"What's the alternative?"

Quitting. Speaking up. Telling him what he can do with his off-color jokes and inappropriate comments. But no. She can't. Mike would fire her. So instead she puts up with it. And I'd wager that she's not the only one putting up with this kind of thing from Mike Fletcher.

I think back on my career, and think of the women who worked in the front office, worked closely with the team, or the few who were in the clubhouse doing post-game interviews. I'm fortunate to have been on a team and part of an organization that worked hard to let the women around us know that we respected them. They had a job to do just like we did.

I'm beginning to realize -- on this side of things -- that this isn't the case league wide. And it isn't the case in other sports either.

Women are still fighting to prove themselves, fighting for a place within the culture of professional sports. Fighting to preserve their dignity. I've seen how Jim and Devon protect Penelope. Speaking up for her in production meetings, making sure that her voice is heard. I've even seen Devon physically step in between Mike and Penelope, putting a large, physical buffer between them. I should have recognized the signs the day that Mike gave me a tour.

That's Penny, the Ice Queen. She produces On the Field. He grinned wolfishly at me, his eyes darting into her open office, Penelope hard at work at her desk, paying no mind to the creep outside her door.

My folks would be disappointed in me, too. For not saying something that day. For letting it go without a word. I'm about to say as much when Penelope barely stifles a yawn, and looks at me apologetically.

I squeeze her hand and gently brush away the hair that has fallen over her eyes. I leave her on the couch for a moment, finding her heating pad nearby and handing it to her to place where she needs it most, and grabbing the ice pack from the bag in her freezer. "Get some rest, Sunshine."

She leans her head on my shoulder, drapes the ice pack across her eyes, and curls her legs up under her. "You owe me," she yawns again, not bothering to hide it this time. "A memory, I mean."

"What do you want to hear?" I ask, wrapping my arms around

her, and pulling a blanket around us both, enjoying the cozy picture we make here on her couch. I kind of like the feeling of her body pressed up against mine, knowing that she trusts me with her pain -- the physical and emotional.

"Hmmm..." she thinks for a moment, eyes drooping as she fights off sleep. "Your favorite memory from spring training."

23
SPRING TRAINING
PENELOPE

"My first spring training. I'll never forget it."

I snuggle up closer to him as he closes his eyes and tells his story. He holds me close to his side, his head leaning against mine as we sit together on my sofa. I could get used to this. This cozy, domestic picture we make. I surrender to his embrace, letting him hold me, adjusting the ice pack on my eyes, and the heating pad on my abdomen as he encourages me to lay my head in his lap. His hand strokes my hair as he tells his story.

"I was feeling kind of down on myself after a bad start and was running the risk of being cut from the forty-man roster. I was discouraged and angry at myself for not performing the way I thought I should have been."

I remember that year. I remember hearing the rumors that he may not make it out of spring training. But he managed to pull off a few memorable starts, cementing his place on the major league roster. My dad was so excited, he'd had high hopes for the kid from his hometown. Dad spent spring training with me in Florida during my first assignment, reporting in Lakeland. He went down to Port St.

Lucie one day to watch one of Jake's starts and raved about him over dinner when he got back to our hotel in Lakeland that night.

"Before one of our games, the veteran players were hanging around and signing autographs, fan favorites, guys with names people knew. The fans blew me off when I walked up, they didn't know who I was. But there was a man there, about my dad's age, anyway he came down to the railing and treated me like I was a star."

My chest aches as he recalls the memory from the spring of his rookie year. The year of my first spring training assignment. I know this story. Or at least, I know the other side of this story. Hearing it from Jake's perspective is like having a piece of my dad right here in the room, and I don't know what to do with that.

It feels like a thousand pounds settles onto my chest, and my breathing becomes shallow. Too shallow. I remember that day like it was yesterday. Dinner with my dad after he got back to Lakeland. Hearing all about the pitcher he watched that day. And then, in an instant, I feel the cold tile under my knees. The smell of antiseptic, acrid and astringent in my nose. I hear the nurses bustling around me, feel arms holding me as I rock and sob on the floor of an unfamiliar hospital room.

I will never forget that night. I will never forget the look on the face of the doctor who woke me up. The cold, impersonal way he delivered the news. *He died on the table.* He turned and walked out, leaving me in the room to gather my dad's things. To call my mom and brother. On the television in the corner, I watched, a dial tone in my ear as I prayed for my brother to answer - a baseball game. A pitcher collapsed on the mound, surrounded by training staff and worried teammates. Then the news that dad's favorite pitcher's career was over.

Finally, my brother answered.

Peter...dad's gone...he didn't make it. Someone has to tell mom.

I held it together until I got off the phone with my brother. And then I was alone in the cold, empty hospital room. Surrounded by machines and tubes and wires. A guttural, inhuman wail escaped my chest as I collapsed to the floor. I heard the sound of shoes slapping the tile floor, a pair of strong arms wrapped around me. Tissue pressed into my hands.

The end of Jake's baseball career will forever be tied to my memory of that night.

My first instinct was to tell my dad.

I wanted to run and find dad and give him the news. I wanted to listen to the Port St. Lucie story for the thousandth time. I wanted to cuddle up beside dad on the couch like I did when I was a kid. I wanted to walk out of that hospital and drive him home. Instead, I drove home alone, with a clear plastic bag filled with dad's clothes. The end of the New York game on the Radio. The announcers were devastated. Everyone was heartbroken that this injury signaled the end of what should have been a Hall of Fame career. Even at twenty five, everyone knew Jake was bound for greatness. And it ended just like that.

Jake's voice snaps me back to the present, hot tears falling down my cheeks as his arms tighten around me.

"This guy was dressed head to toe in my college colors, told me he'd graduated from Michigan too, and made the trip with his daughter who was up in Lakeland, but he wanted to see me pitch. He asked for a picture and I snapped one with him. He shook my hand and wished me well. I took the mound that day feeling more encouraged than I had all spring. He gave me a boost in confidence that I needed. I only wish I'd have asked his name that day."

That night? I wanted to hear this story again. I've always treasured the picture that dad sent me from that game. I wanted to hear him tell me the story again. About the pitcher from his alma mater. The pitcher he just knew was going to do great things. The pitcher who everyone was ignoring but dad just knew. *I have a sense about these things, Nellie Girl. Someday, you'll be reporting on Jake Hutchinson's Hall of Fame induction and call me up. I'll say "I told ya so!"* I wanted to laugh with him again.

The walls of the apartment feel like they are closing in on me. I can't catch my breath no matter how hard I try to control my breathing. I can't fill my lungs. They won't expand. Hearing Jake tell this story about meeting my dad, it's like I can taste the pizza we had for dinner that night. I can feel the scratchy hotel blanket, smell the grass and peanuts and beer from that day. I'm not in my apartment anymore.

I can't escape the memory. All I feel is the weight of my grief.

And then...

A hand on my back. Steady, constant pressure. Right between my shoulder blades. Again.

"What do you see?" A voice whispers from far away.

"What?" I try to wrap my head around the question. What do I see? The field. The hospital room...

"Right now. In *this* room. What do you see?"

"You." I turn to face him. I see his kind eyes and slightly stubbled jaw. His mussed hair and the shadows under his eyes, betraying the lateness of the hour. I see the man who hasn't left my side all night.

"Good." He nods, and his hand starts rubbing in a circle on my back. "What do you feel?"

"Your hand. It's warm..."

He's centering me. Making me focus on where I am, right here and now. He goes through the other senses—taste, smell, hear—and by the end of it, my breathing has returned to normal. My eyes are refocused, and that pain in my chest has turned to utter exhaustion. I haven't had an anxiety attack like that in a long time. And I was alone for my last one.

"Where'd you go just now, Sunshine?" The concern in Jake's voice tugs at my heart as his eyes search mine.

"Port St. Lucie. Actually, *I* was in Lakeland. Dad was in Port St. Lucie."

Jake's brows knit together as I sit up and grab my phone from the coffee table in front of us, opening it to my camera roll and scrolling to the very first picture I have. Everything is a blur as my pictures scroll by and I do my best to keep my tears at bay. I find the thumbnail of the picture and enlarge it, passing my phone to Jake.

"Was this him?" I ask, passing Jake my phone, already knowing the answer.

"It is. How do you..." realization dawns on his face as he looks from the picture to me. No doubt seeing what everyone sees; my eyes and nose are distinctly my dad's. My smile, not always freely given, is my dad's. In this picture, there is no denying that I am Lee Nichols' daughter.

"His name was Lee Nichols," I whisper, wiping the tears from my cheeks and eyes. "And he was so excited to meet you that day."

After dad died, I was so preoccupied with mom and her treatment, making sure she was taken care of, that I never truly grieved my dad. And then mom died. And I was home, making funeral arrangements again, while my brother figured out how to get the time off work that he needed and rearranged his life to come home. Again.

For the first few weeks that Jake worked at ASN, just the sight of him made the telltale signs of anxiety rise in my chest. My mind would drift off to that picture in my phone—my dad's wide smile, the happiness and excitement in his eyes, and my chest would squeeze with grief that I tamped down and hid away. It all came back to me when I was around Jake every day, without a doubt he is the oddest trigger for my grief in the years since my parents have been gone.

He holds me and lets me cry. I know that my tears are a mixture of hormones, grief, and exhaustion; they fall hard and fast and hot against my cheeks. Jake holds me in his arms, one hand rubbing my back in soothing strokes, and with the other, gently wiping away my tears. I've come to realize that I never truly mourned mom and dad. I've carried the grief with me, sure. But I've let that pain define me.

I've let it change the relationship I have with my brother – closing myself off from him, and not truly letting him in. That pain has stopped me from being vulnerable, from trusting people with my heart.

"Get some rest, sweetheart," he strokes my hair and holds me close. I take a deep, shuddering breath as I sink into his embrace and close my eyes, finally letting sleep take me.

I wake from a dream of my dad sitting with Jake and talking about baseball. Rattling of stats and laughing about blunders in games. Talking about Port St. Lucie and *On the Field*. Jake's laugh rings in my head as I open my eyes and try to shake out the cobwebs in my brain. I wake up in bed with a vague memory of him holding me on the couch last night and being lulled to sleep by his steady breathing and the scent of him surrounding me. His strong arms holding me tight, keeping me safe. I know that wasn't a dream. It couldn't have been.

I swing my legs slowly over the side of my bed and stand up, stretching out my sore back, bending down and touching the floor before slowly sliding open the curtain. Jake is on my sofa, glasses perched on his nose, sipping from a coffee cup. I could get used to this.

The only problem is, I never let anyone see me like this in the mornings. I have a routine. I wake up and the first thing I do is shave. I have to. I've been doing it since puberty hit and my PCOS made itself known. Sleepovers were a nightmare back then. Most of the time, I found a reason to come home early. Mom never asked questions, but I suspect she knew. I try to slip quickly to the bathroom, but Jake grabs my hand on my way past and tugs me close.

"Good morning, Sunshine." His greeting sends a shiver through my body, and my heart flutters when he smiles at me, and places a gentle kiss on my cheek. I press my hand to my cheek as warmth floods through me. I feel the scratchy, early morning hair and try to cover my face and slink away from him, but he tilts his head and his eyebrows draw together. As my hands cover my face, he gently takes them in his own, and uncovers my face, planting a soft kiss on my other cheek. When I start to shy away, he releases my hands with a knowing smile, and I step toward the bathroom door.

A voice from the direction of my balcony stops me in my tracks; I groan and turn toward my brother, grinning at me like the cat that ate the canary. All of that just happened in full view of my older brother. And that smug look on his face tells me he saw everything. Great.

"I'll step out...let you two have some privacy," Jake makes his way toward the door, an unreadable look on his face as his eyes dance between me and my brother. Some part of me doesn't want him to leave. Some part of me desperately wishes that he'd stay.

I reach out and snag his hand in mine before he gets too far away, "you don't have to do that. Stay. Please."

My brother tries and fails to hide his grin as Jake squeezes my hand and steps toward the kitchen to place his empty mug in the sink.. I smile at Jake and then turn my head to scowl at my brother, a "play nice" kind of scowl. He makes the "who me?" face and I can't help but smile at him. That smile grows as Sofi bustles through the door with a drink carrier and bag of what I really hope is pastries. She hands Peter a coffee and gives him a kiss on the cheek, then hands a coffee to Jake who looks surprised but grateful that she thought of him.

"Jake," Sofi loops her arm through his and leads him toward the door. "We're going for a walk." It's not a question. They're going for a walk, and Jake has no choice but to follow Sof out the door. Leaving Peter and I alone. Peter sits down on the sofa and indicates for me to continue what I was doing.

I walk into the bathroom and leave the door open as I splash warm water on my face and set to work making myself presentable. I used to be ashamed of this part of my morning routine, but now I find comfort in it. The warm water on my skin. The scent of the shaving cream I've used for years. The lotion I use to calm my skin when I'm done. The confidence the whole routine brings me.

For years I struggled with this aspect of my PCOS. Because it was, is, so obvious. There's no hiding it. The cramps, the pain, the migraines, the bleeding...that is invisible to everyone but me. I can hide those things. I can't hide my face, at least not fully. So I stopped trying.

"He stayed here last night," my brother's voice is quiet, with a slight tremor, as if holding back tears.

"Yes." I nod. My eyes glued to my face in the mirror, wholly focused on the task at hand.

"Why didn't you call me?"

He sounds hurt, and that was never my intention. I didn't call because it isn't the first time I've had a night like that. Or had a migraine. Or gotten sick at work. But it is the first time that I've ever had another person here with me throughout. Someone who noticed that something was wrong and stepped in to take care of me. Normally, I'd have found my way home and muddled through the night with the migraine that is still lingering, the nausea, and the pain. I'd have eventually forced myself to eat, and hopefully gotten some sleep. But Jake stayed here last night.

"Peter, I didn't ask him to stay..."

He comes and leans against the door frame, meeting my eyes in the mirror.

"You misunderstand, I'm not mad that he stayed with you. I'm glad he was here to help you through it..."

He's hurt that I didn't call him to let him know. That he had to find out I was in rough shape through someone else. Again. He's worried that I'm holding him at arm's length. Again. Like I did all those years ago after mom and dad died.

After mom's funeral, we stayed in Michigan long enough to sell the house, pack up the things we wanted to keep or donate or sell, and then we went our separate ways. I went back to work and so did he. We called and texted periodically. I met Sofia before they were married. But I did my best to distance myself from my brother. Part of me was afraid to hang onto the attachment we had as kids, because I couldn't bear the thought of losing him. So, I pushed him away instead.

I wipe my face clean, rinse my sink, and take a long look at myself in the mirror before stepping back out into the room. Peter follows my lead, sitting down beside me on the sofa. I blink back the sting of tears as Peter's arm settles across my shoulders, and I lean into the warmth of my brother's arms.

It's been a long time since Peter and I have been together like this. The night of mom's funeral, we were home together. I'd held it together most of the day, but by the time evening came, I was exhausted. I didn't want to talk to anyone else or look at another flower arrangement. I sat on the couch at home, just like this, with Peter beside me. We just sat in silence and cried. And held each other.

"Peter, I'm sorry." His arm tightens around my shoulder and he drops a kiss on the top of my head. "I'm sorry for pushing you away. For trying to keep distance between us all those years ago. And now. You deserve better."

"No I don't," I can hear the smile in his voice, "I've already got the best sister I could have ever asked for."

He pulls his arm away and sits back to look at me. His eyes search mine, watering with unshed tears, "I just wish you'd trust me with your heart. With your pain and your sickness."

"Peter..."

"Penelope, I was grieving too," his voice takes on a sharper tone than I'm used to from my calm, controlled older brother, "and I didn't have anyone to turn to. It felt like I lost you after mom died. I was in DC, I was working, and you wouldn't talk to me."

"I thought I was protecting you..." I whisper.

"Protecting me from what?" there's a frustrated edge to his voice as he tries to make sense of what I'm saying.

"From me. From my anger and depression and heartache...we'd lost so much Peter, I didn't want to hurt you any more than that."

"Penelope, I *wanted* to be there for you. You're my little sister. I was there for your scraped knees, and your broken bones, and your first break-up..."

Peter beat the snot out of Sam, the first boy who ever broke up with me. All three of us ended up in detention that day. I tried to pull Peter off of him, and Sam's fist caught the side of my head. So, I swung at him myself and broke his nose...next thing I know, all three of us are hauled in front of the principal and spending our afternoon in detention.

"Nellie, we both lost our parents. I felt like I was going through it alone after the funerals; we should have, *could* have, been there for each other. I'm not letting you push me away again, little sister. No matter how hard you try to push me away, I'm not going anywhere. Not this time. I can take your pain and your anger. I *want* to take your pain and anger. Or at least walk with you while you figure out what to do with it."

"Thanks Peter. I don't think I fully appreciated you when I was younger, but I'm thankful that you're my brother."

Peter wraps his arm around me and plants a kiss on the top of my head. A tender moment between brother and sister that soon disappears when he releases me and says with a grin: "So. Let me help you figure out what to do about Jake too."

I groan and whack him with a throw pillow before walking into my "bedroom" and perching on the edge of my bed...far away from my meddling older brother.

"I don't think you understand, Nellie. He stayed with you. All night. Right here on this incredibly uncomfortable couch."

If I acknowledge that statement in any way, it will only encourage him. And he needs no encouragement.

But Peter is right; Jake stayed here last night. He made sure I got home safe, held me on the floor of my bathroom, helped me clean up, and was there when I woke after a few hours of sleep and needed someone to just...be there. I've spent my fair share of time alone; the worst of which being the aftermath of losing my parents. The few times I've had episodes like last night, I've slept on the floor of my bathroom, unable to do much more for myself than drag my exhausted body into the shower and sit under a torrent of hot water. But last night...he held me. He soothed my aching body and calmed my racing mind.

He told me that story about my dad. And held me when I cried.

I bury my face in my hands and roll away from my brother with a groan. Jake stayed with me. He's been by my side through the worst of my migraines, the worst of my pain, and hasn't been scared off yet. He's endured the nights that I'm so frustrated I can't think or in so much pain that I can't speak. And he hasn't left yet.

"What's wrong?" Peter asks with a laugh.

"I'm in love with him," I mumble into my hands, "I'm in love with Jake."

"I know you are," Peter pries my hands away from my face and pulls me into a seated position.

"Why didn't you tell me?!" If I sound indignant, it's because I am. And it doesn't help that my brother looks so...smug.

"Penelope." Peter sits down beside me and pulls me into a hug. "Would you have believed me?"

"No."

"My point exactly. Now...when are you going to tell him?"

For someone whose career is based on communication, I'm doing a poor job of communicating my feelings to Jake. I collapse onto my bed and roll over with a sigh as Peter laughs; I'm sure he's thrilled to be the first in the family to know my true feelings for the man who, just months ago, was the stranger across the hall.

Now I can't imagine my life without him.

24
WHAT IS THIS FEELING?
JAKE

Sofia and I leave the apartment, leaving Penelope with Peter. We walk down to Riverside Park and I scope out a bench overlooking the water. Penelope's favorite spot. She likes to sit here and watch the sun as it sets over the Hudson, and I like to sit here and watch her watch the sunset. As the sun casts its golden light over our little corner of the park and reflects in her eyes, the golden glow makes the auburn in her hair brighter, her freckles more prominent across her nose, and her smile can't be beat.

"Thank you again for being there last night. For staying with her." I can see the glimmer of tears in Sofia's eyes as she looks across the water. "It's hard for Peter, not being in the same city as his sister, but I'm glad to know she has someone looking out for her here."

I remain quiet, not entirely sure of what to say. The silence between us hangs heavy, a lot like when I'm with Penelope; I can tell she has more she wants to say and is trying to figure out how. I'm okay with listening. I'm okay with sitting here in silence until she's comfortable. I've waited for her sister to warm up to me, I can wait a while longer if I have to for her to do the same.

"She's experienced a lot of trauma that Peter and I weren't around for..."

"Yeah. She's shared some of that with me". Her eyes widen in surprise.

"I see..." Sofia is quiet for a moment. "I don't know that she's ever confronted her grief over losing their parents, and Peter harbors a lot of guilt. He feels responsible for her. He had a hard time when she shut him out. That's what she does..."

Sofia is silent for a moment, while I process her words.

"Jake, I don't know what's going on between you two, and I have to tell you that Peter is very protective of his sister, and *I* am very protective of them both. If you are going to commit to her, in any way, you have to know how she handles things. She's going to want to run away. And you're going to have to hold on tight."

"I'll keep that in mind," I glance at Sofia and give her a small smile, "thank you for trusting me. With her."

"I like you Jake. Peter does too, even if he pretends he doesn't. And it's very obvious to me that you love her. So...what are you going to do about it?"

"How much time do you have?"

Sofia throws back her head and laughs, before patting me on the knee and standing up. "I *really* like you Jake."

She pulls me up off the bench and we walk from the park over to the farmer's market where Sofia picks up some fresh flowers for Penelope, and I pick up a few of her favorite things; a wedge of smoked gouda, a loaf of crusty bread, and a few baskets of assorted berries. Sofia gives me a knowing smile as my arms are laden with market bags, and I feel a blush creep into my cheeks. I shrug my shoulders and she grins at me.

"Has she told you what goes on in the office?" Sofia asks as we walk back toward the apartment building.

She tells me about the "Mike File". A record of all the things that Mike has done or said to Penelope over the last two years. The comments, the unsolicited touches at work...and texts outside of work. Sofia tells me that Penelope reported Mike to HR in the beginning, but it became more of a hassle for her, and nothing was being done. So, for the most part she's suffered in silence.

What's the alternative? Penelope's voice rings in my ears.

I've seen the way he looks at her. I've seen the way she tenses up when he's around. I've seen the way she jumps when someone enters her space without warning, the way she flinches anytime Mike crosses a line. No wonder she was so...standoffish the day Mike introduced us. It wasn't me. At least not entirely.

"I'm a civil rights attorney and victims' rights advocate. I've been trying to get Nell to go after Mike. And frankly, Penelope is lucky that Peter and I haven't teamed up on her behalf because we'd nail the guy to a wall."

I chuckle at her comment, but one look at Sofia's face tells me that she's serious. Mike Fletcher deserves to be taken down by the entire Nichols family. But I want a shot at him first.

We head back up to the apartment and after dropping off her flowers, Sofia grabs Peter's hand, insisting that they head downtown for a while, leaving Penelope and I alone in her apartment once again. She's changed out of her sweatshirt and shorts, into fitted joggers and a New York tee shirt that looks fairly new. She looks at me for a reaction, to the shirt I assume, but the heaviness in my chest after my talk with Sofia is nagging at me.

"Have a good chat with Sof?" Penelope asks, wrapping her arms around my waist and leaning into my chest.

"We did. It was enlightening. I think I'm beginning to understand you a little better."

"Sometimes I think, you're the *only* person who understands me," she says quietly as tears form at the corners of her eyes. "I don't let a lot of people in, Jake."

"I know sunshine, I know." I take her in my arms and hold her close, her head leaning against my chest, arms twining around my waist. I press a kiss to the top of her head and she sighs contentedly. "And I promise to pay better attention in the office."

"Sofi told you, didn't she?"

"Yep. I know all about the 'Mike File. I'm sorry I missed the signs. I wish I'd have known sooner."

"There's nothing you could have done."

"That may be true. But I will pay better attention if only so that you have someone to come home to at night who is safe; someone you can vent to, cry to, or work out your frustration in the form of homemade bread with."

This elicits a laugh from Penelope that reverberates through my chest as her arms tighten around me.

"Help me cook lunch," her voice is low, barely a whisper as she releases me and steps into her kitchen. I step up to the counter beside her as she sets out spices and vegetables, cheese and sauce from the fridge, and uncovers a ball of dough in a bowl on the counter.

She hands me a knife and cutting board, putting a green pepper in front of me, and I give her my best "what do you want me to do with this" look. I've cut a green pepper before, she knows it and I know it. But she steps in front of me anyway, taking my hand in hers, and wrapping me around her body. The touch of her hand on mine sends a jolt of heat through my arm. I lean into her partly to see over her shoulder, even though she fits right under my chin, and partly to get as close to her, and her intoxicating presence, as I can.

Penelope wraps my fingers around the knife, her fingers guiding mine. How to rock the blade against the cutting board, slicing and then dicing the green pepper. Once there's a pile of pepper on the board, I let go of the knife, keeping her between me and the counter, my hand strays to her waist and I gently turn her to face me, my other hand sliding through her hair and cupping the back of her neck.

I feel her breath on my neck and lean down to meet her lips with mine. The sound of the door opening causes her to jump away from me so violently, that I have to reach out to steady her. Peter, standing just inside the doorway, cracks up at the sight of us and lightning quick, Penelope grabs a dish towel and lobs it at her brother's head which only makes him laugh more. Sofi, bless her, pulls Peter back out into the hallway, an apologetic look on her face.

The mood is broken, but Penelope steps back into my arms and gives me a gentle, tentative kiss, chuckling against my lips as I draw her in closer. I hug her tight as her family comes back in and she sets her brother the task of setting the table for lunch.

After we've eaten our fill, Penelope finally sends me home, insisting that I shower and shave, and sleep. I'd really rather stay with her, but I have no desire to argue with her. She may be the only non-lawyer in her family, but she can argue with the best of them. So, I head home and do as she says, but the minute I step into the silence of my apartment...I miss her.

She's right across the hall, I was just with her for the last eighteen hours, I shouldn't feel this deep, aching need in my chest to be with her.

I love her. I've known it for a while now, and I know I need to tell her. I have to tell her that I love her. That I have since the day she forced me to apologize on the air for jinxing a no-hitter. And that day we travelled the city together. And every night since that I've worked with her at her dining room table or her balcony or on the floor in front of her couch. And through each cooking lesson and late night movie in my apartment.

I love her.

And it's time I do something about it.

25
A VOICE
PENELOPE

I can't believe I agreed to this.

I can't believe I agreed to go upstate with him to his family's cabin. To meet his family, and be thrown into a long weekend with them. And not just a long weekend, but July Fourth weekend, filled with picnics and games and lots of family time. Something I haven't experienced in years. Something I've desperately missed.

What have you gotten yourself into, Penelope?!

What I've gotten myself into is a much needed trip away. Thankfully we have a long weekend ahead of us, but even the thought of a weekend upstate isn't enough to calm my nerves at the prospect of meeting his family.

All throughout my meetings today, I've been thinking about this extended weekend with his family. Meeting his siblings and nieces, meeting his parents, and spending four days in the same space as all of them? The thought is giving me hives. I'm an introvert. I think it's the curse of having an extroverted older brother and parents. I love people, but they exhaust me. I love living alone because I can recharge at the end of the day. Jake knows that, and respects that. This is going to be a whole new experience for me.

I'm also stressing out more than a little bit about the prospect of three hours in the car with Jake followed by a four day weekend in the same house as Jake. This whole trip is going to be a defining moment in our relationship. Even more than the kiss, this is a turning point for us. I'm meeting his family. He chose to bring me with him. And he understands that it's overwhelming for me.

"If you need to get away, do it. No one will be upset. If it gets too loud or too overwhelming, go outside or to your room, whatever you need to do." He assured me when I first raised concerns to him that his family, particularly his sister Jenna, would be understanding if I needed to excuse myself at any point during the weekend. I appreciate the fact that he's already thought of this, and is giving me the opportunity to take care of myself if I need to.

All month, he's been preparing me, giving me the rundown about his family so that I don't go in blind, showing me pictures and giving me a brief history of each member of his family. I promise to do my best to remember it all, but I'm sure I'll need a refresher. What sticks out most prominently in my mind is his brother Jax. Last month when I was sick, he called Jax to make sure that I'd be okay at home rather than at the hospital, and he told me later on that Jax was willing to advocate for me with doctors as necessary. Which, as a woman who has lived with PCOS for more than half my life, is a huge breath of fresh air.

I know Jake was scared that night. Jax told Jake everything I'd have told him myself if I hadn't been in so much pain. I hope Jax is a hugger, because he's earned one from me when I finally meet him. He also gets a hug for single parenting his two young daughters for the last four years after his wife walked away from them. The guy needs a hug whether he wants one or not.

I call Peter to make my excuses for missing our weekly video chat, but Sofi nudges her way into the frame with a self-satisfied grin and assures me that things will be just fine without me, and that I should enjoy myself over the four day weekend with nothing else to keep me busy.

If I didn't love them both so much, I'd have hung up and ignored them for the rest of...my life.

Even during tonight's live show, I'm distracted. Until Jake does something that stops me in my tracks.

"So guys, I was texting with Penelope about this last night..." He turns and addresses the camera, "for those of you who don't know, Penelope Nichols produces this show, and she's probably the most brilliant analyst you've never heard of."

I'm stunned. I'm hardly ever speechless, but Jake manages it as he sits there on live television giving voice to things I've said. Reading my words and giving me the credit. And then Jim jumps in.

"She and I were talking about this just before we went on the air..."

I can't move. I can't even think. I hear Morgan give a direction into her headset as we move to a commercial break and tears sting the backs of my eyes as I catch Jake's eye and he smiles at me.

"Thanks guys," Morgan quips, "you broke the boss."

The crew laughs and Jake finds me once again, angling his head toward the door.

"What was that?" I whisper, trying not to cry as he wraps me up in a hug.

"I called an audible," he chuckles and wraps his arms tighter around me. "It's about time you get credit for the things you write for us and the ideas you give us for the show. I meant what I said, Sunshine. You're a brilliant analyst. You understand this game better than most people I know, including me. And as much as I hate that your words have to come from three men, you are long overdue for the credit."

I look around us, making sure we are tucked far enough away

from prying eyes, and stand on tiptoe to press a kiss to his lips. "Go, we'll talk about this later."

I've been writing for *On the Field* since I took the producer's job. I thought it came with the territory. I was always writing notes and talking points for Jim and Devon, who are smart guys on their own, and with their playing and announcing experience brought so much to the table. Sure, they'd read the rough sketches of ideas that I'd give them, but they'd fill in with their own analysis.

We've had a group text since my first day as producer. We added Jake after his first night on the show. Sometimes when I'm watching a game on my own, I'll text them a running commentary. As we move closer and closer to the trade deadline, we always text each other our thoughts and sometimes those thoughts aren't television appropriate. But when this news broke? I had more than a few thoughts on the subject.

A veteran player, sure to be a hall of famer, was released by his team out of the blue. The news broke late last night. We'd already been off the air for hours but I knew I wanted to cover this story first thing on tonight's show. It's *huge* news. I fired off a string of angry texts to the guys letting them know they needed to come to today's meeting ready to discuss the news and how to handle it on the air. Jake and Jim especially, as former players; one whose career ended unexpectedly and the other who walked away on his own terms. I knew that they would be able to offer their unique perspective on this news.

After I sent the first text, there was a knock on my door and I opened it to find Jake, hair sticking out in every direction like he just climbed out of bed, wearing nothing but a pair of gym shorts and his glasses which confirms my suspicions that I woke him up.

"Let me hear it," *he tries, and fails, to stifle a yawn. And I practically have to restrain myself to keep from launching into his arms.*

"Hear what?" *I ask more than a little defensively.*

"Ideas for the show." *He pushes past me and sinks into my couch, throwing an expectant look in my direction.* "I know you have them and if you don't get them out of your head, you won't sleep. And Penelope-hopped-up-on-caffeine is not the Penelope we want running the show tomorrow..."

He humored me for an hour. Listening to every thought that was jumbled in my brain, letting me work out the questions to ask for the show, and vent my own frustration. Then he kissed me, tucked me into bed, and left my apartment, locking the door behind him.

I had no idea that he was going to give voice to my words on the air like this. I've never expected it of him. And to say I'm humbled is an understatement. I have to wipe tears from my eyes for the rest of the show. I've missed doing reporting and analysis. As much as I love producing this show, and I really do love it, I've missed spending my days on analysis; talking about stats and trades and injuries and what teams need to do to get to the playoffs.

For the first time in almost a decade, I find myself wishing I was sitting at a desk talking about the game I love, instead of behind the cameras, tucked away in the safety of the control room. That's why working on *Shattered Glass* was such an incredible experience, regardless of if it goes anywhere; I worked on it. I had Jake's support, and I worked through that lingering fear that comes with being on camera.

I don't know that I'm willing to walk away from *On the Field*, but it wouldn't hurt to polish my resume. To look for places willing to hire a woman as a baseball analyst. Jake and the guys banter to close the show and something squeezes in my chest at the thought of leaving them. I can't say that I'd mind leaving the network, but leaving *On the Field*? I don't know yet.

The rest of the show is uneventful. I slip up a few times, still a bit distracted by what the guys have just done for me; I apologize to

Morgan on our way back to my office after the show and she just laughs. "Don't worry about it. Jake was right, it's about time you got the credit you're due."

"Thanks, Mo," I hug her before grabbing my overnight bag from just inside my office door, slinging it and my work bag over my shoulder before meeting Jake in the parking structure. He throws our bags in the back of his SUV and expertly navigates the streets of New York City, getting us out of Manhattan before we stop and pick up a bite to eat at a retro-style drive-in restaurant.

"Thank you for this," I lean my head against the headrest behind me, stretching out my legs and closing my eyes while we wait for our food to be delivered. "I don't take time to rest as often as I should, and I'm really looking forward to this chance to get away."

"Thanks for saying yes," there's a hitch in his voice, almost as if he's not sure what to say. "I enjoy spending time with you, and after the last few weeks, I figured you could use the time away as much as me. My folks have plenty of space, and I'm looking forward to spending time with you outside of the city. Outside of the office and planning for *Shattered Glass*."

Silence hangs between us for a moment and I quirk open one eye, catching him watching me. A slow smile spreads across his face when he realizes he's been caught staring. I close my eyes again, my thoughts turning to tonight on the set. And another set, almost a month ago.

"Thank you, for tonight. And I know I've already said thank you about a thousand times, but I still don't know what kind of favor you had to call in to get Susan Walters to be a part of *Shattered Glass*, and I will never, ever be able to thank you enough for that."

"For a minute there, I was afraid you were going to run out of the room..." he laughs, the tension in the car eases almost immediately.

"Oh believe me, I wanted to. We're all lucky I didn't burst into tears on the spot." I open my eyes and sit up straight. My attention fully on the man sitting beside me. He shifts to drape his arm around my shoulders as much as he can, and I find myself leaning into his touch.

"I meant what I said. You do so much for us, give us so much insight and bring an incredible amount of knowledge to the show. You deserve so much more than your name being buried in the credits at the end of the show."

Tears. Lots of them. I dig in my purse for tissue and come up empty. I turn toward the window and hope he doesn't see me using my sleeve instead. Without thinking, I shift in closer to Jake, as close as the center console between us will allow, his arm tightening around my shoulders as I lean against him.

"Beyond getting my childhood idol to come that day...thank you for being there with me, and every night for the last month. I couldn't have done this -- *wouldn't* have done this -- without your support. And tonight? It means the world to me, Jake."

"Penelope, it's a joy to work with you." He plants a kiss on my cheek and it sends a jolt of electricity through my body. After a moment, I pull away from him, sitting back against the door and watching him. My heart flutters when he smiles at me. The corners of his eyes crinkle in the cutest way, and his smile is slightly lopsided. The things this man's smile can do to me.

I have to tell him. This is probably terrible timing, because if this doesn't go over well, I'll be stuck in Saratoga with someone who doesn't reciprocate my feelings. But my gut tells me this is it, this is my opening.

"Jake..." I hedge, "You've been with me through a lot over the last few months, you've seen me at my very worst, and I can't tell you how much it means to me to have you nearby...to be able to lean on you. To spend time with you. *This* means something to me. *You* mean something to me."

I pause and he watches me. At this point, we know each other well enough that he knows my pauses usually mean I'm trying to gather my words together in a way that makes sense, and considering I'm about to bare my soul to him, I want my words to make sense. And I want to make sure he knows how I feel about him. This is so much more to me than just weekends exploring the city, dinners at my apartment, and kisses goodnight. I love him. I need to tell him, but if I tell him now I could ruin everything.

"I've fallen pretty hard for you. I can't quite pinpoint when it started, I think I was already head over heels for you before I realized what was happening. And when I woke up that morning and you were still there? I hadn't scared you away; you stayed with me, took care of me. No one has ever done that for me before."

He stares at me. For a long time.

A ridiculously long time.

Too long to sit in silence after a person lays their heart bare like that.

I start to think that this was a huge mistake. A "let me out so I can walk back to Manhattan in shame" kind of mistake. I don't want to seem desperate, but I have to break this silence. The tension is too much.

"Say something. Please." My voice is choked with emotion despite my best efforts, but I just handed my heart over to him and he's...

Kissing me.

He closes the short distance between us, gently taking my face in his hands and kissing me. I thread my fingers through his hair and pull up to meet him. I lean into his kiss, my hands threading into his hair as he wraps me tighter in his arms. I pull back for a moment, my hands moving to either side of his face, his eyes fully focused on me.

"You mean something to me too," his voice is low and gravely when he responds, his eyes alight with desire as he pulls me close again. I press my lips to his one more time before a knock on the window interrupts us and we fly apart as if we were teenagers being caught by our parents. The poor carhop stands there with a tray of food and a slightly exasperated look on her face. I smooth out my hair and clothes as Jake rolls down his window and accepts the food after digging out his wallet and tipping the girl *very* generously.

After our food is delivered and we devour our burgers, we head back out on the road for the rest of the drive to Saratoga Springs and the Hutchinson family cabin on the lake.

26

A TRIP UPSTATE
PENELOPE

I doze on and off for most of the three hour drive, and am gently shaken awake when we stop and pull off the road in front of the cabin. Though, cabin isn't exactly the term I'd use. Not for the house in front of me. The cabin stands two stories tall, with a balcony wrapping around the whole second floor. Large windows face us, glowing gold from the light inside the house, and I can only imagine what it must look like on the other side, facing the water. I step out of the car and admire what I can see of the house. It's unreal. Certainly not what I was expecting for this weekend.

The door is thrown open and two young girls race down the path, one with braided pigtails that fly behind her as she runs, the other with curly blond hair that hangs in messy tangles around her shoulders. They both have chocolate smeared on their faces and my heart does flip flops when Jake leans down to catch them and scoops them up into his arms, kissing each little one on the cheek, before depositing them back on the ground.

The younger one peers up at me with a curious look on her face. "Who are you?"

Jake looks ready to step in and make introductions, but before he has the chance, I crouch down to meet her green-eyed gaze and hold out a hand. "I'm Penelope."

She shakes my hand, her smaller one slightly sticky with marshmallow residue. "I'm Alice."

"Nice to meet you, Alice."

"Come on," she says, taking my hand and tugging a bit, "we're having s'mores."

I throw a glance at Jake, a grin spread across his face as he watches me trail behind the little girl right up the path to the door. It strikes me as I follow her inside that I'm a stranger to everyone inside these walls, we've never met, and I was kind of banking on the fact that Jake would be there to ease my nerves when we finally met.

Alice continues tugging me behind her until we come to a stop in the kitchen where the family is gathered around the kitchen island laden with all kinds of s'mores supplies; a variety of graham crackers and cookies, all kinds of chocolate choices, and fresh berries piled high. At our entrance, the family turns to stare at Alice and me, the stranger in their kitchen.

"This is 'Nelope," Alice announces. A few confused looks pass over the faces of the people looking back at me as I raise a hand in greeting. There's no doubt that the two young men currently burning their marshmallows are Jake's brothers, all three of them bear an uncanny resemblance to each other. Jenna stands nearby, a grin on her face as she sees Alice tug me into the kitchen. She greets me with a warm hug before taking Alice's hand, leading her over to the sink and helping her wash before tossing a damp rag in my direction to clean the secondhand marshmallow mess from my own hands.

"Thanks," I catch the rag out of the air and wipe down my hands, grateful for the distraction. It doesn't last long. Alice bounds past me, shouting something about Uncle Jake, and leaving me with the rest of the family. "So...as Alice told you...I'm Penelope."

"It's nice to finally meet you," Jake's mom, I assume, wraps her arms around me in a warm hug. A hug that brings an unexpected bit of emotion. I feel tears well up behind my eyes and will myself not to let them fall. I haven't been hugged like this in a long time. Sure, I've been hugged...but mom hugs are different. They hold a different kind of power. I hang onto her a little bit longer than I probably should, but she doesn't seem to mind.

"Sorry," I say, letting go and stepping away. I wipe the corners of my eyes and she squeezes my hand, giving me a knowing smile. I love her already. One by one, the rest of the family introduces themselves. I meet Jax—the oldest of the siblings, and the one that Jake called last month to make sure that I wasn't going to die under his supervision. I wrap him in a tight hug, thanking him for all that he did for Jake that night. Thanking him for all he does for women like me.

Alice and her sister, whose name I learn, is Mackenzie, are Jax's daughters. Jenna, the second born, and only sister in the bunch gives me a hug just as warm as her mom's. She's an environmental scientist and professor, and according to Jake, she can throw a mean fastball. James, the youngest, is an ER doctor who just finished his residency. And finally, I officially introduce myself to Jake's parents—Claire and Benjamin.

As I'm pulled further into the family group, welcomed in with hugs and handshakes, I look up and spot Jake watching us from a distance, leaning against a wall near the back of the room, a smile on his face, eyes glittering in the soft light as he watches me being pulled into the family fold. Alice watches me too, her gaze following mine to Jake. She walks over and takes his hand in hers, pulling him behind her into the family fray until he's standing right beside me at the island. We toast our marshmallows and build gourmet s'mores, and standing there side by side with him, I fall into a rhythm that doesn't normally come naturally to me. I laugh and joke with his sister. I talk baseball with James, and Jax's girls hug me before their dad shepherds them up the stairs for baths and bedtime.

As we wind down for the night, Jake takes my bags upstairs, and

I jump in to help Claire and Jenna clean the kitchen. They try to insist that I go upstairs and settle in for the night, but I want to spend more time with them, getting to know them and allowing them to get to know me. Although it is late, and my batteries are drained, I'm oddly energized as I laugh and talk with them as we clean. With hugs for them both, I allow Jake to take my hand and lead me upstairs. At the end of the hall is a door with my name written on a tiny chalkboard that hangs from a hook on the door.

"Looks like this is me," I smile and stretch onto my tiptoes to plant a kiss on his cheek.

"Mom put me in the basement," he laughs, wrapping me up in a hug and taking a cautious look down the hall before giving me a much less gentle kiss than I just gave him. "Goodnight, Sunshine."

"Goodnight, Stormcloud." He turns with a grin and heads down the stairs, back to the first floor, and eventually to the basement. He assures me that it's not as bad as it sounds, but a part of me feels guilty that my being here means he doesn't get a proper room for the next four days.

That guilt vanishes as soon as I open the door to my room.

It's like something out of a fairytale; a rustic, wooden, four poster bed with a gauzy canopy draping down the posts, a plush rug under my feet, that I instinctively curl my bare toes into, and the softest sheets I've ever felt. A basket of extra blankets sits in the corner, and heavy curtains are drawn over the windows, the only light is from a small table lamp by the bed. I take a quick shower in the ensuite bathroom to wash off the day before slipping into the silky soft sheets covering the cloud-like mattress.

When I wake in the morning, I pull open the curtains to find the sun rising over Saratoga Lake. The water is still as glass, early morning sunlight glimmering across the surface. I throw on a sweatshirt and open the door to the balcony, stepping out into the crisp morning air. There's a dock jutting out into the water from the edge of the Hutchinson's property, a small fishing boat moored on one side, and a pontoon on the other. I watch as the rising sun dissipates the fog from the surface of the lake, and hope to myself that I'll get many more opportunities to spend time in this house. With this family.

27
INTENTIONS
JAKE

As I round the bend from the trail, the house comes back into view and with it, Penelope, standing on the upstairs balcony in shorts and a sweatshirt, her hair mussed from sleep, glasses perched on her nose, gazing out across the lake. I could well and truly get used to seeing her here. I lift a hand in greeting when she sees me, and the closer I get to her, the better I can see the smile lighting up her face. I pick up my pace a bit and come to a stop under her balcony.

"Morning, Sunshine!"

"Good morning, Jake."

In a move that I hope looks as cool as it does in my head, I jump up and grab the floor of the balcony, straining to pull myself up far enough for her to lean down and meet me for a kiss. She turns a brilliant shade of red when she realizes what I'm doing, but kisses me anyway. I jump down, satisfied, and let her know that I'm going to get cleaned up but plan on meeting her in the kitchen for breakfast.

I get cleaned up more than I normally would for a weekend with my family. Jeans and a thin flannel button down, sleeves rolled up because I like the way it brings out the blush in Penelope's cheeks anytime I roll up my sleeves around her. I head upstairs when I smell coffee and bacon, and find Penelope in the kitchen with my dad. They're making pancakes. I see the recipe card on the counter between them, as he explains a step and watches as she whisks a bowl of egg whites.

"Consider yourself lucky," I step up behind her and bend to press a kiss on the ticklish spot behind her ear, "he doesn't share this recipe with just anyone."

"No," dad laughs, pushing me out of the way, "I just didn't share it with *you*."

That's fair.

Or it was until I met Penelope.

They will all eat their words when I wow them with a full meal this weekend. I sit down on one of the stools at the island after pouring myself a steaming mug of coffee and I watch as Penelope and dad work side by side in the kitchen. Penelope skillfully, almost artfully, mixes and pours the pancakes, watching them intently, waiting for the precise moment to flip them. Her nimble fingers pinch up a handful of mini chocolate chips and sprinkles them on top of the ones she just poured.

Little feet pound down the stairs, and soon Mack and Alice are in the kitchen with us and a bedraggled Jax sits down beside me, taking my coffee and draining the mug. I pour myself a refill and give Jax a fresh mug. Penelope picks Alice up and sets her on the counter, letting her and Mack help place the chocolate chips in the next round of pancakes. They munch on a few too, a grin on Alice's face as she is given a task and gets to help with breakfast.

Penelope tames Alice's curls, smoothing out the unruly bedhead. Jax turns to me with a look that's hard to read. He nods toward the patio door and we take our coffees out to the patio table and sit down on the same side, facing the lake. I watch as the water laps at the shore, a few boats in the distance, fishing lines in the water. Jax breaks the silence.

"What are you going to do about that?" He asks, hiding a smirk behind his mug.

"About what?"

"Seriously, man? She's in there making pancakes with dad. Dad, who never lets anyone else make his pancakes. She let Alice help without Alice even needing to ask. And did you see what she did to her hair?! It takes me almost an hour to do her hair some mornings and Penelope just..."

"Worked her magic?"

"Yeah."

"I know. Watching her last night with Alice and the rest of you, and this morning with dad and the girls. I've fallen in love with her, Jax."

"First things first: Tell her. And then go from there. I know I'm probably not the one you want advice from..."

"Don't say that," I stop him with a hand on his arm, turning to look him in the eye. "You *loved* Angela. You did. We all saw it. You loved her with all that you had, Jax. It is not your fault that she left."

Jax was devastated when Angela left him and the girls. We all were. He has sole custody of the girls, which, aside from the girls themselves, is one of the only good things to have come from that situation, the problem is their mother will have nothing to do with them. I watched how Jax loved his wife through all of the turmoil of their marriage, through the ups and downs, the good days and the rock bottom days. But it wasn't enough for her. He gave her every bit of his heart, and had it broken.

In spite of that, I will always listen to his advice on love.

"Thanks Jake. I'm serious. Tell her how you feel, she deserves to know. She's entrusted you with a lot of vulnerable, emotional parts of herself. You risk hurting her the longer you wait."

I'm just about to respond when Alice runs outside to announce that breakfast is ready. She takes her dad and me by the hands and pulls us along into the dining room, pointing me to the open chair closest to Penelope before crawling up into Penelope's lap, where she stays for the duration of the meal.

"I think she likes you," I stretch an arm over the back of Penelope's chair, leaning in close to whisper in her ear, and inhale the sweet scent of strawberry and mint.

Penelope turns her face toward me, leaning in for a quick peck on my cheek before kissing the top of Alice's head. "The feeling is very mutual."

I can't explain what happens to my heart when I watch Penelope with my nieces, especially with little Alice who took to her immediately. I watch her with the girls—this morning in the kitchen, and now as they take her downstairs to show off their playroom—and that Sunshine smile never goes away. She's at ease here. She was worried about this weekend being overwhelming, but so far she's slipped in as if she's always been a part of our family, and I find myself thinking that I wish she was.

I've got to clear my head. And nothing does that better than being on the water. I grab the keys from the hook on the door and let dad know I'm taking one of the boats out. I jog down to the dock and hop in the fishing boat, which gets the attention of the rest of the family. Before I know it, we're planning a family outing on the boat.

When Jax mentions staying behind with the girls, Penelope steps up and volunteers so that Jax doesn't have to miss out on time with the family. "Besides," Penelope says, looking every bit the part of Jax's annoying little sister as she shoves him playfully toward the rest of us, "you deserve a break."

So much for my own quiet time on the boat.

I think the best in silence.

Connecting with nature has always been an outlet for me, which is hard when you live in the middle of New York City. Sure, I can wander Central Park, or walk along the Hudson. But out here? On the lake? It's quiet. Peaceful. Which is what I need when my brain is a mess.

Instead, I'm confined to a boat with my family. At least through lunch.

"Are you sure you don't mind," I ask one last time, wrapping Penelope in my arms and planting a kiss on her forehead.

"I'm sure, Jake. Go. Fish. Have fun."

"Okay. As long as you're sure."

"I can handle it," she laughs and pulls herself out of my arms, shoving me toward the dock and my family waiting for me on the boat.

I board the pontoon and take a seat behind dad. As he backs the boat away from the dock we wave at Penelope and the girls who wave back to us from the shore. We head out onto the lake with our fishing gear ready for us, lunch packed in the small cooler, and my head filled with thoughts of Penelope.

Alice is taken with her, that much is clear. Mack took some time but is warming up to her. And Penelope has been so good with the girls, right from the moment we got here. I wasn't entirely sure what to expect, throwing Penelope into my crazy, sometimes overwhelming, family, but she's acclimated beautifully, and everyone is quite taken with her.

We drop anchor in our usual fishing spot, each of us moving to our usual spot in the boat. Dad drops his line over the side, no bobber. He's a tightline fisherman, something that I picked up from him when I was about thirteen, and something I still do today. We set our lines to the right depth, and drop them over the side of the boat. When a fish bites, I set the hook and lift my line straight out of the water. If it puts up a fight, I'll reel it in.

Mom and James cast their lines with bobbers as close to the shore as they can, and Jenna and Jax cast their bobber-less lines on the other side of the boat, in the direction of the open water. With our lines in the water, a silence settles over the boat, nothing but the sound of the waves, the birds overhead, and the occasional splash of a fish coming out of the water.

Dad breaks the silence. He settles back in his seat, rod held between his legs, and crosses his arms over his chest. He casts me a sidelong glance and a smile tugs at the corner of his mouth.

"Son, what are your intentions?"

I sputter and cough as I sit up and try not to lose my rod over the side of the boat.

"Ooh, I want to hear this!" James reels in his line and turns from the other side of the boat to face me, a sly twinkle in his eye.

"Me too."

"Yup, let's hear it."

Mom, bless her, is the only one who leaves me alone. She keeps her line in the water, eye on the bobber while I'm interrogated by my family.

I know what my intentions are. I don't know that I need to share them with my parents and siblings. I've already talked to Peter, and that's enough for now.

"Is this a conversation you'd have had with my dad?" he asks, his voice choked with emotion.

"It is." From everything she's told me, I know I would have loved getting to know Penelope's dad. I'd like to think he would have liked me. I've had the chance to get to know Peter since that weekend he and Sofia came up to visit, I've joined a few family video calls since then, and have corresponded with Peter a bit as well. I've enjoyed getting to know Penelope's brother, the man in her life that has been there for her throughout adulthood. Peter has been an older brother and father figure for Penelope for her adult life. It means a lot to me to have his blessing.

"I'll tell you what he would tell you if he were here: you don't need my permission. Penelope is a strong woman. An independent woman. You don't need my permission to ask, and she doesn't need my permission to

say yes. All I ask is that you respect her. And treat her with kindness," he swallows, and sniffs. I give him a moment to collect himself before he continues. "And give her the love that she deserves."

"I will Peter."

"Yeah. I know you will."

"Thank you Peter," I have to choke back tears of my own as I hang up the phone and look across the open office floor and see her pacing her office, scribbling notes in her notepad, shoes discarded, hair disheveled, glasses slipping down the end of her nose. Morgan intercepts Mike, redirecting him away from her office, and I see an opening for myself.

I roll up my shirt sleeves, loosen my tie and open the top button of my collar. I'm not blind, I know what that does to her. It fills her cheeks with a light blush, sometimes the tips of her ears too.

I cross the office and knock lightly on her door. She turns to face me, a smile lighting up her features. She waves me inside and I shut the door. When I turn around, I bump right into her, or rather she bumps into me. I wrap her in my arms, admiring the pink tinge in her cheeks, as she stretches and lightly kisses my cheek.

"Hi Sunshine" I kiss her on the corner of her mouth. She smiles against me and the pink in her cheeks darkens. I've done my job. But, there's more to ask. "I'm heading upstate for the long weekend. My siblings and I are all going to be there with mom and dad, and I wondered if you'd like to join me. With all the work we've been doing - you've been doing - I thought since we're off Thursday and Friday anyway, we could make a long weekend out of it."

She stares at me for a long, charged moment.

"I'd like that," she says with a small smile, "I really could use the time away."

"Yes, you could." I wrap her in another hug, but we jump apart at a sharp knock on the door. Morgan sticks her head in to give the ten minute warning, surprise registering on her face as she sees me standing in Penelope's office. I nod in her direction and she gives me a knowing smile.

I head back to my office as Penelope makes her way to the control room. I fix my sleeves, tighten my tie, and throw on my jacket. Shutting myself in my office, I dial mom on my cell phone.

"Honey! It's great to hear from you!"

"Hey mom. Do you still have grandma's ring?"

I have the ring.

Mom gave it to me last night after I got Penelope settled into her room. She knows. That's why she's keeping herself out of this particular conversation. I know. Peter knows. My intentions are to marry her. I just have to ask her first. But there are other conversations that Penelope and I need to have before I ask her to commit to spending the rest of our lives together.

On the ride up here last night, Penelope said that whatever this is between us means something to her. It means something to me too, and as much as I tried to avoid it at the outset, I've fallen in love with her.

I've fallen in love with her smile. Her frown. Her laugh. The little line that forms between her eyebrows when she's deep in concentration. The way she talks about her family and friends and people she loves. The way she herself loves deeply. The way her hair falls in her eyes when she kneads bread dough. The handprints on her jeans because she doesn't know how to use kitchen towels.

I've fallen in love with Penelope Nichols. Deeply, hopelessly, madly in love.

"I intend," I take a deep breath and steel myself against what I'm sure will be a number of questions, "to make her a part of this family."

"YES!" Jenna shouts, raising her hands in the air before high-fiving James.

Jax smiles and nods before turning back to his fishing rod. Dad claps a hand on my shoulder and mom gives me that knowing smile of hers.

I explain to them that beyond knowing I'm going to ask, I have other things to talk to her about first. But I assure them that when the time is right, I will ask her the question. For now, I'm happy having the ring. And Peter's blessing.

We eat lunch on the boat, and after a while the fish stop biting. Rather than pulling anchor and finding a new spot on the lake, we pull anchor and head back toward the house. As we pull up to the dock, I hear one of the girls wailing not all that far away. Jax hears it too, and jumps out of the boat, nearly breaking into a sprint up the dock.

I tie down the boat for dad and jog quickly up to the house, but by the time I get there, the crying has stopped, and Jax is standing in the lawn, staring at a heap in the grass a few feet away. Penelope is sitting in the grass with a red faced, tear streaked Alice in her arms. Penelope looks up and says something to Jax, he nods and heads into the house. Returning a few moments later with a couple of bandages in his hand. He hands them to Penelope.

Her focus returns to the little girl in her arms. She pulls open a little package that Jax gave her, wiping Alice's knee and elbow with what I assume is an alcohol wipe by the way she scrunches her face and starts to cry again. Penelope quickly covers each spot with a bandage and then kisses the bandages. She wipes away Alice's tears and the little girl throws her arms around Penelope's neck, snuggling into her and holding on tight.

My heart flutters as I watch Penelope with my niece. Holding her and taking care of her. Loving her. Comforting her.

This woman who has spent so much of her life taking care of the people that she loves, now taking care of the people *I* love. Penelope is one of the most nurturing people I've ever met - between cooking and sharing her food with a stranger, making sure that her hosts are taken care of each night, and giving up her own plans to take care of her parents while they were sick. I look at her there, holding Alice, and know beyond a doubt, that I want to take care of her.

For the rest of our lives.

I want her to be nurtured, loved, and cared for.

I want her to know how important she is to me. That her needs are as important as the needs of those around her. From that night in her apartment, when I was terrified I'd have to rush her to a hospital, to this morning with the pancakes, and now something as simple as a bandage. I want to care for her the way that she cares for me. For everyone around her.

I want to give her the love she deserves.

28

SHE LOVES ME
JAKE

I head outside after cleaning myself up from the fishing trip this morning, and I find the family in the middle of a soccer game, Dad and my brothers against Penelope and my nieces. I watch as Penelope runs the length of the yard, holding her own against dad and the guys, while also allowing Mack and Alice opportunities to score.

Jenna sits down next to me where I've landed on the patio, handing me a bottle of ginger ale from the cooler. She watches me as I watch Penelope, a smile tugging at the corners of her mouth as I take a swig of the spicy ginger brew and try to hide the fact that I'm openly cheering against my brothers in this pick-up game.

"Have you told her yet?" Jenna asks.

"Told her what?" I hedge.

"That you're hopelessly in love with her?"

I watch Penelope, out in the yard with my brothers, and nieces. She looks at home here, surrounded by my family, laughing, and trash talking James and Jax. She stops running and gathers my nieces close to her in a huddle, she points down the lawn to the makeshift goal, and after a team handshake, she kicks the ball to Mack who streaks across the grass, juking past her dad, and passing the ball to Alice who shoots it straight into the goal before James can even think about getting close to it.

My heart flutters when Penelope opens her arms out wide and wraps the girls up in a hug, celebrating their teamwork, and the girls throw their arms around her neck. They high five James, Jax before they all collapse into the grass for a well-earned break. When I swing my gaze back over to Jenna, she is waiting patiently for an answer.

"No," my voice is barely above a whisper, "not yet."

"You need to…"

"I know."

"She has trust issues, you know that. You also know she's confided a lot in you…"

"I know."

"Jake…"

"Jenna," I snap, "I said I know. I know I have to tell her. I know that I am probably falling too hard too fast, and that I haven't given her any reason to *fully* trust *me*, and I know that I'm scared that telling her means I'm risking losing even her friendship. And frankly, I would deserve that."

"No, you don't deserve that. You deserve to have someone who loves you just as much as you love them. And I think that person is Penelope."

I wish the thought of that didn't make me so deliriously happy. The idea that Penelope could love me as much as I love her.

"You think she loves me?" I ask, even though I'm sure I know the answer. She said as much in the car on the drive up here. She said it all without actually saying the words.

"I see the way she looks at you. I see the way she laughs at the stupid things you say. She talks about you as if you hung the moon just for her. Don't screw this up little brother."

"I'll try not to."

Penelope and I take a trip into town so that we can pick up ingredients for tonight's dinner. Apparently mom has relinquished control of her kitchen for the night, which is not something she does lightly. It's the ultimate sign that Penelope has made an impression on the family. But what mom doesn't know is that Penelope isn't going to be the one cooking tonight.

When we get back to the house, I get to work.

For dinner tonight, I'm making the first dish that Penelope taught me to make: Pasta Primavera. Penelope helped me pick out the vegetables, pasta, and cheese, but is otherwise not lifting a finger for this meal tonight.

I lay out the vegetables and grab a knife and cutting board, slicing everything the way that Penelope showed me all those weeks ago. I heat olive oil in a pan and sauté garlic first before adding the rest of the summer vegetables. The smell of garlic brings the whole family into the kitchen, and it's hard not to register the shock on everyone's faces when they find Penelope watching me from the kitchen island. She looks so proud, and it does wonders for my confidence in the kitchen. Knowing that she believes in me is all that I need.

"It smells amazing in here," Jax sits down beside Penelope. "I thought you were cooking tonight?"

"There was a change of plans," Penelope answers, picking at the heel of a baguette that we bought today to serve with dinner and handing a chunk to my brother. "Jake wanted to show you all what he's been learning."

"He told us you were teaching him," Jax bites into the bread as mom and dad inspect the pans on the stove, hovering over my shoulder as I work. "You've done a number on him."

Penelope regards me for a moment, a question in her eyes. Then she looks at my family gathered in the room, breaking bread together and harassing me for finally learning how *not* to burn food. I laugh along with them, and am startled to find Penelope not laughing, but crying, and trying really hard to hide it. Jax notices too and suggests to the family that they take their bread out to the patio, leaving Penelope and I in the kitchen. James seems determined to stick around and see what unfolds until mom grabs his ear and pulls him behind her. Penelope tries and fails to hide her smile.

"Jake...." She sucks in a breath, her eyes breaking away from mine and focusing on the chunk of bread in front of her. I so desperately want her to look at me. I drop the spatula in my hand, turn down the burners and give her my full attention.

"What's going on, Sunshine?"

"I lied to you before," she whispers as tears slip down her cheeks. "I haven't just fallen for you. I *love* you, Jake. You were the curveball I never saw coming. And I realized just now that if I didn't tell you, I'd end up regretting it. I needed to put it out there despite my fear and despite the fact that the logical part of my brain is telling me that it's way too fast..."

I silence her with a kiss. Closing the distance between us and gently framing her face with my hands. I press my lips to hers, and for the first time since I've known her, her overly-logical brain shuts up long enough for her to kiss me back. She wraps her arms around me, pressing as close as she can to me. Penelope breaks the kiss, taking a deep breath and wiping her tears.

"I love you too, Penelope," I wipe away her tears with the edge of my apron. "Truly, deeply. And you're right, we haven't known each other for very long, but I know that I love you, too. I love everything about you. I love that you came up here and made yourself a part of the family. I love that you love my nieces. I love to watch you from the desk during the show, and the sound of your voice in my earpiece during commercial breaks. I love the way that you distract me so badly that Jim usually has to throw to commercial or bring us back when I'm supposed to. I love how you fall asleep in my arms on the couch during movies, or how you stream baseball games to your tablet when I'm trying to watch a movie with you, and that you're a tiny bit superstitious..."

She laughs as she wipes away her tears. And I keep going.

"I love that you have a video call with your brother every week, and I love that you've let me be a part of that. I love your routines. I love your smile. And your frown. And that face you make when you're concentrating really hard on something. I love that you stole the only New York hoodie I have from my playing days and still haven't given it back. I love..."

She closes the distance between us, cupping my face in her hands, and kissing me. Soft and gentle. I thread my fingers into her hair and pull her against me, wrapping my other arm around her waist and falling even further into her kiss. She pulls back at the sound of muffled cheering coming from the other side of the sliding glass door. She laughs, pressing her forehead to my chest as a blush creeps into her cheeks.

I'm gonna kill my brothers. But that can wait until after dinner.

29
WHAT THE FUTURE HOLDS
PENELOPE

After a morning and afternoon spent doing typical family picnic things—another game of pickup soccer, a cookout, and a swim in the lake—Jake and I pack up and get ready for our drive back into the city. He holds my hand as he drives, our fingers intertwined, the warmth of his hand in mine grounding me, giving me the security I need as we head back toward the busyness of Manhattan.

I watch out the window as we drive further and further from Saratoga Springs. As my heart gets further and further from the feeling of home that surrounded me these past few days. A part of me has always longed for the sense of belonging I felt with Jake's family. Sure, I have my brother and Sofi, but being with Jake's family felt different somehow. It just felt...right.

"You're awfully quiet over there," Jake's voice cuts through the silence of the vehicle, as he gives my hand a squeeze.

"Have you ever thought of moving out of the city?" I ask, keeping my eyes glued on the scenery outside my window. "Getting a house upstate and commuting?"

"Sometimes," he answers, an air of dreaminess in his voice. "Not as far as mom and dad's place, but far enough outside of the city that I could have a yard, some quiet."

"This weekend reminded me of why I loved where I grew up. Why I loved some of the smaller stations I worked for. It reminded me of my need for quiet; time for myself, or spent with the people I care about."

I grew up in a small-ish neighborhood in Michigan. Not all that far from where Jake grew up. We had a front and backyard, a small garden, trees for shade. We were ten minutes away from my grandma's house, and spent a lot of weekends and holidays with her. My brother and I would ride our bikes everywhere in the summer, and in the winter we traipsed around the neighborhood with shovels, clearing driveways for anyone who needed it.

Up until taking the job at ASN, I'd worked in small towns. Nothing like Manhattan. It took some adjusting once I moved to "the city that never sleeps". For one thing, when I get one of my frequent migraines, it's a lot harder to block out the light and the noise of the city. Walks in the park are crowded, and the wail of sirens is a regular part of the day.

I miss having a yard to mow. A garden to tend. A quiet neighborhood to take walks in. And I wouldn't mind having those things, and sharing them with Jake. This weekend, more than ever, I've found myself thinking of a future with him. The two of us in a cozy house upstate, close enough to his parents and the city that our drive either way wouldn't be too terribly long. A yard for kids or a dog…or both… to run around in. A little plot that we could till into a garden. A neighborhood where we could walk together, hand in hand.

Watching Jake with Mack and Alice this weekend had me thinking about the future of our relationship—watching him with our own children. As great as he is as Uncle Jake, this weekend, I could see him as Dad. Teaching our kids to fish, to tie their shoes, to play soccer or baseball. To dream big, to do whatever they set their little hearts on. I know that the reality is, I may have a hard time conceiving, if I'm able to at all.

The sun is just starting to set as we round the bend back toward the house. As the house comes into view, Jax and the girls are visible on the lawn, right back to kicking the soccer ball around. I stop and turn toward the water, sitting down and drawing my knees up to my chest. I tug Jake down next to me and he wraps an arm around my shoulder.

For a long time, we just sit in silence. He doesn't push me to speak or ask any questions. He lets me sit and gather my thoughts. Finally, as tears slip past my defenses, I break the silence.

"You want kids, don't you?"

Surprise registers on his face for just a moment. But is quickly replaced by an unreadable expression.

"I do."

"You know that with my PCOS, I may have trouble getting pregnant and carrying to term, if I can conceive at all."

"I know. Jax gave me a bit of a crash course that night when you were sick."

I figured as much. Jax probably also gave him the hopeful news that a lot of women with PCOS find success with fertility treatments. That while pregnancy is difficult, it's not an impossibility.

"I want you to know," *he shifts so that my back is pressed against his chest, his arms now wrapped fully around me,* "that this doesn't change anything. I love you, Penelope. No matter what. If and when the time comes, I will support you. If that means we try on our own, or with the help of fertility treatments, or even adoption, I will support whatever you choose."

I wipe away my tears and turn in his arms to look at him more fully. "You know we just made this official the other night, right?"

"I know," *he chuckles and kisses the tip of my nose.* "But I've been in love with you for a long time Penelope. I just had to work up the courage to tell you."

"I love you too, Jake."

"I'd love to live outside of the city," he says, thoughtfully. "I'd love to live *with you* outside of the city."

He squeezes my hand again before lifting it and softly kissing my knuckles. We drive in silence a while longer. As we approach the city, I see the skyline in the distance, the iconic view that I fell in love with years ago, but am slowly realizing isn't for me. I long for the peace and quiet we just left, the peace and quiet I remember from my childhood, from my early days as a sports reporter.

I could live outside of Manhattan. If it meant a life with Jake, I'd live anywhere. The silence of the drive is broken up by the pinging of both of our cell phones. I look at mine and see that it's a text from Morgan for the both of us. I read it aloud.

It's ready. Want to watch?

I inhale a sharp breath as tears prick the back of my eyes.

Shattered Glass. It's ready. Morgan finished the editing. I sent her my notes, worked on it with her late most nights for the last week. It's finally finished. Do I want to watch it? Part of me does. The other part of me is terrified. For so long, it's lived as a rough list of notes in my tablet and a series of old notebooks. I don't know if I'm ready to see it come to life.

"I don't know," I whisper. "I don't know if I'm ready to see it."

We meet at my apartment, the four of us - Morgan and Dan, me and Jake. I pace the kitchen as Dan sets up his computer and streams to my television. I make sure everyone has what they need -- snacks, drinks, a handful of tissues shoved into my pockets...just in case. I wave Jake off as he tries to get me to sit down. I can't. Pacing is fine. For now.

At the end of the hour, I hug Dan and Morgan and thank them for their work on the show. Morgan presses a USB drive into my hand as tears fill her eyes, and mine too. I give her another hug as they leave and then I collapse into Jake's arms.

In one month, I'm going to go into the executive pitch meeting with a fully produced episode to share with them. Finally. I'm nervous. More nervous than I've ever been for the monthly pitch meeting. But I feel good about it. Dan and Morgan polished the episode way better than I ever could have done on my own. And Jake's confidence in me does wonders.

Jake plants a soft kiss on the top of my head as he holds me in his arms. He assures me that the meeting will be great. That *I'll* be great. I wish I had the same confidence in myself that he has in me. But tonight, I choose to believe him. We sit on my sofa, Jake scanning the channels while I cuddle up next to him, dozing on and off after the excitement of finally seeing my dream made a reality. And recovering from some of the craziness from a weekend with Jake's family.

"It's getting late," he unwraps me from his arms and pulls me in for a tender kiss, the kind of kiss that steals my breath away.

"Thank you," I pull back and look at him, sleeves of his flannel shirt rolled up, a couple days of scruff and a smile on his face as he leans against the open door of his apartment. That fluttery feeling is back as I look at him. I cross the room and take his face in my hands. "Thank you. For everything."

I softly kiss his lips, before stepping past him and crossing the hall back to my own apartment.

"Goodnight Sunshine," he grins at me.

"Night Jake. I love you."

"I love you too, Penelope."

30
SHARDS OF GLASS
PENELOPE

I smooth the lapels of my blazer, adjust the bow tied at the neck of my blouse, and run my clammy hands down the length of my skirt before checking the time again. Ten minutes. Ten minutes until the meeting starts. Until I stand before that imposing group of men *again* and give them a piece of my heart. Give them the most vulnerable part of me I've ever offered them.

Jake stops by my office for a good luck kiss and a promise that he'll be waiting for me when the meeting is over. He takes something from his pocket and tucks it into my hand, telling me to take a look at it any time I need a boost of courage during the meeting. Morgan squeezes my hand as I walk past her desk and make my way to the conference room.

I take my seat among the usual crowd of men who make up the network's executive team. To bolster my courage, I look at what it was Jake gave me, and my breath catches as I see two pictures, side by side: me and my dad. The same picture I have in my office. And one of me with Mack and Alice, a picture I didn't realize was being taken as I stood with them in the yard, playing a pickup game of soccer.

Written across the bottom of the picture are the words: *If you can do it, so can they.*

I take a deep breath and tuck the pictures into my jacket pocket and steel myself for the meeting ahead. After all the usual pitches, it's time for mine. For *On the Field*...for *Shattered Glass*. I throw out a possible road trip and location shoot for the All Star Game, something that everyone seems to be on board with. And then. I take a deep, steadying breath.

"There's something I've been working on," my voice sounds foreign to my own ears. "I've looked at the data, audience demographics, and ratings, and I think it will be perfect to air during the off-season, after the playoffs are over. I have a fully produced -"

"Not again," Mike groans, cutting me off. "Penny. How many times do we have to tell you no before you understand it?"

I take a few calming breaths.

"No. At some point you have to understand, this just isn't a fit for our network, am I right?" He looks to the other men in the room for validation. They don't meet my gaze. They also don't outright tell him he's right, which is progress I guess. "Besides, you wouldn't be able to host."

His eyes bore right into mine. I do my best to stay in the moment, not slip into the memories of years' past. I block out the memories as best I can, staring Mike down from where I'm sitting.

"Why not, Mike?" I challenge him the way he's challenged me so many times in this very room. "Why couldn't I host?"

He looks from me to the men seated around the conference table as if it should be obvious to all of us why I shouldn't be the host. But I want to hear him say it. I want to hear him, in this room filled with men who control both of our jobs, tell me exactly why he thinks I shouldn't be on camera.

"Come on Penny, you've seen yourself."

And there it is.

The men around the room look to me for a reaction. But I won't dignify them with an emotional outburst. "Yes, I have. And while I've struggled for many years with my appearance I've come to the conclusion that if anyone has a problem with me, it's *their* problem to deal with, not *mine*."

For the first time, I look at the other executives. Mr. Fields meets my gaze and gives me a small nod. So quick I almost missed it. But it was a nod. It had to be. He scribbles something on the pad in front of him as I stand and address the room one more time. "Forgive me if I don't stay for the rest of the meeting. I have a broadcast to prepare for."

I pack up my things, and for the first time in the two years that I've worked here, I leave the executive pitch meeting before it's over. I walk out with my head held high. And then I sit in the stairwell and sob. I'll never get my pitch passed as long as Mike is in those meetings. Maybe I should send it to other networks. ASN is small compared to other national sports networks. I could shop it around, see if anyone else would take it. I just don't know if I can stand being shot down again.

I think back to that night Jake read my texts on the air. Polishing my resume when I got home that night. I'm clearly not valued here at ASN as anything more than a producer. I don't have a voice in these meetings anymore, if ever. With Mike undermining me, I've lost the respect of my colleagues, he's made me a laughing stock. As long as I continue working under Mike Fletcher, I won't be taken seriously. Today proved that.

Once I've composed myself, I head back down to my office where Jake is waiting with Morgan. I shut the door behind me, and wrap my arms around Jake's waist, burying my face in his chest and letting him hold me for a minute. I feel safe in his arms. Secure. Stable. All the things that I wasn't feeling in that meeting today.

I give Morgan the flash drive with *Shattered Glass* on it, asking her to keep it safe for me. She excuses herself and leaves Jake and me together. He tells me not to give up, and I assure him that I won't but right now, I really want to. Right now I want to go home and bake something. Or take a walk through Riverside Park. Or...escape to the house in Saratoga Springs. Surround myself with people I love, people who love me.

When my parents passed, I shut myself off and that made it harder for me to deal with the grief and the pain. Therapy helped. Therapy, and a few hard conversations with my brother. Which is why I'm not going to do that this time. This time, I'm going to let people in. Let people close. Let myself be loved and cared for. And I'm starting right now, with Jake's arms wrapped around me as I cry into his chest. He'll have to change his shirt before the show.

"I need to get ready for the show," I pull away and wipe my face with the sleeve of my blazer. "But, this isn't me shutting you out. Please know that."

"I know," he kisses my temple and excuses himself from my office, leaving me to make preparations for tonight's broadcast.

I pull up an old document on my computer. A file I haven't looked at in a long time. I change the date to today's, I update a few lines and I save it. I don't want to use it, but if I have to, I will.

To whom it may concern,

I humbly submit my resignation...

I don't want to. Not without a job to fall back on. Not without some kind of financial support to keep me afloat. But these are things to worry about later. For now, I have a show to put on the air.

The show starts in a few minutes, which means I need to be heading to the control room. As I step into the corridor and lock my office, I notice Jake is still seated at his desk. I head toward him to give him the time, and make sure he's ready for the show.

"She just won't stop. No matter how many times we tell her no, she keeps bringing this 'women in baseball' idea. And come on...she wants to host? What kind of image would that present of the network?" Mike's derisive voice stops me in my tracks. I wait, stepping away from Jake's door. I don't want either of them to see me, but I do want to hear more of this conversation.

"It's a good idea. It'll grow our audience, appeal to a new demographic, it might even introduce young women and girls to the game, show them what they are capable of," he pauses for just a minute, looking at Mike with a deadly expression, "and you're kidding yourself if you think people won't watch her."

Mike scoffs. I step toward the door and knock, poking my head in to give Jake a five minute warning. He nods, and stands, donning his sport coat and passing me on the way toward the studio. Everyone else has headed to their post for the night, and I intend to follow Jake to the studio, but Mike stops me. He grabs my wrist and pulls me close. I shake myself free of his grasp.

"You're wasting your time on this. You're wasting *my* time, and network resources."

Wrenching myself from Mike's grasp, I brush past him and head to the control room. My hands shake as I scribble a few last minute notes for the show. Jake, Jim, and Devon are at the desk ready to start the show, and Jake looks past the camera, making eye contact with me. At his furrowed brow, I shake my head, I can't get into any of it right now. Mike's advances up to this point have always been verbal. This is the first time, other than the occasional wandering hand, that I've ever felt threatened. There was something in his eyes tonight when he grabbed me, something that rocked me to my core.

But I can't think about that right now. I have a broadcast to focus on.

Before the cameras roll, I see Jake huddle with the other hosts. They nod, and he passes them notecards that he draws from the pocket of his jacket. I give them their cue. And Jake starts the show discussing Amy Kim, the first female general manager. I don't have to look at my notes to know that he has completely changed the direction of tonight's show. We don't have graphics prepared for this. Or clips. Anything. I tell Morgan to get ready to cut to whatever game is currently in progress. Just in case.

At the first commercial break, the studio doors burst open and

Mike strides in, a scowl on his face. He stands at the threshold between the control room and the set.

"Penelope," he shouts, no doubt hoping everyone on this floor will hear him. "I know this is your doing. I told you no and you hijacked my show? Of all the unprofessional things..."

"It wasn't her Mike," Jake rises from his seat and takes a step toward Mike. I abandon my post and put myself between them, waving Jake off. He stops, but I can tell he wants to do more. "This story was my idea."

"Jake, please." I plead with him, turning and pushing him back toward the set. "It's not worth it. The show must go on, right?"

Jake gives me a tight nod, and a squeeze of the hand before heading back to his seat. I look at the clock, we have about thirty seconds before we have to be back on the air. I step toward the control room, and once again Mike grasps my wrist in his hand. He's never done this in front of other people before, I worry that even this many witnesses won't deter him. The clock is counting down. Morgan meets my gaze. I nod.

We're off the air. We've just cut to a game in progress.

"Take your hands off of me. Now."

"Or what, Penny?"

That's all it takes. I can't hold back any more. Too bad a kick in the shins won't do the trick here.

"My whole career I've been told how I should dress and style my hair so that I look friendlier. That I should smile more. Tone myself down to be taken more seriously in this industry. I've been asked on multiple occasions to "prove" my knowledge. To prove that I know the rules of the game. The history of the game. In countless meetings with you Mike, you've asked me these things."

His eyes search mine, and I can feel my anger bubbling close to the surface. I do my best to keep my tone even, my words measured. The eyes of my colleagues are on me as I address Mike, doing my best to keep my voice down.

I think of all the interactions I've had with Mike since I've worked here. All the things that I didn't report because I didn't want to be a nuisance. All the encounters that we had, away from prying eyes...eyes that could have reported him just as easily as I could have. I think of all the veiled remarks in staff meetings. All the times he's asked me to prove my knowledge.

I think of all the times he's tried to silence me.

31
I WON'T BE SILENCED
PENELOPE

"When I started at this network I was a production assistant. I made coffee runs and did a lot of copying. Eventually I was promoted to the editorial staff, apparently the network hotshots had finally gotten ahold of my resume and realized that I was too qualified to make their coffee. They liked me and liked the idea of having a woman in that office. So I became the token woman. I ticked a box.

"When I applied for the open producer's job, I got it based on my merit. Based on the ways in which I'd proven myself over the years to this network and on the references of every single local and state network that I've worked for in my career. So please, forgive me if I'm not very happy right now with the man whose first impression of me was that I got this job because I *must* have slept with someone from the network. That I got the promotion because of the way I look in a skirt. Or that I got this promotion because it makes the network look "good to have a woman leading a national sports broadcast five nights a week, even though they never miss an opportunity to sideline her."

I stop and take a breath. Pressing the heels of my hands to my eyes. I turn away from him. The last thing I want right now is for Mike to see me cry and I can feel the tears forming behind my eyes.

I'm aware that we have an audience now. I look around and see that all eyes are on us. Jim and Devon look ready to step in, Jake is fuming. Morgan and the rest of our team in the control room are figuring how to run the show with chaos on the set and their EP right in the middle of it all. And the irony is, as Mike has just accused me of ruining his show, he is the one *actively* ruining tonight's broadcast. This show that I have dedicated my career to. He calls it *his* show, but he doesn't put in the work, he doesn't have a claim on this show. This show belongs to the people on this set. Not him.

I don't hear anything else through the pounding of my pulse in my ears. I feel heat creep into my cheeks and glance away from Mike. And that's when the dam breaks. "Ironic that you want to talk about professionalism, Mike."

"Excuse me?" He crosses his arms over his chest and nails me with a steely glare.

"Every pitch meeting, every time I try to get something of mine on the air, you remind the room of my appearance. You joke about no one wanting to listen to a woman who looks like me talk about baseball," John Fields, the network CFO, steps into the room and I briefly register the shock on his face as Mike scoffs at me. "Have you ever wondered, Mike, why I look the way I do? No. Of course not. Because it's easier for you to judge than to try and understand. I've been dealing with small minded men like you for most of my life."

"When I was a teenager, and hair appeared on my face, I was laughed at and teased and made fun of. I missed so many days of school for debilitating cramps and heavy bleeding that I fell behind in all of my classes. As if the hurtful words weren't enough, I began to doubt my worth as a person. I shut myself off from friends and family. I started to believe the things that were said about me. But not anymore Mike."

I'm done holding back. I'm done being worried about what any of the people in this room think of me, least of all Mike Fletcher. I'm done allowing this man to control me. I'm done letting him have any kind of power over me. Thankfully, I have a family full of lawyers. Because I'm done being silenced.

"I'm done, Mike. I'm done putting up with you belittling me and my work. Done with you judging my body, my work, and my worth. I'm done letting you make me feel like I am nothing. Consider this my two weeks' notice."

I hear the gasps and whispers of the crew. I see the look on Jake's face and Devon and Jim's faces. Mr. Fields turns and walks back out of the room. Jake looks proud. Jim and Devon look ready to throw down. But Mike? He takes a breath to respond but I beat him to the punch.

"You have five minutes, after that I'll have you thrown out."

As I try to brush past Mike on my way to the studio doors, he grabs my arm and pulls me toward him. From the corner of my eye, I see Jim holding Jake back with a hand on his arm and something squeezes in my chest. Something primal deep within me really likes the idea that he'd fight for me. Mike whispers something about me never working in this town again and his breath is hot against my ear.

I wrench myself free from his grasp and make my way to my office with Morgan on my heels. With shaking hands, I start shoving things into my briefcase and packing up the box that someone handed Morgan. All my pictures, all my books, all of my sports memorabilia from over the years.

My heart races and I do my best to steady my breathing, knowing that if I can't get myself under control, I'll have a full-blown panic attack right here. I have to get out of here. Morgan senses my distress and drops the box in her hands, crossing the room and standing in front of me, hands on my shoulders. She takes a deep breath and I mirror her breathing. I'm so thankful for this friend of mine; this friend who understands me without a word and knows how to get me out of my own head. Once I'm steady and my heart rate has slowed to a slightly more normal pace, I continue to pack up my office.

I grab everything I can from my shelves; I can hardly look at the picture of my dad and me at my first baseball game. The memories of that day, the memories of learning to keep score and him teaching me the history of the game are so overwhelming that if I look at that picture I *will* lose my composure. I will not give Mike anymore ammunition to use against me. I grab the extra outfits and shoes that I've stashed in my office. I clean out my desk.

"Morgan," I look up to find Mike glowering in my doorway and feel my panic rising again. "I'd like a moment with Penelope before she leaves."

Morgan shoots me a worried glance and takes a protective stance in front of me, "I can't let you do that, Mike."

"Out. Now. Or you'll be out of here with the Ice Queen."

Morgan closes the distance between us, putting herself between me and Mike, a fire burning in her eyes. I squeeze her hand and give her a little nod. "Morgan, you're my best friend, and I refuse to put you at risk. You have to go. Please."

She reluctantly lets me go, and as she steps into the hallway, Mike closes the door behind you, turning to me with something sinister in his eyes. "You know I'm right. You can stand out there and spout whatever self-love crap you want to, but you ultimately know that I'm right."

He is so calm as he stands across from me, knowing exactly what buttons of mine to push. Isolating each of my insecurities and zeroing in on them. He crosses the distance between us, and I instinctively take a step back. He laughs. "Yeah, right. Like I'd waste my time on *you*."

His words hit their mark, and try as I might, I can't keep my tears at bay. The voices that flood my head are those of faceless commenters on social media. Faceless letters and notes sent to stations where I worked. People whispering at lockers in the hallways of my high school. It's easy to *say* that those things don't affect me anymore, but they do. I suspect that in some ways, they always will.

Mike leaves me standing in the middle of my office, opening the door to reveal Jake waiting on the other side of the door, and he turns to fire off one more shot. "He doesn't love you Penelope. He *pities* you."

Time slows to a crawl. The world stands still as Jake takes one look at me, registers Mike's words. "What did you just say?"

"Can you honestly tell me you want to be with *her*?"

Jake is not a violent man.

In all the time I've known him, he's been restrained and even tempered. When he played professional ball he never threw at a hitter, he stayed toward the back of the melee if the benches ever cleared. It's one of the things I love about him. He helps me keep an even keel, but even the most measured, peaceful person has a line in the sand. And if you cross it, they'll let you know. Mike just crossed that line.

A muscle in Jake's jaw ticks as he watches Mike, his gaze narrowed. "Penelope, go out and find Morgan. She was asking for you. And shut the door on your way out."

I once got involved in a fight between my brother and my ex-boyfriend in high school. I remember seeing a similar fire in Peter's eyes that day that I see now. That day, I walked away with detention and a bruised eye. "Be careful," I whisper to Jake, squeezing his hand on my way out the door.

"I'm always careful, Sunshine."

32
WE FIGHT FOR WHAT WE LOVE
JAKE

I'm not a violent person, never have been.

Even when I played.

I wouldn't throw at a guy unless I had a good reason.

I'd say tonight I have a good reason.

It's been building up for a while. His jabs at Penelope and her appearance. The way he talks about her ideas and her desire to host again. But when he looked at her and told her that I didn't love her? That's what did it for me. That was the vinegar on the baking soda.

I take a step toward him, pull my fist back and swing. He doesn't see it coming. His hands fly to his face, and he shouts in pained surprise.

"What'd you do that for?" At least...I think that's what he said. It's a bit muffled.

"Who? Me?" I open the office door and step out. "I didn't do anything."

"You punched me in the face!" He shouts, his face turning red as he thinks through what I've just done. He tries to take a swing at me, but the man is all bark and no bite. I block his punch and press him up against the nearest wall.

"Let's get one thing straight Mike, you ever treat her like that again and you'll be lucky to be left standing afterward." I have never in my life had this kind of confidence. An absolutely foolish, "punch your boss in the face and then threaten him" kind of confidence. And I have no idea where it came from. I think I was possessed by the spirit of a long-dead mob boss.

The elevator nearby dings, and when the doors open, we're greeted by John Fields, CFO of American Sports Network, and two police officers. I wasn't expecting that. Mr. Fields points the officers in the direction of a still sputtering Mike Fletcher and they make quick work of him as Mr. Fields gives me a long look. "What happened to Fletcher's face?"

"Self-defense." Preemptive self-defense, that is.

He nods, looking around the room until his gaze lands on Penelope. She's standing near the kitchen, a cup of tea in her hand, a sweater pulled tightly around her body. She gives me a small, sad smile, and Mr. Fields calls her and Morgan over, indicating that we should step into Penelope's office.

"Ms. Nichols, I was appalled at what I heard tonight," so far, I'm not sure we're off to a good start. If Fields thinks he's going to reprimand Penelope for what happened in the studio tonight, he'll have to find a new host, because I will walk out those doors with her tonight and not look back. "I've been in the meetings you talked about, I've heard the things Mike has said. And please, let me say how sorry I am for not doing anything about it sooner."

Okay. That's better.

"I can assure you, Ms. Nichols, Mike Fletcher will not be returning to ASN. Ever again."

It's about time.

Mr. Fields explains that tonight only confirmed something he'd already suspected. Turns out Mike has been having all HR reports buried; he and his cronies in HR have since been fired, and the executives will be convening soon to handle the aftermath. I don't envy him the decisions that have to be made in the days ahead. But I am grateful for the decision he made tonight.

"Ms. Nichols, I'd like to offer you the chance to take your job back. You are an important part of why this show is a success, and it wouldn't be the same without you. I know tonight has been emotional, please don't answer me tonight. Take all the time you need to think about it. In the meantime, Morgan, I'd like you to step in and cover the post."

Mr. Fields dismisses the three of us, shaking my hand and reminding Penelope to take time to think about her answer. I pick up Penelope's bag from the floor near her desk and take her hand in mine. We walk in silence, I don't want to push her to talk about any of it. I don't want to push her toward a decision one way or the other. I want her to take his offer. The show wouldn't be the same without her, but I know that it isn't my decision to make.

When we reach our doors, Penelope's hands shake as she tries to find her key. I take her in my arms, drawing her into my chest and step toward my own door. With one hand, I unlock and open my door and lead Penelope toward my couch. We sink into it, her head against my shoulder as she curls her body up next to me.

The fact that she is so close to me right now is unexpected. I know that this is going against her instinct. Sofi warned me, Peter warned me. When things get hard, Penelope runs. She pushes away the people she loves, afraid she's going to hurt them. But, here she is. Next to me. I know this is new for her. Letting someone experience her pain. She's used to running away. I need to give her a place to run away to. With me.

"What do you say we go up to the lake tonight? Spend a few days away from the city?"

She nods and stands, wiping away the tears from her cheeks. I watch as she steps across the hall into her apartment, leaving the door open as she walks around and packs a bag. She stops for a long moment in front of the bookcase, her hands reaching out toward a picture frame. One I've seen countless times. It's a picture of Penelope and her parents on the day she graduated from college. She clutches it to her chest and another little sob escapes her. This one is different. This one is filled with sadness instead of pain. Exhaustion clouding her features.

Somehow, without realizing it, my feet have carried me to her doorway. Close enough to hear her whispered words. "I'm sorry. I'm so, so sorry."

I close the distance between us and take her in my arms again. Holding her as tightly as she'll let me. I don't know her grief, other than what she's told me. I don't know what to say at this moment, but I know that I can hold her up. I can be her strength when she doesn't have the legs to stand. So, I hold her. And after a few minutes, she breaks the hold, kisses me on the cheek and continues to pack her bag.

Soon, we've packed our bags and are on our way out of Manhattan. Penelope reads on her tablet while I drive, neither of us saying much. We stop for dinner at the drive-in. Burgers and fries and milkshakes for us both, and I start to see a little bit of the light returning to Penelope's eyes.

It isn't until we reach the house that Penelope looks like herself again. She sighs contentedly when we pull up in front of the house, silvery moonlight illuminating the path to the front door. I carry our bags inside and send Penelope upstairs to the room she stayed in last time, insisting that she get some rest and we can talk in the morning.

My parents are in the living room with Jax and James, they all look startled to see me, and are even more surprised when I tell them Penelope is upstairs. I tell them the basics of what happened tonight. "She needs a place to run away to without isolating herself. I thought this would do the trick. I didn't realize it would be a full house this weekend."

"Don't worry about us," James says, in a rare serious tone, "we'll give her the space she needs, as long as she knows she can lean on us. We're family."

My parents and Jax nod their agreement and affection swells in my chest. I love my family. And I know they love Penelope and will take care of her up here for as long as she needs. She can have her space, she can have time to think, but at the end of the day she'll have family surrounding her. A loud, rowdy, wild family that loves her and wants to take care of her. It's going to be a shock to her system.

I walk our bags upstairs and pause outside her door, raising my hand to knock. I hear the sound of muffled cries on the other side of the door and without thinking, I let myself in. She's curled up on top of the bed spread, a pillow hugged to her chest. Her face is red and tear streaked. It breaks my heart to see her like this.

I kneel down beside the bed and gently brush hair away from her face and wipe away her tears with the corner of the pillowcase. When she looks at me, I see the sadness in her eyes. The hurt. The brokenness.

"I don't need pity," she whispers, so low I almost didn't catch the words. Of all the things that Mike did tonight, making Penelope doubt my love for her was his worst offense. Making her think that she isn't worthy of my love. If given the opportunity, I'd punch him again.

"Penelope. Look at me." I sit on the edge of the bed, and she sits up, not quite making eye contact with me. The pain in her eyes is a punch to the gut. "Do not *ever* doubt how much I love you. You brilliant, beautiful, incredible woman. I know how hard it is for you to accept love, to allow yourself to love and be loved...Penelope I've never pitied you, I never would. I fell in love with you. I *am* in love with you. I don't ever want to stop loving you."

She falls into me, her arms twining around my waist, "I love you too," she whispers against my chest. I hold her here until she falls asleep, tucking her into bed once I'm sure she won't easily wake up, and then I head downstairs for a few hours of sleep before I drive back into the city first thing in the morning. I ask mom to make my excuses when Penelope comes down for the day and I hit the road.

There's an emergency meeting today, in the wake of the firing of Mike Fletcher. All of the higher-ups will be in attendance and this is the perfect opportunity to get *Shattered Glass* in front of the people who could decide its fate. I stop at Morgan's desk and ask about the flash drive. She tells me Penelope entrusted it to her before we left.

"Morgan. We have a meeting to crash."

33
THROWING A CURVE
JAKE

When I was twelve, I told my dad I wanted to be a pitcher.

I'd been playing baseball for six years at that point, and this was the first time that I felt I knew what I wanted to do on the field. There was something powerful in holding that ball in my hand. Knowing that I could control the speed of the ball, its location, and what would happen to its movement.

As a twelve year old, I didn't have a lot of control over my pitches. But I knew I could get the ball in the strike zone and that's what was important. I was striking kids out and it felt good. I wanted to do it for the rest of my life. So with dad's help, I put in the work. I broke a few windows and hit my dad more than a few times, but I improved.

As I got older, I learned how to throw different pitches. I gained velocity on my fastball. And I had a sinker that was effective in striking out a lot of batters. In college, I was first in the rotation. I was in the minor leagues for a year before my call up. Five years in the majors, a career 2.55 earned run average, and I led the league in strikeouts until my elbow problems.

I pitched in back-to-back world championships. I was rookie of the year. I have two Cy Young awards under my belt. I've pitched in high pressure situations. But *this* might be the most important pitch of my life.

Morgan and I enter the conference room, all eyes turn toward us as we intrude on the meeting. Morgan sets up her computer and I stand in front of the room full of men in suits, suddenly hyper aware of why Penelope has always hated this monthly meeting.

Good grief.

Morgan is the only woman in the room, and that's because I dragged her in with me. And if this isn't the exact reason that the world needs *Shattered Glass*, I don't know what is. This is what Penelope, Morgan, and countless other women—in sports and other professions—have been putting up with for far too long.

I'm ashamed to say that I never noticed it until it was right under my nose, and even then it had to be pointed out to me. I think of the world that my nieces are growing up in, the world that—if we're able —Penelope and I will raise a daughter in. I want them to have the confidence to follow their dreams. To reach for every goal, and not be told that they can't do something because of their gender.

It's time to shatter the glass for good.

One year when I came home from college, I'd just learned to throw a changeup. It was working for me at school and I was eager to show my dad how my command of the pitch was coming along. We went out in the yard and he tossed me a ball. He crouched low in a catcher's stance while I paced off the distance to the "mound". I wound up, and just as I was almost to my release point, James came bounding up behind me, startling me. My release point was too high. And there was nothing any of us could do but watch.

I heard the glass shatter and a moment later I looked up to find my mom on the deck with a baseball in her hands. I cleaned up the shards of glass, dad and I replaced the window, and I stopped pitching toward the house. I'll never forget the sound of the glass breaking. Or the slightly amused look on mom's face. But what stopped me in my tracks that day was the look that passed between mom and dad, and dad jogging out to where I was standing. He crouched low, readied his mitt, and nodded.

My mom, Claire Hutchinson, looked at that ball in her hands, lined her fingers up with the lacing, wound up, and hurled a split-seam fastball right into dad's mitt. If James or I had been holding a bat, I don't think either of us could have made contact with that ball. No one would have dared tell mom that baseball wasn't for her.

The glass ceiling was made to be shattered. And I'm here to help it along. Penelope has been chipping away at it for her whole career when what it needs is a well-placed changeup.

"Can I help you?" Mr. Fields asks.

"Yes. You can listen to this pitch. But let me be very clear, this is not my pitch, or Morgan's. This project belongs to Penelope Nichols."

Mr. Fields looks to the men around him, and they agree to hear us out. Much to my relief. And surprise.

I cut the lights and Morgan starts playing a truncated version of *Shattered Glass*. She whittled the hour and a half special down to fifteen minutes of highlights. It ends with Penelope's conversation with Susan Walters. At the end of the fifteen minutes, the room is silent.

"Penelope wanted to be here to do this," Morgan says, standing at the head of the conference table. "This is her passion project. It's what she's been pitching to you for months."

"We decided to do it on our own," I add. "So that the next time you met she could have something to show you; something other than the research and data that she would usually bring with her."

We brought the data anyway. Morgan passes it out as the men in the room start to ask questions. Without Mike in the room, there is actual discussion about what this could mean, not just for the show but for the network. And what it could mean for Penelope. We spend the next forty five minutes in the conference room with a whole bunch of men who control our jobs and paychecks.

"You've given us a lot to think about, Jake. Morgan..." Mr. Fields stops her as she packs up to follow me out the door. "We'd like you to continue to produce in the interim."

Mr. Fields stops and looks to the men around him, "I'll be reaching out to Ms. Nichols. Originally we—I—asked her to come back and step into her old role, but what you've just shown us was compelling, and I'd like to air it. If it's alright with you I'd like to offer her a seat at the desk. If she accepts, Morgan, we'd make you the executive producer."

Holy crap.

They accepted it. Her special is going to air. I can't believe this.

Morgan's eyes go wide. I'm sure mine do too. This is more than I ever expected would come from this meeting today. I came in here on a whim, hoping to get *Shattered Glass* the recognition it deserves. And now Penelope might be getting the recognition *she* deserves.

Mr. Fields asks if we can stick around to film a few additional pieces for the special, and Morgan runs off to call Jim and Devon.

When Devon and Jim arrive in the studio, they talk my ear off about the work that went into making *Shattered Glass*. I answer as many questions as I can, relying on Penelope's own words and work to explain to them what this show means to her. I also tell them what I told Mr. Fields just this morning, and they agree that Penelope would be welcomed at the desk any time. For good.

Morgan directs us and produces the whole recording, taking over Penelope's usual role, and in no time we have an intro and outro filmed to accompany *Shattered Glass*. I take the outro, recording my own message, specifically for the woman I love. I put the ball in her court, let her know that whatever happens next is going to happen on her terms. Not mine.

I feel good about what we've just done. I can only hope Penelope will too.

34

A DREAM REALIZED

PENELOPE

It turns out that spending a week in Saratoga is exactly what I needed to get my head on straight after that disastrous night in the studio. I wasn't sure that night if being around Jake's family was going to help, but I'm glad he knew to bring me here. Being surrounded by people who love me is so much better than running away from them.

My instinct that night was to run. To hop on a train to DC and hide away with Peter and Sofi. Get myself away from the city, away from the studio. Away from Jake. But he held me that night, on his sofa, after walking me home. He held me without a word. Just like he did on the floor of my bathroom weeks before. He held me and let me feel the emotions that were threatening to overtake me.

He kept me steady. Kept my head above the water.

He gave me a place to run *to*, without running *away*. He brought me to this place of peace. Of comfort and family and…belonging. I climbed the steps to the guest room that night in something of a daze. Mike's words echoing in my brain.

"He doesn't love *you, Penelope. He* pities *you."*

"Can you honestly tell me you want to be with her?" *Mike's words hit*

their mark. I open the door to the guest room, just as warm and inviting as I remember it. I kick off my shoes and curl up on the bed, clutching one of the pillows close to my body, using it to muffle the sound of my crying. The last thing I need is to call attention to myself.

The sound of footsteps on the stairs startles me. They pause for a moment, and then the door opens. I try to shy away, but Jake is too quick. He's seen me. He kneels down on the floor beside the bed, wiping my eyes with a corner of the pillowcase. The tenderness in his gaze...I've seen it before. But tonight? Tonight it feels different. Tonight, my brain is telling me that it isn't love and warmth in his eyes. It's pity. Derision.

"I don't need pity," I whisper the words so softly I hope he misses them. But he doesn't. Anger and hurt flash in his eyes as he stands. I close my eyes, expecting to hear the door open and shut behind him. Expecting him to realize that I'm more trouble than I'm worth.

Instead, I feel the dip of the mattress beside me. He takes my hands in his and when I open my eyes to meet his gaze, he pulls me up so that I'm seated, facing him. Jake's eyes search mine, filled with an earnestness I've never seen from him. "Do not *ever* doubt how much I love you."

I want to believe him. But I've internalized too many years' worth of comments and insults and tonight, Mike's words pushed me to the brink. To the boiling point. Who could love me? Who would want to?

"You brilliant, beautiful, incredible woman. I know how hard it is for you to accept love, to allow yourself to love and be loved..."

He holds me close, his arms coming around me and holding me to his chest, his fingers twisting in the curls at the back of my head, cradling me ever closer. His warmth envelopes me and for just a moment, the events of the last few hours are a distant memory. Mike's words are replaced by Jake's, from tonight, and all the nights we've spent together up to now. The days spent on Shattered Glass and On the Field. The countless ways that he has shown and told me that he loves me. That he considers me worthy of that love.

I fell asleep in Jake's arms that night, and was more than a little confused when I woke in the morning and he'd already taken off, but his mom assured me he'd be back that night. He had some things to take care of in the city, including taking a week's vacation. So, here we've been for the last week, in this house that has brought me so much comfort, with these people who haven't pushed me for answers or explanations.

Peter and Sofi have checked in with me, Jake informed them of my employment status and they've been supportive. They were also more than a little happy to hear about Mike being fired and subsequently arrested. The biggest shock though, was the call this morning from Mr. Fields, offering me a spot at the desk, as co-host of *On the Field*. When I told Jake, he asked me what I wanted to do. And…I don't know.

I want to be on television again. Creating *Shattered Glass* reminded me of what I loved so much about my days as a sports reporter. Telling stories, elevating voices to a platform where they could be heard…talking about the game that I love.

But then I remember the hard days. Nights that I'd cry on the phone to my dad. Nights that brought more pain than fulfillment. I remember the comments and the letters and the tags on social media. I don't know if I want to go through all of that again. Which is how I find myself here, on the shore, watching as boats cut swaths across the water, leaving white capped waves in their wake.

This is a decision that I have to make on my own. A decision that could be potentially life changing. *What's life without a little risk?* Diane from Florida's voice comes back to me in the most inopportune of moments. I took a risk when I opened my heart to Jake. And when I filmed *Shattered Glass* on my own. And when I didn't run away a week ago. Even though I wanted to. So far, my risks have paid off.

Dad would have wanted me to do it. I think of what he'd say if he were here. *Nellie girl, it's your dream.*

"Nelope?" A sweet voice interrupts my thoughts and I swipe away my tears before Alice can see that I've been crying. "Why are you crying?"

Oh, this sweet child. She's stolen every bit of my heart. She climbs into my lap and throws her arms around my neck in a tight hug. I put my arms around her and squeeze her to my chest. I love this little girl. And her sister. And the rest of the Hutchinson family. I can't thank them enough for opening their home and their hearts to me and I don't know what compels me to do it, but I tell Alice exactly what's on my mind.

"I've been offered a new job. One that I've always wanted. But I don't know if I should do it."

"Why not?" Her inquisitive little face looks up at me, full of all the innocence of a five year old. A five year old with dreams. A five year old who is told by her dad, and her uncles and aunt, and grandparents that someday she can do anything she sets her mind on.

I tell her the truth. A truth that I don't think I've ever admitted but have been living with for years. The truth that has kept me from following my dreams. Putting myself out there. Trusting in myself and my abilities.

"Because...I'm afraid."

"Nelope," she shakes her head, blonde curls bobbing around her face. "When I'm afraid, uncle Jake tells me not to be, you know why?"

"No, why?"

"Because. He leaves in me."

"He what?" I try not to laugh. There's an earnestness in her voice, and in her eyes as she stares into mine. All the earnestness and intensity of a five year old who can't imagine anyone not believing in her.

"He leaves. It means that he knows I can do anything, even if I don't think I can."

"He *believes* in you," I say, pressing a kiss into her hair.

"That's what I said. And he leaves in you too, Nelope."

With that, she's off. Running back toward the house. Leaving me alone again, watching the waves on the water. My thoughts are significantly less jumbled than they've been over the last few days. Knowing that Jake believes in me, even when I don't believe in myself, is all I need right now. All it took was the wisdom of a child to show me what I have been afraid to see.

I take my phone from my pocket and dial Mr. Fields. Letting him know that I'll take the hosting job, as long as it means that no one gets pushed out. He assures me that I'll be an addition to the current team, in fact, it seems they've all insisted that I be added, and no one wants to leave. Next month, I'll need all the belief Jake can muster...as I join him at the desk.

"Nelope!" Alice comes bounding up the stairs after dinner, grabbing my hand and tugging me behind her. "Come on! My favorite show is on!"

I follow her down to the basement where the family is gathered, spread out on chairs and sofas, a place has been saved for me between Mack and Alice. I sit down and they snuggle into my side, eyes wide with excitement as a hush falls over the room, and the opening graphics for *On the Field* fill the screen; the familiar music bringing the sting of tears to the back of my eyes. The screen fades to black before transitioning into a title card that I designed, a title card that for years was just a pipe dream—pitched and shot down over and over again. A title card that has been animated to reflect shards of glass falling from a ceiling, broken by a baseball that falls among the shards. *My* title card.

I look around for Jake and if the blush in his cheeks and sheepish look on his face is any indication, this is his doing.

Then, Jake, Jim, and Devon are on the screen.

"Tonight, *On the Field* is going to look a little bit different," Jim announces, before throwing to Devon. "Tonight we are sharing with you a passion project from our producer, Penelope Nichols."

My heart flutters in my chest, my pulse picking up and I try really hard to choke back my tears, knowing that once they start, they won't be stopping. When Jake speaks, my tears silently spill over.

"Penelope Nichols is one of the most talented baseball analysts you've never heard of. Most of what the three of us cover on this show comes from her brain. We fill in with our own analysis and commentary, but for a long time Penelope's voice was silenced. Beyond her knowledge of the game, Penelope has a *heart* for baseball. And for the women who enjoy the game as much as she does. Knowing that there is a need for inclusivity in the media that covers the game, in executive positions, coaching staffs, and in everyday conversations. Some of you may have heard Penelope's name in the news recently, not for the reason she would have wanted. She's not with ASN at the moment, and we here at *On the Field* miss her dearly..."

The Jake on the television screen trails off and even through the television, I can see tears glittering in his eyes. Jake, here in the room with me, comes over and sits down on the floor in front of me, leaning his weight against my legs. A touch that says *I believe in you.* A graphic appears on the lower third of the screen, and I have to laugh at my former production assistant turned interim producer: *We really do miss you, Nellie! - Mo*

"Tonight, *On the Field* presents *Shattered Glass: A Conversation on Women in Baseball*", we hope you enjoy the show."

Suddenly my face is on the screen. My voice fills the silence of the room, and everything fades away. Alice gets as close to me as she can, climbing onto my lap and taking my hand in hers, holding on tight.

I watch myself interview the baseball writers and announcers that I looked up to as a young woman just starting out. I cry when my interview with the first female general manager plays, and the roundtable I had with women who are fans of the game. I am stunned as I watch my dream come to life. This show that I was so passionate about, conversations I've wanted to have since my days as a young, local sports anchor.

I remember the first time I was asked to prove what I knew about baseball. I was always asked to prove my sports knowledge, but the day I had to prove myself about the sport that I loved, was the day I decided to create a baseball show about women, for women, and by women. The network didn't believe in my concept, but Jake did. And most importantly, he believed in me. And now I'm watching my dream come true.

The hour and a half flies by. I cry through the whole thing.

I can't believe Jake did this.

I know it was him, it had to be him. I think back to that call with Mr. Fields, the day after everything blew up. *Mr. Hutchinson made an impassioned plea...* He put me on the air, put *my heart* on the air. I watch as the credits roll, and fade out. And then there he is, alone on the screen.

"I spent a lot of time over the last few weeks with Penelope Nichols, watching as she conducted these interviews, learning as we went along about the places where I still need to work on myself and the way that I approach this game and the spaces that we create for voices other than our own. Penelope learned this game from her father, he reminded her as she worked her way up the ranks to keep chipping away at the glass ceiling. Penelope will never be satisfied until that glass is shattered. Until women are welcomed and valued in all spaces."

Hearing my dad's words from Jake's mouth brings a fresh round of tears to the surface, that and the picture on screen behind Jake. The picture of me and dad at my first baseball game, a scorecard on my lap, my head bent over it as he leans in and helps me score the action that was taking place on the field. I remember that game like it was yesterday. Jax reaches over and places a supportive hand on my shoulder, reminding me of my brother.

After a cut to commercial, the show reopens with Jim and Devon, and Jake, at their usual desk. A chair has been added between Jake and Devon.

"Penelope, there's a seat at the desk for you," Jim looks to the camera, and Devon jumps in, "we'd love to have you join us."

Jake, sitting in front of me, gives an almost imperceptible nod, and as Jake on the screen closes out the show, the room slowly empties, leaving only the two of us behind. Then on-screen Jake closes the show.

"Sunshine, you already know how I feel about you, but in case you need the reminder: I love you. I've loved you since the day I jinxed that perfect game on the air," Jim and Devon's laughter burst from off camera, and I can't help the laugh that escapes as I continue to listen to Jake's voice. "Penelope, it would be an honor to have you join us at the desk as co-host. And if you would join me as my broadcast partner and co-host...for as long as we both shall live."

The credits roll and Jake turns around, down on both knees in front of me, and takes my hands in his. "What do you say?"

35
YES
PENELOPE

Pulling a small leather box from his pocket, Jake watches me expectantly.

Tears roll down my cheeks as I nod. Extracting his hands from mine, Jake pulls me in for a kiss, kissing away the tears from my cheeks and tucking an errant curl behind my ear. I sink to the floor beside him and wrap my arms around his waist.

"I can't believe you did this," I whisper, leaning into him. "I can't believe you got it on the air."

"*You* did it, Penelope," he reminds me of the work that I did to make *Shattered Glass* happen. All the years of planning, all the pitch meetings, all the rejections. "This was all you, Sunshine."

I shake my head and start to argue with him, but he silences me with another kiss, this one leaving me breathless. Breathless, and more than a little nervous.

"Are you sure about this?" I ask, searching his gaze for any sense of doubt.

"I've never been so sure about anything in my life." His smile sets something aflame in my chest, and I pull him in for another kiss. A kiss that is interrupted by little feet pounding down the stairs. Those little feet are attached to a precocious five year old with red cheeks and curls that bounce as she shuffles from foot to foot. Mack, ever the older sister, is right behind Alice, trying to get her to come back upstairs.

"Nelope?" If anyone ever corrects Alice on how to say my name, they will get a kick in the shins. It's effective. Just ask my brother. "Are you going to be our aunt?"

"Would you like that?" I ask. And she nods her smile growing.

"I'd like that too. Which is why I told your uncle Jake yes."

I have to stop myself from laughing when her intense little eyes meet mine…and Mack's roll back in her head; the sign of an older sister who is *over. It.* Alice puts her little hands on either side of my face, "I told you he leaves in you!"

"Yes, you sure did."

Alice turns and runs up the steps, shouting "she said yes!" all the way up the stairs. Mack stays behind though, looking like there's more she wants to say. "Is it too soon to call you Aunt Penelope?"

"Not at all, kiddo."

Mack quickly closes the distance between us and wraps me in a hug.

"I thought it was really cool what you did. Not just the show tonight, but standing up for yourself the way you did." Mack throws her arms around the both of us. "I'm really glad you're going to marry her, uncle Jake."

"Me too, Mack," Jake looks at me over the top of Mackenzie's head, his eyes filled with the promise of a lifetime.

It was a long night of celebrating. Peter and Sofi called to check in after seeing the show tonight, and ended up on a video call meeting every member of the Hutchinson family, including Jenna who arrived in time for dinner. We ate a meal cooked by Jake and myself, with help from Claire and the girls, enjoyed a bonfire down by the lake and now, I'm sitting in the silence of the balcony outside my room. Enjoying the sound of waves lapping at the shore, crickets chirping, and the occasional bark of a dog from somewhere across the water.

Propping my feet on the railing in front of me, I think back over the last several hours. Over the last couple of months, really. From the moment I met Jake Hutchinson, I knew I was a goner.

I knew when he came into that conference room on his first day, all sure of himself and full of confidence. When he noticed Mike's behavior in that meeting a little wrinkle formed between his eyebrows. Then we started hanging out and all of my prior judgement of him flew out the window. And somehow we ended up here.

I fire off a quick text to my brother: *I know you knew. I don't know how you knew, and that's not important. But you knew. About all of it, I'm sure. Thanks for always looking out for me. And for mother-henning me when I'm too stubborn for my own good. I love you Peter. I don't tell you that often enough.*

His reply is quick: *He talked to me a week ago about the show. I knew about the ring before you left for your first trip upstate. I love you too, Penelope. We all do. Mom and dad would be incredibly proud of you.*

Followed by: *And I KNOW they'd love Jake. Welcome him to the family.*

Tears roll down my cheeks as I read my brother's words.

It's times like this that I miss mom and dad more than usual. I always feel their absence, not always prominently, but on a day like this? When I've just agreed to marry the love of my life? The love of my life who was also Dad's favorite baseball player? Yeah. I'm missing Dad today.

I glance at the ring on my finger. A simple white gold band, with Celtic knots on either side of a solitaire sapphire. I assume, based on the age of the box Jake presented it in, it's a family heirloom, making it even more precious. I wrap the blanket tighter around my shoulders, as a light clicks on and spills out onto the balcony from the room next door, and the sliding door opens.

"I thought I might find you here." Jake kneels in front of me, pressing a kiss to my forehead. "This family can be a little overwhelming. You're not reconsidering are you?"

His eyes dance as he watches me, a smile tugging at his lips. There's no way I'd reconsider. Sure, the family is loud and overwhelming, but that's how they love. And they didn't mind that I slipped away tonight to sit in the silence of my room.

"Of course not."

Jake pulls me to my feet and wraps me in his arms, holding me close. I lean into his embrace, soaking in his warmth as the cool breeze kicks up around us. Jake holds me tight and I feel safe in his arms. Sheltered and protected. Loved.

Jake loves with an intensity that I've never known before. Jake loves me. He *knows* me. He knew, a week ago, that my instinct would have been to run, and he gave me that option. He gave me a place to run to, and came with me. He says that *Shattered Glass* was all me, but I never would have done it if he hadn't pushed me to do it. If he hadn't believed in me, and pushed me to believe in myself.

I'm standing here on this balcony because of him. Because he loves me, and I love him. I look forward to more days like this. For the rest of our lives.

36

FOR LOVE AND THE GAME
PENELOPE

"Good evening, and welcome to *On the Field*. The playoffs are over, and the off-season is in full swing. We're talking trades, free agents, and universal designated hitter tonight." I see Morgan in the control room, a grin spread across her face as Jim, Devon, and Jake kick things off for tonight's show. I'm standing in the wings, hands shaking, pulse pounding, and a smile that won't leave my face. "But first, we'd like to introduce you to the newest member of the *On the Field* team."

I watch the monitor, waiting for my cue. Just as we did for Jake, a highlight reel plays, though in my case it's a handful of clips from *Shattered Glass* and my early, *early* days as a sports reporter. A few pictures of me and dad, now that our audience knows that part of my story. And then, a video that I thought was long buried.

Jake glances at me and throws me a wink that sets my heart a flutter and heats my cheeks.

There I stand, in the batter's box, wide legged black trousers, black stilettos, and my favorite purple blouse. I hike up my pant legs, kick up my leg, and knock the ball out of the park, shocking everyone around me as I trot around the bases. The cheer that goes up from the hosting desk is exactly the kick that I need to get my nerves under control.

"Please join us in welcoming Penelope Nichols!" All three men stand to greet me. I hug Devon and Jim, and when I look at Jake, the pride in his eyes, I press a soft kiss to his cheek. He squeezes my hand as I take my seat beside him at the desk.

"Thank you Jim, Devon, and Jake. It is an honor to be seated at this desk with you." I address my new co-hosts before turning to address the audience. "I grew up watching this show every weeknight with my dad. As a kid, I'd sit next to him and work on homework while he watched, stopping every now and then to ask him a question—not about my homework, but about the game of baseball. As a young woman, on my own for the first time, *On the Field* was still how I connected with my dad. We'd watch together, from afar, texting the whole time. Everything I know about this game, I learned from him."

The last picture I ever took with dad flashes on the monitor, I blink away my tears, and look straight into the camera. "Dad, this one's for you."

The show goes by in a blur. After a while, I forgot the cameras were on us, we were having a conversation. There was no self-consciousness, no insecurity creeping in, and best of all...I was supported by the men at the desk with me; never once did they make me feel like my opinion was invalid, or that I didn't belong at that desk. I earned my seat at this table.

At the end of the show, Jake stops by my office, leaning against the door frame, watching me as I adjust the dress I've just changed into. He's dressed in a gray suit, crisp white shirt, and navy and orange striped tie. My dress is tea length, ivory, gauzy and lacy with long sleeves to keep out the early autumn chill. "You ready?"

"Yeah," I take his hand, and together we head toward the elevator. "I'm ready."

On the way back to Manhattan from Saratoga two weeks ago, Jake and I discussed what we wanted for a wedding. I was honest with him. I told him that I wanted something small. If it could just be the two of us, that would be perfect. I spent so much of my adult life alone that being around lots of people for big life events gives me anxiety. I was also struggling with the thought of getting married with my family there…and not Mom and Dad.

As a kid, my dream wedding always included dad walking me down the aisle. Mom tagging along while I dress shop, and helping me get ready, doing hair and makeup and being by my side on the day of. Without them, it feels wrong to have a big wedding, even if it means depriving my siblings and Jake's family of a big wedding.

One night, in the midst of making plans, panic started to set in. I recognized the signs right away: a tightening in my chest and narrowing of my vision. I couldn't take a deep breath or form coherent sentences.

"Sunshine," *Jake sounds like he's underwater even though he is sitting right here beside me on the couch.* "You okay?"

He takes my hands in his and stares into my eyes. All I can do is shake my head. No. I'm not okay. I'm not.

"Okay, hey. I'm right here." *His arms close around me, one hand exerting constant pressure on my back, the other rubbing soothing circles between my shoulder blades.* "Tell me what you can see. Right now. What can you see?"

"The view. Lights…from the balcony."

"Good. What can you hear?"

Not much aside from my pulse pounding in my ears. But the sound of the baseball game on TV is starting to become clearer.

"The game…'"

"What do you feel?"

"You," *I don't even have to think about it. The tightness in my chest is lessening.* "Your arms. Your strength."

"That's right, Sunshine. I've got you."

I can't get married without my parents there. I can't do the big cere-

mony and dress and reception thing without them. If the thought of that is enough to send me into this kind of anxiety spiral...we need to figure something out.

"What if," Jake holds me at arm's length, still close enough that his arms are sort of around me, but now we're looking right at each other, "we get the license and someone to marry us and we just...do it? Do the vows and the legal stuff first, just you and me? And then later we have something for our families. I know mine will understand, and Peter and Sofi will too."

"You'd do that for me?"

"You have to know by now, I'd do anything for you."

So tonight, with an officiant and two witnesses, we're getting married. We'll have a big family affair in a few weeks—with food and cake and celebration. We'll eventually tell them about this, but for now we want our marriage to just be...ours.

This morning, we moved Jake across the hall into my—now our—apartment. His lease is up at the end of the month, and so is mine. Devon's wife Terri is getting us started with house hunting. She sent a number of listings into the office with Devon this morning and we promised her we'd look them over. But not tonight.

Tonight is for us.

We stand on the bank of the Hudson River, Morgan and Dan stand with us, and the officiant stands across from us; she leads us through our vows, we all sign the marriage license, and from his jacket pocket, Jake produces a small bakery box.

He holds it open to me, revealing two, snowy white macarons, the words "just married" intricately piped across their tops. We each pick one up, offering it to the other. Morgan and Dan congratulate us, Emily offers to take care of the paperwork. And then the two of us are alone in the park, surrounded by people walking home, kids playing ball, and boats on the river...but right now, the world is ours.

When the sun sets and the chill sets in, Jake takes my hand and we walk hand in hand back to our building. Upon entering our apartment, Jake tells me to make myself comfortable while he gets dinner ready. I start to argue, but he shuts me down with a look. I watch as he steps into the kitchen, ditching his jacket, rolling up his sleeves, and donning one of my aprons.

There's no use arguing with him, so I change out of my dress into a pair of shorts and my well-worn Jake Hutchinson tee shirt...and as I step out of the bathroom I find my husband...*my husband!*...at the kitchen counter. Cooking.

He doesn't let me help, in fact he insists that I sit on the sofa and let him take care of everything. He's helping me learn that it's okay to be taken care of, so I have to let him do this. I turn on a baseball game, and make myself comfortable, while trying really hard not to go behind him and clean up the kitchen. This is...the ultimate test of my patience.

Up to this point, Jake's experiences in the kitchen have been heavily supervised. By me. I've directed him, or stood beside him and helped him. I've shown him almost everything I know, and now I have to trust that he's learned from me. That he can be trusted in my kitchen. Alone. Without my help.

My curiosity gets the better of me, and I tiptoe as silently as possible into the kitchen, attempting to peek at whatever Jake is doing, but he catches me in his arms and unceremoniously lifts me off my feet. With his mouth pressed to mine in a series of playful kisses, he deposits me on the balcony with a chuckle and heads back into the kitchen, but not before I hear the faint click of the lock on the sliding door leaving me out here and Jake grinning at me from the other side of the door.

All I can do is laugh. And enjoy the glow of sunset as it falls over the city and the thought of my husband inside the apartment cooking dinner for us. *My husband.* I still can't believe that Jake is my husband. The thought of it makes my insides all fluttery. I have a husband, someone to share my life with, to share my love with. To wake up next to and rant about baseball with.

I can't believe how lucky I am.

Before long, we're seated together on the balcony, with a

wedding meal of steak, roasted potatoes, bread, and salad. And everything is delicious.

"I'm impressed, Mr. Hutchinson," I bend down and kiss him before taking our dishes into the kitchen. "You surprised me, and I don't surprise easily. That meal was perfect."

We sit together on the balcony a while longer, my old fears and insecurities playing in the forefront of my mind as Jake holds me in his arms. Tears prick the backs of my eyes as I think about what comes next. Jake presses a soft kiss to the tender spot behind my ear and despite myself, I flinch. I feel him tense beneath me as a hand strokes down my back.

"What's wrong Sunshine?" His voice is choked with emotion, and I wage silent war with myself. This is my husband. I've trusted him with so many other parts of my heart...I need to give him this too.

"What if you hate it? What if...I hog the blankets? Or snore..." My next words come on a whisper I wish would get lost in the din of the city. "What if you get bored with me?"

Jake gently turns me so that I'm facing him. That calming hand taking mine and holding on tight. His eyes search mine and I cast my gaze down to my hands. Jake tips my chin so that I'm looking at him once more.

"If you hog the blankets, I'll buy more. If you snore, I'll get earplugs..." his mouth quirks up in a smile, "or, I'll buy you those sexy little nose strips."

He pauses and watches me, his expression turning serious once more. "As for the other two? Something tells me I'm not going to hate being married to the woman I love. And...I want to be bored with you."

"That's not what I meant and you know it." He chuckles and softly kisses my forehead as I try to pull away from him. He gathers me closer in his arms and presses another gentle kiss to my temple before I settle into his arms again.

"I lived most of my life on the road. Traveling from one city to the next, one ballpark to the next. Even during the offseason I never had a place to call my own. And then I met you, and I realized I want a boring life with you. I want to settle down with you and do boring married people things. This past year with you has been...nothing short of a dream come true. You've given me something I haven't had in a long time. Stability. A place to call home. You're my home, Penelope, and as long as I'm with you I'll never be bored."

"Are you sure?" I know it's my fear and insecurity talking. Making me doubt myself even as I sit here wrapped up in Jake's embrace.

"Positive."

We sit there a while longer, in each other's arms until the chill sinks in. I stand and take Jake by the hand and he follows me into the kitchen, filling the sink with our dinner dishes. With hands no longer filled with dishes, Jake wraps me in his arms and kisses me. Really kisses me. He walks me backward until my hips are pressed against the countertop, fingers toying with the hem of my shirt before drifting to my back. I untie his tie and toss it over his shoulder as his hands drift lower down my back, my fingers working the uppermost buttons on his shirt.

Everything else can wait.

37
READY FOR ANYTHING
PENELOPE

"Are you ready for this?" Jake asks, tucking me in his arms, and giving me a squeeze.

I'm so ready.

I've been ready since the night I woke up and looked over to see him asleep on my sofa, a book splayed across his chest, glasses slipping down the bridge of his nose, and worry lines marring his brow even as he slept.

I was determined that night to keep my pain away from him. Not to let him get too close to me, let alone let him into my world so intimately. I've learned how to deal with my pain, how to manage my symptoms and manage my migraines at work so that no one would see or think I'm weak. But Jake, in all things, has always seen right through me. He saw right through my mask that night and stayed with me through the worst of my symptoms.

I may never have children of my own, Jake. I made my teary-eyed confession as we walked along the lake after an afternoon spent with Mack and Alice. We'd just defined our relationship and I was already beginning to feel the pull of my heart toward his, toward a future with him, and he needed my full honesty, needed to know what he would be getting on board with. He slipped his hand into mine, stopping our walk and pulling me into a tight hug, flooding my body with warmth.

I know, he said. *Jax gave me a crash course. We'll cross that bridge when we get to it.* With a tender kiss to my temple, we turned and headed back toward his parents' house. The house where our families are gathered right now. Waiting for us.

I've been ready since the day he said yes and put this ring on my finger...two months ago. I've been ready since the night we stood along the bank of the Hudson and said our vows to each other and went home legally married.

There is something comforting in having someone to share my life with, and sure, we were already sharing life together. So many days spent eating and hanging out at my apartment...or his, after his confession at the Saratoga House. Cooking together, sitting on my balcony until late in the night, walking through the park and exploring the city together.

Quite literally, we've been spending every waking hour together. And I've loved every minute of it. Of getting to know him and falling deeper and deeper in love with this man who invaded my life and made himself a presence that I never want to live without.

It's been kind of nice to have our marriage just be ours for a little while. To establish a routine and to get used to being around each other all the time, learning each other's annoying habits. Getting used to sharing a bed and bathroom and moving around each other in the kitchen. The apartment feels a lot smaller with both of us and what belongings of Jake's didn't get put into storage.

Hand in hand, we walk the snow covered trail. Taking a few minutes for ourselves before standing in front of our families and making our vows to each other. I glance over at Jake, looking as handsome as ever in his slate gray suit, crisp white shirt, and purple tie that matches the purple canvas of the sneakers that peak out from the hem of my dress.

He stops and pulls me into his arms, the way he has so many times over the last several months, and wraps his woolen coat around us both. We stay here for a while, wrapped up in each other. The lake is starting to freeze over and we are enveloped in the whisper of the falling snow. Birds sing in the trees overhead, and Jake's heart beats strong and steady in my ear as I press myself against his chest and melt into him.

"We probably shouldn't keep them waiting," he whispers, dropping a kiss on my forehead. "I don't want to wait anymore, either."

When we reach the house again, we split off. Jake makes his way toward the area around the dock where our families have gathered, and I head into the kitchen to find Peter waiting for me.

With every passing day, Peter looks more and more like dad. A few gray hairs, thanks to a career in politics he says, are starting to show up around his temples, lines around his eyes from years of laughter, and a smile that reduces me to tears. I wrap my arms around my brother's waist and he draws me against him, kissing the top of my head as he does.

"I hope you know how proud I am of you," he whispers, fighting tears of his own. I can only nod in response.

Sofi slips in through the patio door with a bouquet of flowers from the florist in town. One look at me and she dissolves into tears too, pulling me away from Peter and into her embrace.

I think of mom and dad. As I stand here with the people I love most in this world (minus a few), I think of the parents who raised us. Who instilled in us the importance of family, who showed us each day how to love. More than anything, I wish that they could be here today. But as I cling to my brother, I'm surrounded by the memory of mom and dad, and surrounded by their love.

"I hope you don't mind we're doing a small ceremony," I laugh as I break away from them and wipe away my tears.

"Of course not," Peter laughs. "In fact, this is perfect for you and Jake. Besides, I know you guys are married already."

We've been so careful to keep it between us -- and our few witnesses -- up to this point. Leave it to Peter to figure out the truth.

"I...what...?" Peter stops me with his hands on my shoulders, looking right into my eyes the way he used to do when we were kids and he wanted to know what I got him for his birthday. He could always get me to crack.

"Don't even try it," he laughs, pulling me into a hug. "You're my sister, you've never been able to keep secrets from me. Now come on, let's get you married....again."

Turns out, Jake and I aren't as great at keeping secrets as we thought we were. Everyone knows, and after our explanation of my anxiety and the night we lovingly refer to as "wedding panicking", everyone is understanding. That, and Jake confided in Jax that we'd already done the legal stuff. And the fun stuff.

Today we're surrounded by our families and a few close friends -- Devon, Jim, and their wives, and Morgan and Dan -- standing in the most gorgeous setting, on the shore of a semi frozen Saratoga Lake with the sun just starting to set, casting shades of pink and orange across the sky and the snow covered ice. I see the girls standing near Jake, he's crouched down talking to them and pointing to the house. After a moment's deliberation, Alice breaks away and runs toward the house, kicking up a flurry behind her.

"Aunt 'Nelope!" Alice tugs on my hand and I crouch down close to her. She cups a hand around her mouth and leans in close, her breath a whisper against my ear. "Uncle Jake wants to know if you're ready yet."

"Go tell your Uncle Jake that I'm on my way."

Alice runs through the door and down the lawn, shouting, "Uncle Jake! She's on her way!"

Sofi and I share a laugh while Peter turns and tries to wipe away his tears without either of us seeing. I wrap Sofi in a hug before she heads back into the yard with the rest of the family, leaving Peter and I alone again in the kitchen.

He walks me through the dining room, exiting through the sliding door, and down the makeshift aisle. My family stands to one side, and Jake's to the other. The girls have sprinkled flower petals between the families. As Peter and I approach Jake on the dock, our families and friends close ranks behind us, joining as one group, gathering around us rather than taking sides.

With a kiss to my cheek—and tears in his eyes—Peter leaves me standing on the dock with Jake, the pastor between us. Jake wipes away tears and I have to do the same, he grins when I reach for his hands, handing my bouquet to the nearest family member. I think it goes to Jenna but I'm not sure, I'm too distracted by my husband watching me.

I barely make it through our vows. At some point, someone comes up and tucks a handkerchief into my hand and I wipe my eyes in an attempt to clean myself up, but the tears don't stop. Soon, we're pronounced husband and wife. Again. Jake cups my neck with one hand, the other rests on my lower back as his mouth meets mine for a kiss. I thread my fingers through his hair and sink into him and deepen the kiss.

At the sound of cheering, we break away, barely containing our laughter. Jake rests his forehead against mine, his eyes gazing right into my soul.

"I love you Sunshine."

"And I love you, Stormcloud."

38
WHERE THE HEART IS
PENELOPE

After indulging in the food that Claire and I worked on for the better part of the day, and the cakes that Jenna and Sofia made, our family and friends wish us well, and start to make their way out, Jax tucks the girls in upstairs before heading off to his shift at the hospital, and Jake and I stick around for a bit with his parents and Sofi and Peter who are staying the rest of the weekend here at the Saratoga house.

I love seeing my family getting to know Jake's family; Claire and Benjamin welcomed them all with open arms, and have been treating them like family from the moment they arrived. This time with them, with the whole family, is so precious...and overwhelming. I sit back and let the conversation flow around me, the laughter, the stories everyone shares. I couldn't have asked for a better end to this day.

Finally, Jake and I take our leave. We head south, our final destination a mystery to me. I don't know what he has planned, and right now, I'm content to sit beside him, my hand held tightly in his, as he watches me from the corner of his eyes, a grin stretched across his face.

We've technically been married for two months, but doing it again today in front of our family and friends was the icing on an already pretty incredible cake. And I know that Jake is happy. He'd have been happy if our wedding was that simple ceremony in the park, and I would have been too. That one was just for us. Today was for everyone else.

And tonight is ours.

After a few hours of driving, Jake pulls off into a subdivision. I'm not exactly sure what he's got planned but this is a surprise. We'd looked at a few houses in this neighborhood over the last couple of weeks, but agreed that nothing seemed to fit what we were looking for.

He pulls into the driveway of a two story ranch. Blue-gray siding, white shutters and trim and a red front door. Flower beds in the front. A wrap around porch, perfect for a swing on one end and rocking chairs near the door. The front yard is expansive and needs some landscaping—perennials and ground cover by the porch and lining the walkway. I could do that myself.

Neighbors on both sides, but not so close that we'd be in each other's business all the time. Close enough to greet in the morning when we're on the porch or in the afternoon when I walk to the mailbox to get the mail. There are trees in the yard. I think my time in the city made me forget what it was like to have trees so close. And it's December, so the neighborhood is awash in the glow of Christmas lights. I think of wrapping Christmas lights around the rails of the front porch. This very front porch, where Terri Wilson—Devon's wife, and the best residential realtor in the county—happens to be standing, waiting for us.

This is the most excited I've been to see a house since we started looking at listings. This is the most excited I've been all week, save for a few hours ago when Jake and I exchanged vows...again.

The only problem is, there's no for sale sign in the yard, nothing around to indicate that this house is on the market. I ask Terri about this, and she explains that the owner is allowing her to give us first dibs before it's officially listed. I didn't know this was a thing, but I'm not about to argue when my dream house is being served up to me like this.

Still in our wedding finery, Terri gives Jake and me a tour of the house. I'm hit with the smell of fresh paint as soon as we walk inside. Terri explains that the owner has just finished renovating the kitchen, which is where she takes us first. Apparently this house is a flip. The owners bought it to renovate it and resell it, and the kitchen was the last bit they had to finish. While the outside of the house has been restored to its former glory, the kitchen has been updated and modernized.

I'm in heaven. I died somewhere along the house hunting journey and this kitchen is heaven. That's the only explanation for this absolutely *perfect* kitchen. The flow. The vibe. It's all...right. An island, a breakfast bar, an open concept from the kitchen to the dining room to the living room. The kitchen is the heart of this house. With a set of doors in the dining room that lead to the back deck and the backyard. I can see everything from the middle of the kitchen which is obviously what I have in my apartment, but this is the dream right here.

I test the "flow" like I have in every single house. And it feels right. All of it. It just *feels* right. The cabinets and counters and appliances are brand new. Jake watches me with a smile on his face. An odd smile. One that tells me there's something he's not saying. In the span of about thirty seconds we have a silent conversation in which I interrogate him with a series of brow quirks, smirks, and one well timed frown.

Terri looks between us with a laugh and leads me down the hall toward the master suite and additional bedrooms and bathroom. Then she takes us to the finished basement with its living space, two more bedrooms, a full bathroom and an office space. There's room in this house for us to host all of the siblings and in-laws. We could host everyone, and I mean *everyone* for Christmas if we wanted to.

I can see myself decorating every inch of this house for Christmas. Or Thanksgiving. I can see us having movie nights, game nights, picnics and cookouts and family celebrations. The office space is big enough for both of us to have a desk and our own space to work. I'd have a place to write and work on things for *On the Field* and *Shattered Glass*...and all of the other ideas that roll around in my brain on a daily basis.

This house is perfect. So perfect that it feels too good to be true.

"What's the catch?" I ask, turning to Terri as I give the basement another once over.

"What do you mean?"

"I mean, it's like someone got into my brain, read my mind, and created this house just for us."

Terri smiles at me, nods at Jake—which seems odd, but again, I'm not questioning anything while I am standing in the physical embodiment of my dream house—and then she heads upstairs, telling me that the owner is here to see us.

Jake heads up the stairs behind Terri while I take one last look around the basement. I close my eyes and picture a Christmas tree set up down here, piles of presents under it as Alice and Mack race down the stairs on Christmas morning, and all of our siblings, and Jake's mom and dad.

I picture the two of us in the office together, Jake and I working at our own desks, on our own projects, a ball game on television. Music playing. Or Jake and I cuddled on the couch watching a movie. This house feels like it could be our home. No other house we've visited has felt like this one.

Trudging up the stairs, I convince myself that something is wrong with the place. A pest infestation. Mold somewhere. Or, and even worse, it's drastically outside of our price range. I walk upstairs to find Jake standing in the upstairs living room with...his siblings? James, Jax, and Jenna all grin when they see me.

"What's going on?" I ask, approaching the group.

"These are the owners," Terri says, gesturing toward Jake and his siblings.

"For now," James says, looking at me with a sly smile. "It depends on what you think, Nell."

"I'm sorry. What?"

Jake laughs and slips an arm around my waist, drawing me into his side. He explains to me that he, Jax, and Jenna went in on the house with James about a year ago with the intention of flipping the house and selling it. James completely restored the place; he took the walls down to the studs, redid every single room, moved the laundry room from the basement to the first floor, finished the basement (complete with the added bathroom), and just finished the kitchen last week.

Apparently my husband has been paying close attention to all of my daydreams over the last year. When he realized that he was falling for me, and decided to propose, he sent a list to James. And James worked his magic. The reason the kitchen felt like it was perfect for me is because it was tailor made to my daydreams. It was tailor made to what I have always wanted in my home kitchen. Because of Jake. And James. James did the physical work on the house while Jake gave him direction.

The reason, Jake tells me, that we've spent the last week on a wild goose house hunt, is because James needed time to put the finishing touches on the kitchen.

"So...if the four of you own it, what does that mean for us?"

"It means," James grins from ear to ear, "that if you love it, Jake has to pay up."

James sticks his hand out expectantly and Jake shakes his head with a laugh.

Jake pulls me away from his siblings, taking me into the kitchen for a moment of privacy. "I didn't want to make this decision without you. But Penelope...Sunshine...this house? It's perfect. For the both of us. For us to start a family. The commute is relatively short, considering the distance. The neighborhood is great...."

I silence him with a kiss. My hands frame his face and I pull him toward me as his hands wrap around my waist and he draws me into his embrace. After a moment, I pull back and search his eyes with mine. "It is perfect. Do it. Go buy them out."

He laughs and kisses me again, chuckling against my lips. "I've already written the checks."

Terri and my new siblings clear out pretty quickly after we make the decision to keep the house, and Jake and I are left alone in the sparkling, fully stocked, perfect kitchen. I leave Jake at the kitchen island and do one more walk through the house on my own. When I make my way back down to the kitchen, Jake has shed his jacket and tie, the sleeves of his crisp white shirt are rolled up revealing those arms of his, and his collar hangs open. He grabs my hand and draws me out onto the back deck. We have a deck!

Two chairs wait for us, between them is a small table with an ice bucket and two bottles of our favorite ginger ale. He sits down, pulling me onto his lap and wrapping an arm around my waist. I take care of opening the bottles and hand one to him, taking a look at the note:

10D --
Here's to forever.
Love you, always.
10C

"Here's to forever," I kiss him, tasting the spice and sweetness of the ginger ale on his lips as his arms wrap around my waist and hold me tight.

"Here's to forever."

39
ONE YEAR(ISH) LATER
PENELOPE

Middle of the night phone calls used to strike me with panic. Fill me with dread. But, since connecting with the adoption agency nearly six months ago, this middle of the night phone call could be the one we've been waiting for. I turn on the bedside lamp as Jake sits up and groggily answers his phone. In an instant, his sleepy, groggy eyes brighten as he turns to face me.

"Yes....okay. We have one, yes. That too....yes, passed all inspections and interviews. We'll be there." When he hangs up the phone I realize I've been holding my breath. He takes me in his arms and plants a kiss on my forehead. "She's gone into labor and asked if we'd be there."

We dress quickly and make our way to the hospital. I run through the checklist in my head: we have a crib, diapers, some clothing gifted by family and friends, bottles, a car seat. I have no idea how we're going to do this. I have no idea how we're going to just be thrust into parenthood. Jake grabs my hand and intertwines our fingers, pressing a soft kiss to the back of my hand.

We'd had hopes that the fertility treatments Jax was helping with would take, that eventually we'd conceive on our own, and while that hope is still there, we decided to look into adoption. I've spent a lot of late nights crying into my pillow, Jake's arms around me as he softly kissed my neck and held me tight. We've spent a lot of time in and out of appointments with specialists. There've been a few losses. But finally, we started to feel a bit of hope. A mom chose us. And now we're on our way to meet our baby. We understand the immense privilege that we are afforded by being able to adopt and do not for a moment take for granted the sacrifice and courage that got us to this point.

We take the elevator up to the labor and delivery floor, riding silently, hands tightly wound together. My heart is racing and tears are welling behind my eyes, but I do my best to pull myself together. I have to. The doors slide open and a doctor stands in front of us, startled to see us. It barely registers in my brain that my brother in law is standing in front of us, eyes and face conveying a thousand unspoken questions.

"What are you two doing here?" He asks, clearly confused to see us in the middle of the night.

"Having a baby." I say as Sharon, our social worker, meets me in the hallway and whisks me off to the delivery room to be with Katie. She's asked if I'd be with her during labor, and there's no way I'd have told her no. I stand beside her and hold her hand through the whole ordeal. Wiping her brow and encouraging her, all the while trying my very best not to cry.

When it's all over, Katie decides to let me be the one to hold the baby first. And that's when the tears come. I'm taken to a room down the hall and pointed toward a chair. The nurse suggests that right now what the baby needs is skin to skin contact, she hands me a gown to throw on, allowing me to bare my chest and neck. I do as she says and cradle the baby against me. And finally let my tears fall.

Jake is shown to the room, and he kneels down on the floor, laying one hand across our baby's back, a hand so large that it covers the infant's entire tiny body. His eyes meet mine, glittering with tears as he watches the two of us.

"Jake," I take his free hand in mine and squeeze. "Meet your daughter."

He smiles as tears fall from his eyes and he presses a gentle kiss to the top of her head before claiming my lips in a soft kiss. "We have a daughter," he breathes, his voice filled with wonder.

Jax joins us, with Sharon close behind. Tears prick at my eyes and roll down my cheeks as Jake presses a kiss to the top of my head and together we look down at our baby. Our daughter. Jax squeezes my shoulder and hugs Jake, both of them wiping away tears of their own. The social worker returns with paperwork for us to sign. Katie signed what she needed to sign. Now it's up to us.

We sign everything, passing papers back and forth, all the while I hold onto my baby girl -- *our* baby girl. I think of the bravery it must take to do what her mother did. To allow us, complete strangers, to take on this precious little life as our own. To love her and care for her. To be her mom and dad.

"Last thing you need to do," the social worker looks at us with a smile, "what's her name?"

I look at Jake, and we already know. We've thought about it and discussed it over and over.

"Leigh," I stare down at my -- now sleeping -- daughter, and my heart constricts. "Her name is Leigh."

It honors my dad, her grandfather. And Leigh means "one who brings healing". This little sleeping bundle has brought healing to my heart in ways that she could never imagine. This precious baby is an answer to so many prayers, a miracle I'd only ever dreamed of. I spent so many years wondering if I'd ever be a mother, and even though I didn't carry and give birth to this precious life, she has been entrusted to me, to us. I consider myself luckier than I deserve that I get to be her mom. And that I get to walk this road with Jake by my side.

When everything is filled out and ready, and uncle Jax has had a chance to hold his new niece, we head home. We carefully take Leigh out of the car and transfer her to her bassinet that is set up in our room. Jake and I stand watch over her for several long, silent moments just watching her breathe. Watching her eyelids flutter and her little lips move. Every now and then one of her feet twitches and I feel myself falling more and more in love with each passing second.

Eventually, we tear ourselves away. I change back into my pajamas and crawl into bed, settling myself into the crook of Jake's arm as he wraps it around me and presses a kiss to my lips. As I lay beside my husband, my daughter only a few feet away, I think back on everything that brought us to this point—all the pain, the grief, the love and healing that I found along the way. All of it leading us here, with our daughter.

"What are you thinking?" I feel Jake shift behind me, his breath a warm whisper against my ear. "I can practically hear your brain whirring."

I'm thinking about how happy I am. How I can't wait for Leigh to grow up in this crazy, loud, loving family. I can't wait for her to meet her grandparents and aunts and uncles. I can't wait for Mack and Alice—the first little girls to steal my heart—to meet their cousin.

I want to teach her about baseball. And following her dreams. I want her to know what a wonderful man her dad is. I want her to know that this world is her's for the taking, and that her dad and I will always believe in her.

"I'm thinking about all the glass ceilings she'll shatter."

I turn to face Jake, and even in our darkened bedroom, I can see the smile on his face. Jake's arms tighten around me as he pulls me closer to him. "Of course she will," he grins "you're her mom. She's going to shatter all the glass ceilings if you have anything to say about it."

Look out, Leigh. Nothing is going to stand in your way.

ACKNOWLEDGMENTS

I don't know what to say other than thank you. To friends and family who have encouraged my writing over the years, have read early drafts and short stories and blog posts.

To Mom and Dad. Thank you for teaching me everything I know in the kitchen and about baseball. And even more than that, for being there. For walking with me through the good days and bad. Dad, thank you for still listening to my baseball rants. Someone has to. And mom, thank you for letting me experiment in your kitchen. I love you both. And I promise it's nothing personal that Penelope's parents are both gone...it was necessary to the plot!

To Brittany. The best sister this only child has ever had. For reading my messy drafts and insomnia-fueled brainstorming sessions.

To Emma. For previewing this while it was still under construction. Your feedback was incredibly helpful, and very entertaining. Thank you for your encouragement throughout this process. And most importantly thank you for your friendship.

To Lindsey. Fellow baseball lover, and quite possibly my biggest cheerleader (outside of my family). You gave me the push I needed. Your encouragement and support throughout this process was invaluable, and your friendship a blessing.

To my home team. I will forever be loyal, no matter the win-loss record. Thank you for inspiring more than a few of Penelope's rants... and this love letter to baseball.

ABOUT THE AUTHOR

Megan is a daughter, student, office administrator, and Michigan native who loves books, board games, baseball, and her family—not necessarily in that order. She loves books with wit and banter and scenes that wouldn't make her grandma blush...so she wrote one.

Megan's stories are filled with humor and heart, sometimes obscure baseball references, swoon-worthy heroes, and heroines who aren't afraid to speak their mind.

And keep an eye out for more of the Hutchinson Family and The Wild Pitches Series COMING SOON!

instagram.com/authormegancousins

Printed in Great Britain
by Amazon